D1020046

Taxed to the Max

TAXED TO THE MAX

CHERYL B. DALE

FIVE STAR
A part of Gale, Cengage Learning

Detroit • New York • San Francisco • New Haven, Conn • Waterville, Maine • London

GALE
CENGAGE Learning®

LIBRARY OF CONGRESS CATALOGING-IN-PUBLICATION DATA

Dale, Cheryl B.
  Taxed to the max / Cheryl B. Dale. — 1st ed.
    p. cm.
  ISBN 978-1-4328-2600-0 (hardcover) — ISBN 1-4328-2600-X (hardcover)
    1. Tax assessment—Fiction. 2. Georgia—Fiction. I. Title.
PS3604.A3536T39 2012
813'.6—dc23   2012029014

First Edition. First Printing: December 2012.
Published in conjunction with Tekno Books and Ed Gorman.
Find us on Facebook– https://www.facebook.com/FiveStarCengage
Visit our website– http://www.gale.cengage.com/fivestar/
Contact Five Star™ Publishing at FiveStar@cengage.com

Printed in Mexico
1 2 3 4 5 6 7 16 15 14 13 12

ADDITIONAL COPYRIGHT INFORMATION

CHAPTER 1

The burly guy wearing a do-rag and one hoop earring leaned a beefy elbow on the high counter separating us and glared. "You don't understand, lady. All I need's a tag for my pickup."

"I realize that." I tried not to stare at the EAT ME tattoo on his forearm. "Unfortunately, there's nothing to prove the truck is yours. The state computer shows it belongs to a J. P. Basquil."

"Like I told you twice already, this Basquil use'ta own it." He shook his temporary insurance binder at me. "See that? I got insurance on the car. Why the hell would I pay for insurance on something that ain't mine?"

Tact was called for. "Maybe the dealer you bought it from hasn't changed the title yet."

"Didn't buy it from no dealer." He looked at my name badge. His tone became confidential. "Look, Miss Corralie Caters, I bought it from this Basquil guy hisself. He's gotta get the title from his bank before he can give it to me. I can't put it in my name till I get a hold of it. *Capisce?*"

All too well. "I'm very sorry, but until the title is changed, nobody can buy a tag except Mr. Basquil."

His eyes narrowed. "So you ain't gonna sell me a tag?"

"I wish I could but I can't. The state computer won't let me. The vehicle isn't in your name. The state computer thinks Mr. Basquil still owns it."

Not for the first time I blessed the State of Georgia for putting us online. When we blamed their computers for making us

7

follow the law, most people didn't get upset with us peons.

This guy was one of the exceptions.

His fist slammed the counter so hard, I almost fell backward. I had to slide down and put one foot on the floor to stop my stool from tottering.

Oh, Lordy, I thought, please let Delores call 911.

If she didn't, I was pretty sure Mr. Jethro, the tax commissioner, wouldn't. He was back in his office where he took his morning (or afternoon) nap. On the shady side of eighty but scoffing at the idea of retirement, he usually remained oblivious to any commotion outside his office, including the fire alarms that went off sporadically in the ancient courthouse for no reason except that they felt like wailing.

"This is the sorriest excuse for a tag office I ever seen," my customer hissed. He thumped the counter again.

I flinched.

"I'll go up to Fannin County, that's what I'll do. They know me up there and they'll sell me a tag, by gawd."

They wouldn't break the law any more than we would, but I didn't say so. Offering a tentative smile, I pushed the useless bill of sale toward him, real careful not to get my hand close enough for him to reach. "Maybe by that time, the state computer will show your name on the title."

My smile didn't help. He grabbed his paperwork and slammed the door so hard on his way out, it was a wonder the glass pane didn't shatter.

"Try not to get customers so upset, Corrie," Delores Kineely said from behind me where she sat at her desk eating her favorite chocolate Devil Dunky cupcake and thumbing through the latest copy of an entertainment magazine. "We're here to serve the constituents, you remember."

Clamped teeth stopped my hot retort. Demon Delores, as we called her behind her back, had little room for talk. Her own customer service skills were nonexistent, which was why I bore the brunt of dealing with the public.

But that was Delores. She'd worked here nearly as long as Mr. Jethro McCartery had been tax commissioner, and she acted like she was boss instead of him.

I pulled out my statistics textbook to study for a big test. After reading the same page three times, I gave up, pushed it aside, and laid my forehead down on the counter. That bully with the tattoo had shaken me up bad.

I hated this job. I really, really hated this job. After three years as a tag clerk, I was to the point of hating my daddy for making me take it. There had to be something better for me to do out there somewhere.

Delores noticed my despair. "What's wrong? Are you sick? If you are, get the disinfectant spray out and use it around your counter. I don't want you giving anything to me."

I raised my head. "No. I'm just resting."

She looked at me suspiciously. "From doing what?"

From waiting on all these nutty people with no help from you. I swallowed. Hard. "Stayed up late studying last night. Got a test I need to ace."

"Huh." She glanced at the clock. "Nearly time to go."

I looked, too. Twelve twenty-five.

Thank goodness. It was Wednesday, the day we closed at twelve thirty. After this morning's cantankerous crowd, I needed an afternoon off.

Since Delores won't abide anything left on the counter, I put away letter opener, stapler, Scotch tape, pens, pads, and paper clips. Then I pulled out the drawer holding my purse so I could grab it and leave at twelve thirty sharp. Man, was I ready to get out of here.

Suddenly, the door flew open so hard it banged the wall.

One of the local rednecks stomped in.

Oh, shoot, I thought. A last-minute customer who wants a tag, and he won't have anything to prove it's his car and he won't have insurance, to boot. Or else he'll need to change the title or have some other problem that'll take forever to straighten out. He might even yell at me.

Then I saw who the redneck was and my heart sank.

Yell or worse.

Billy Lee Woodhallen is the meanest man in Ocosawnee County, Georgia, and everybody knows it. They couldn't pin it on him, but my dad and his cronies are pretty sure Billy Lee was responsible for firebombing the local charity the past year. Its head, Sister Ursula, had refused to give Billy Lee's momma free groceries because her income was too high.

Billy Lee went in and cussed the nun out, but she stood her ground. The following weekend, the building burned to the ground with all its contents, including food, clothing, and other miscellaneous donations for the needy, like a barely used john my grandmother wanted to buy for her garden after the sisters priced it for the thrift store.

The verdict was arson, by person or persons unknown.

Sure. Like everyone in the county didn't know who the unknown person was.

On top of that, Billy Lee got sent to prison some years back for something or other. Now gossip says he's running drugs for the Mexicali Mob, a kind of southern Hispanic mafia. Whether true or not, his dark beard and bulky figure in flannel shirt and mud-spattered jeans made him as scary-looking as his reputation.

He came right up to my window. "Need to see Mr. Jethro."

Jubilant, I silently squealed. He doesn't want a tag! He doesn't want a tag!

Before I could fetch Mr. Jethro, Delores beat me to it.

"Mr. Jethro!" she hollered toward the back office. "Billy Lee

Woodhallen wants to see you out here."

The minute hand nudged the six. Twelve thirty. Freedom. At long last.

I slid off my stool.

In the rear, I heard Mr. Jethro's chair plop down hard from where he had leaned it back against the wall while he napped. "Tell him I ain't here."

Billy Lee glowered. "I hear you, you old sumbitch!"

He went over and rattled the door leading back to the area where we worked.

It was locked. I crossed my fingers, praying the lock would hold.

Then Billy Lee came back and started to jump the high counter. Fortunately for us, he was so large he couldn't quite make it.

He tried again.

Not wanting to be in his way if he somehow managed to throw his ample poundage over the counter, I scrambled off to the side.

From her desk in the rear, Delores noticed my quick retreat. "What're you doing, Corrie?"

Billy Lee missed his second jump, too. The third time, to my consternation, he was able to heave his big butt up onto the twelve-inch ledge over the space where I worked. There he sat on his precarious perch and caught his breath.

I wanted to run outside, but my purse was still in its drawer.

And the drawer was directly below where Billy Lee's blue-jeaned bottom drooped over the counter edge.

While I considered the situation, Billy Lee got his wind back. He hoisted his tree trunk legs up and slid them over the counter top where his big feet could rest on my work desk. Then he eased down, kicked my stool aside, and jumped off. The heart of pine floor shifted under his weight as he landed.

Not too agilely, I might add.

Dolores finally caught on and shot up from her desk. "Just what the heck do you think you're doing, Billy Lee Woodhallen? You could of broke that counter, big as you are."

He snorted and, after stumbling and recovering, headed straight for Mr. Jethro's office.

Delores got out of his way.

So did I.

In the meantime, Mr. Jethro had moved faster than I ever knew he could. The door to his office, original in the century-old courthouse, was solid cherry and thick enough to withstand a battering. As Billy Lee reached it, Mr. Jethro shoved it to. "You ain't getting in here."

Billy Lee managed to catch the edge and stick one work boot between the door and casing. Then he yelled, "Owww!" as he grabbed one hamlike hand with the other.

I reached for the phone.

"Goldammit, that hurt!" Billy Lee bobbed up and down as if jumping, but kept his foot wedged firmly in the door opening. Holding his smushed hand, he yelled from between clenched teeth, "You slammed that door on me, you damned old thief. I think you broke my fingers."

Mr. Jethro's retort was muffled from behind the not quite closed door. "Shouldn't have put 'em where they don't belong."

Delores finally got her wits back and started screaming, "Call nine-one-one, Corrie! Call nine-one-one! You can't come back behind the counter, Billy Lee!"

Yeah, right. Like Billy Lee wasn't already back here.

I punched in 911.

Billy Lee forgot his wounded hand and tried to force the door opening wider. "Let me in, you lily-livered coward!"

"Nope. Ain't gonna do it. Go on now, get out of here, Billy Lee." Mr. Jethro's door, still ajar with Billy Lee's foot caught in it, didn't budge an inch.

"Get help! Call nine-one-one!" Delores spluttered, "Y-you'll be in a lot of trouble for this, B-Billy Lee Woodhallen! We're a state office! A *state* office, you hear me? State! *State!* Corrie, call nine-one-one!"

"The hell I'll get out of here!" Billy Lee bellowed to Mr. Jethro. "I know what you're trying to do, you weaselly snake in the grass! You ain't gonna git away with it!"

He beat on the door with his injured hand once more, snatched it back, and bobbed in pain again—his foot lodged in the door opening all the time—then switched hands to pound some more.

Despite his breached shield, Mr. Jethro stayed calm. "You're crazy as hell to come in here like this, Billy Lee. You're fixing to get yourself arrested again, is what you're fixing to do."

For his age, our tax commissioner was real spry, and he must have been stronger than he looked because he held the door steady against Billy Lee the whole time Billy Lee kept pushing. The younger man had at least a hundred pounds on the older, but Mr. Jethro acquitted himself well.

The emergency responders, stationed upstairs, took forever to pick up. A dispatcher I didn't recognize answered.

"Weneedhelp!" Slow down, be coherent. Big breath. "Billy Lee Woodhallen is trying to kill Mr. Jethro. Send somebody down here, quick." I remembered I hadn't told her where. "Downstairs in the tax commissioner's office. Right now. Hurry." I remembered my manners. "Please."

Behind me, Mr. Jethro remained reasonable, if still muffled behind his door. "I ain't gonna talk to you till you compose yourself, Billy Lee."

By now, Delores was flat out shrieking. "State! We're a *state* office!"

Billy Lee remained oblivious. "I'm gonna beat the crap out of you!"

"Who is this?" the woman at 911 asked suspiciously.

"It doesn't matter. Listen, send somebody down now."

"What's your name and address? I have to have a name and address. I can't send anybody anywhere till I have a name—"

"Corrie Caters! We're in the blooming tax commissioner's office right down below you, you twit! Same building! Same address! First floor! *Help!*"

Between the two combatants and Delores's screeching and my yelling at the 911 dispatcher, we made quite a commotion.

The two tax assessors in the adjoining office heard and rushed in. When they saw Billy Lee, they hesitated.

I'd have hesitated, too, but they were men, and the younger one was built like an ex−football player. "Do something," I fussed between screaming at the 911 clerk. "He's gonna hurt Mr. Jethro."

Of course it was the shrimp who came to the rescue. Calvin Dredger, the hulking oaf, stood there in the door with his mouth open and his eyes bulging, while skinny little Fred Bauers took a big gulp and approached the problem.

He gamely tapped Billy Lee on the shoulder.

"Now Billy Lee," he said in his prissy way, "let's just calm down here. This isn't the way to settle any disagreements you might—"

Billy Lee promptly hit him in the schnoz.

Fred felt his nose, looked at the blood on his hand, and turned white. The other assessor's eyes and mouth grew wider, and he hightailed it back to his office, the coward.

Fred sank down in Delores's chair and held his hand up, studying the blood. His head drifted down toward her desk pad like he was passing out.

Delores quit screeching. She snatched up some paper towels

by the microwave and scurried over to wipe up any blood Fred might drip. Demon Delores never could stand a messy desk.

I gave up on 911. There had to be something around here to bop Billy Lee with.

By now Billy Lee had switched his attention back to Mr. Jethro's door, but the wily old tax commissioner had taken advantage of Fred's diversion and Billy Lee's foot removal to wedge the door closed.

Billy Lee banged on it anyway.

Was the cast-iron dachshund boot scraper holding open the vault door too heavy to hit him with?

Probably. I wanted to slow him down, not kill him. Still . . .

Billy Lee backed up a few steps. "You stinking coward! You piece of dog shit! You open that door! You wait'll I get my hands on you!"

He got a running start so he could use his shoulder against the door. The move might have been effective in a thinner man, but Billy Lee's bulk acted like a rubber ball. He bounced back into a file cabinet and nearly lost his balance.

Mr. Jethro's protection held.

Infuriated, Billy Lee returned to the fray and started to kick at the cherry door.

I stopped debating the pros and cons of using the dachshund, and snatched it up. Its unexpected weight threw me off balance. I staggered back. Good grief, it was heavy. Could I raise it high enough to hit Billy Lee in the head?

About that time, a couple of deputies arrived from the jail next door. Thank heavens. I dropped the dachshund to let them behind the counter, then stood aside.

They were big men, but so was Billy Lee. The three scuffled for several minutes before the deputies could subdue Billy Lee enough to snap on handcuffs. As they wrestled him out the door and carried him off toward the jail, he hollered like a stuck pig. We could still hear him as they went down the courthouse hall to the exit.

Mr. Jethro peered out, then brought his lean six-foot, five-inch frame out from his makeshift stronghold. He looked pretty pleased with himself. "Well. My gracious goodness. That was kind of exciting, wasn't it, ladies?"

"Huh." A shaken Delores blew her nose. "Exciting ain't the word for it. I swear, if I could afford it, I'd retire this very instant."

Mr. Jethro carefully stroked his thin white hair back into place. "Aw, now, Delores. There ain't many folk as feisty as old Billy Lee. Besides, ain't you noticed people retire and then die right off the bat? That's why I don't mean to do it, and you better not either." He adjusted his plaid shirt as nonchalantly as if he dealt with hooligans all the time. "Reckon it's a good time to call it a day. I got to go on home and take a nap so's I can get Miss Jeanie to church on time tonight."

Delores and I exchanged disbelieving looks.

She was the most frazzled I'd ever seen her. Her dyed black hair with its unintentional purple tints flopped down over her eyes. Her mascara had somehow gotten smeared. Even the cardigan sweater she wore over her starched blouse hung off one shoulder like someone had caught her by the collar and yanked.

I guessed I didn't look much better, so I retrieved my purse and statistics book and scurried out.

One thing was sure. I had to find another job. Nobody with any sense would work in a tax commissioner's office.

The next day as I drove to work, daydreams about moving down to Atlanta and taking a job with less stress filled my head. Maybe I could be a cable TV clerk or a telephone customer service person or a waitress or something.

Pipe dreams. I'd been born in Medder Rose and grew up here and would probably die here. I loved the foothills with their tall forests and rushing trout streams. This morning the green of spring tinted the landscape, while the dogwoods were beginning to pop out white blossoms. Some were big as saucers.

Their masses against the sloping hills made my heart swell with gratitude that I lived in the area the Cherokee had once called the Enchanted Lands. I knew exactly how fortunate I was.

Sometimes, though, like yesterday . . .

In the courthouse entry hall, smelling of age and dust and lemon oil, the high arched windows over the exit spilled sunshine on Delores Kineely as she stopped to get out her office keys. With a blue shirt buttoned primly to the top and creased gray slacks, she was back to her usual neat self.

She displayed her usual sour attitude, too. Had she smiled, she might have been attractive.

Then again, maybe not. Her long face with its high forehead and square chin always reminded me a horse. An ill-tempered nag with big teeth ready to bite.

I put on a wide fake grin. "Good morning."

"Huh," she grunted.

The old bat. I bet for a dollar, she'd ram the keys right down my throat without remorse. Today wasn't going to be any better than yesterday.

Of course, with Demon Delores, no day was a good day. My mom blamed her grouchiness on menopause, but my dad had gone through school with her sister and said the whole Jemson family was like that. "Always have been. They're bipolar or schizoid or something," he opined. "The lot of 'em. Take after their Grandmother Williston, and I hear she was a doozy in her day. They say she used to take a rolling pin to people trampling her flowers. Hurt one man pretty bad."

After working with Delores for three years, I leaned toward my daddy's theory.

"Huh," Delores said again, but this time it was a surprised grunt. She put her keys back in her purse without using them. "Door's already open."

"Really? You think Mr. Jethro's here?" The whole time I'd worked in the office, Mr. Jethro had never come in early. He relied on Delores to open up and get things started. Usually he ambled in about nine or ten o'clock, smiling and chipper, in time to get a cup of fresh coffee from the second pot and head back to his desk where he read the paper from back to front before dozing till lunch.

Delores snorted. "Mr. Jethro here before eight o'clock? That'd be a first." She pushed the glass paneled door open and led the way inside.

"That ruckus with Billy Lee Woodhallen yesterday might have upset him enough to get him out early this morning," I said. Then, after looking toward the back office: "Guess not. His light isn't on."

Delores had probably forgotten to turn the lock on the door when she left because of all the excitement yesterday, but I wouldn't dare suggest that.

Demon Delores did not take kindly to criticism.

Throwing my statistics book onto the counter, I stowed my purse and closed the drawer. It slid back out as it always did, so I ripped off a piece of Scotch tape and taped it shut.

Nothing in the ancient courthouse worked properly. The Romanesque Revival building might be impressive from the outside, but in my opinion, it needed tearing down and replacing. Or at the least, renovating on a big-time scale.

Fat chance of that happening. Voters in our part of the country don't like to spend their money on government offices. They prefer investing it in baseball and football fields.

While Delores flipped on the office lights, I headed to the break area where I made coffee every morning. The coffee-maker sat in the corner beyond Mr. Jethro's door, so naturally I glanced into his empty office as I passed.

Something lay on the floor by his desk. A piece of plaid cloth or scarf or . . .

I stopped short. It looked like the plaid shirt Mr. Jethro had worn the day before.

Then, submerged in the murky interior, something pale and distorted stuck out from the end of the cloth.

"Mr. Jethro? Is that you? Are you okay?"

One tentative step forward was enough to see that the plaid cloth was a sleeve and the pale thing was a hand.

Easing around the desk, I found the other arm pillowing a snowy head like its owner had fallen asleep on the floor.

He wasn't asleep though. Dark crud mingled with the white strands of hair. Somebody had hit Mr. Jethro on the head and left him on the floor in his office.

I backed up, screaming.

"What the heck do you think you're doing? All that caterwauling—" Delores came to push me aside and look. "Well, shit. What happened to Mr. Jethro?"

Eventually we got some help, but it was too late for poor Mr. Jethro. He was stone-cold dead.

CHAPTER 2

After the deputies arrived, they immediately banished Delores and me to the tiny assessors' office that adjoined ours.

Painted a dispirited beige like every other room without paneling in the courthouse, the walls held a large county map and several framed assessor class certificates. Two metal desks and mismatched wall-to-wall filing cabinets left scant room to maneuver.

Like us, the assessors used every available flat surface, but unlike our office that Delores ruled, their place was messy. Real messy. It smelled of paper and dust and . . .

Was that sausage? No. More like dirty socks.

I sat in Calvin Dredger's chair frowning at bread crumbs and two empty sausage biscuit wrappers on a desk pad filled with doodles. A signed baseball in a plastic case stood beside a pair of binoculars and a mason jar holding pens and pencils. The binoculars lay on what looked like a pair of athletic socks. Used athletic socks. Yuck.

Delores gingerly sat down in Fred's chair, careful not to touch the untidy stacks of files and half-empty coffee cups that littered his desk. "This is a pigsty," she muttered. "Mr. Jethro hadn't ought to allow—"

She stopped, both of us reminded again of Mr. Jethro's body that the EMTs still hovered over.

We waited to be questioned, me sniffling and Delores's usual belligerence muted.

"I can't believe it," I said.

"Me neither," Dolores agreed. She sounded annoyed that her routine had been disrupted, but I charitably put her grumpiness down to shock.

"Do you think they'll question us?"

"Duh!" The old Dolores was definitely back. "We found the body. Of course they'll question us."

Sheriff Garimond "Duke" Duval did the honors in person. He had graduated high school with my uncle, but got elected sheriff of Ocosawnee County ten or twelve years ago after two decades spent as an Atlanta policeman. I shifted my feet over against the filing cabinets so he could get through the door. Once his big-boned frame in its neat uniform entered, the assessors' small space overflowed.

He was all sympathy and commiseration for what we'd gone through.

Of course, we spilled our guts about Billy Lee Woodhallen.

"Yeah, I already heard about the disturbance. Billy Lee bonded out right after we picked him up yesterday, so now we're trying to chase him down for questioning," Sheriff Duval said. His stance was military, his manner levelheaded. "What was he so aggravated with Mr. Jethro about?"

I didn't know.

Delores did. She always knows everything. "Billy Lee hasn't paid his taxes in over two years, and Mr. Jethro is transferring the tax liens to Arvin Smelting."

Arvin Smelting is the richest man around these parts. He got that way by being miserly, conscienceless, and a cheat. His only friends are people who don't know him well.

The sheriff perked up his ears at the mere mention of Arvin's name. "You mean Arvin's gonna get a hold of Billy Lee's property?"

Delores shrugged. "Maybe. First he has to give Billy Lee a

chance to redeem it. If Billy Lee doesn't pay the overdue taxes plus attorney fees and advertising fees and all the other expenses Arvin pays to get the property ready for sale," Delores recited as if reading off a paper, "then yes, Arvin can sell his property."

After thirty-odd years, Dolores knew the tax laws backward and forward.

Another thought struck her. "Oh, and Billy Lee'll have to pay twenty percent interest on top of everything else. Comes to a pretty good chunk Billy Lee'd have to cough up if he wants to redeem his land. That is, if Arvin gets hold of the tax liens."

The sheriff leaned back against the door frame. "How much does Billy Lee owe in taxes?"

"Right now?" Delores looked toward the ceiling as if toting up sums. Her head snapped down. "About eighty-four thousand six hundred or so. Interest changes the sixteenth of the month though, so the total will go up again next week."

My eyes grew wide. "Good grief!"

The sheriff whistled. "Eighty-five thousand dollars? Ho-boy, that's a right smart dab of change. You mean to say Arvin can charge Billy Lee that much plus another twenty percent on top?"

Delores nodded vigorously. "Yessirree. Billy Lee was fit to be tied when he heard what Mr. Jethro intended to do."

"I can see why." Sheriff Duval studied his knuckles. "I didn't realize Mr. Jethro transferred liens."

"He won't usually, but Billy Lee made him mad. Instead of paying his taxes, Billy Lee bought a new truck and one of them expensive bass boats and a brand new tractor last year. Then this year he put up a big metal building for those classic cars he collects. He owes over two years' back taxes on his farm and his strip mall with the package store and some other stuff he owns. But he won't pay up. Mr. Jethro didn't think it was right."

She added piously, "I don't either. Everyone else in the

county has to pay their taxes. Including me."

"Yeah. And me, too." The sheriff looked through the open door into the tax office where several of his people continued to mill.

Holding back tears, I remembered the plaid shirt Mr. Jethro had on when I found him. "Billy Lee must have come back here before Mr. Jethro left work yesterday. Mr. Jethro would never have worn the same shirt two days in a row. He was real particular about his clothes."

"Huh," Delores scoffed. "Couldn't have happened like that. Mr. Jethro and I went out the office door together before one o'clock. He left in front of me. I pushed the lock in on the door and followed him out like I always do. When I started my car, he was already in the road heading home."

I snuffled. "Then he must have come back for something. Billy Lee must have seen his car parked outside and come in and . . . If only Mr. Jethro had stayed away . . ."

"Did Mr. Jethro have an appointment with anyone yesterday afternoon?" The sheriff wanted to pace but the office was too little. He kept taking a step and having to turn around. Step and turn. Step and turn. "Could he have come back to the courthouse to meet someone?"

"How would I know?" Demon Delores snapped, reverting to form. "He never tells—told me anything. Half the time he'd arrange to meet somebody here at a certain time and forget. Then I'd be the one having to chase him down." She remembered he was dead. "Not that I minded. Poor old soul."

I volunteered what Mr. Jethro had said before leaving yesterday. "He was taking Miss Jeanie to church last night."

"Miss Jeanie?" The sheriff switched his attention to me.

"Jean Ogletree," Delores clarified. "She was married to Bill Ogletree till he died last year. She and Mr. Jethro been seeing each other for the past few weeks."

Mr. Jethro was a widower, but he surely liked the ladies. I knew of at least four besides Miss Jeanie he squired around to socials and potlucks and dances. All the senior ladies would miss him.

My eyes teared up, and I dove for another tissue.

The whole miserable mess was my daddy's fault.

No sane person would want to work in a tax commissioner's office, but Daddy didn't care about that.

"You got a choice, chickadee," he had told me three years ago when I was busy working at a fast food place and recovering from being jilted at the altar. "You can sulk over this thing with Bodie and flip burgers and work weekends and nights, or you can get on with your life and find an easier job with benefits. Thing is, with your burning up our kitchen at Christmas and then knocking down the garage wall last month, we've got unexpected expenses. Your mother thinks it's only fair you help pay for them. In fact, it's probably not a bad idea for you to pay us rent."

"You want me to pay rent?" I couldn't believe my daddy, my own father, was asking me to pay rent in the house where I'd lived all my life.

He nodded vigorously. "You got it, chick. That associate degree you just earned won't get you much of a job here in Medder Rose. You know yourself if you don't teach or get on with the county or city, there's not much work to be found. Now Sam Blanken says there's an opening in the tax office he can help you get. Working for Mr. Jethro's a good opportunity to hold down a real job for a while."

"A good opportunity? The tax office?" What in heaven's name was my father thinking? "Daddy, I was in there last month to change the title on my Hyundai, and this lady pitched a hissy fit when she found out how much her new car's tag cost. The old bat behind the counter talked to her so mean I nearly saw a cat fight. You want me to work *there?*"

"I know Delores Kineely's not good with people." Daddy sighed. "In fact, she run the other clerk off." He brightened. "But that's why there's an opening for you."

He was clearly out of his mind.

I put my hands on my hips, repeating, "And you want me to work *there?*"

Daddy flapped his hand. "Aw, you can get around Delores and her moods. Listen, I talked to Mr. Jethro, and he says they ain't too busy except for tax time. The rest of the year it's pretty slow. Eight to five, no weekends. Half day on Wednesday. Except maybe in property tax season, but you get paid overtime then. Easy job."

Easy job, hah. If I'd known then what I found out later, I'd have gone back to the burger joint.

I tried to protest. "I don't want to sell tags. I don't want to work in a tax office."

"Won't be forever." My dad was an optimist. "Go back to school at night, get your four-year degree so you can teach or something. Jethro says he don't care if you study in the office anytime you ain't busy. He says Delores reads magazines most of the time 'cause there ain't much going on. Look at it this way, it'll pay the bills till you can get a real job."

So there I was, twenty years old and jilted at the altar right when I was about to say my vows, working for Mr. Jethro Mc-Cartery, who was already in his late seventies and who'd been the tax commissioner in Ocosawnee County for forty years.

Besides me, the only other fulltime employee in the tax office was Delores Kineely. Around fifty, Delores had been with Mr. Jethro since she graduated from high school. She was a widow whose only child must have been halfway smart because as soon as he was old enough, he joined the army and left home. From what little Delores said, he came back as seldom as possible.

The woman whose place I was taking corroborated my suspicions in the couple of weeks she stayed to train me. When I asked about Delores, her upper lip curled. "Mr. Jethro's a big teddy bear, but that Delores Kineely is the pits. She thinks she's the queen bee, and if you don't do what she says, she'll sting. I been here two years and would of stayed on if it hadn't been for Demon Delores."

That didn't bode well, but Mr. Jethro was an old sweetie, and he seemed so pleased I wanted to work for him that I figured I could handle it for a while. As a plus, I did get a lot of time to study when I started back to school. Except for property tax seasons, we weren't that busy. But when property taxes came due, I worked my butt off taking payments and posting. We had two part-time people come in to help during that time, and even Demon Delores was forced to pitch in.

Besides me and Delores and the two part-time people, Mr. Jethro oversaw the two assessors in their office next door. Delores and I didn't have much to do with them.

Neither did Mr. Jethro. "Let 'em do what they gotta do," was his mantra regarding the assessors. "We don't appraise property in this office. All we do is collect taxes."

The public didn't see it like that, of course. They complained mightily to us when their property values went up by a third or a half, or occasionally even doubled. Most people were smart enough to understand that a higher assessment meant their taxes might shoot up accordingly, so they wanted their homes valued as low as possible.

Unfortunately, due to the influx of Atlantans and northerners snapping up second or retirement homes in our mountains, land prices had shot up out of sight. Even the economic downturn hadn't brought prices back to what they'd been ten years earlier. That meant the assessors had to adjust values up, or open the door for the state to come in and do it for us. If the state fined Ocosawnee County for failing to turn in an accurate digest, everyone knew who'd eat the cost.

Us Ocosawnee taxpayers, that's who.

So when people fussed about their high assessments, Mr. Jethro's stock answer was that he had no influence over appraisals, since the assessors answered only to the board of assessors. Most of the irate property owners went away angry with the board and not us, even though Mr. Jethro was technically in charge of the assessors and on occasion had been known to make them back down when he thought they were wrong.

Anyway, I worked there for three years, going to school at night and learning how to sell tags and collect property taxes and sales tax on cars during the day. I even learned how to do several insignificant jobs with lots of paperwork that had nothing to do with taxes. Liquor license issuance, dynamite permits, you name it. Whenever nobody else in the county wanted to do something, it got foisted off on us.

So when Mr. Jethro died, things were going along about like I expected. I'd learned about auto titles and property digests and mobile home decals, and I was through my third year of college, starting on my fourth. I even had a boyfriend of sorts, or at least somebody to run around with: a deputy sheriff I'd known since elementary school.

Looking back, despite Demon Delores, I didn't have a bad life until the unthinkable happened.

Well, not literally unthinkable. I mean, Mr. Jethro was already over eighty, wasn't he? At his age, dying wasn't out of the question. But though he said more than once he intended to die in office, no one took him seriously. Everyone figured he'd give up the job eventually and retire.

He certainly wasn't supposed to go like he did, with somebody bopping him over the head with a lead pipe he kept in the office for his personal protection. As far as I knew, despite the number of angry customers we had, the pipe had never once been used till somebody hit Mr. Jethro with it.

Maybe if he hadn't kept the pipe so handy, he wouldn't have got killed.

When the sheriff finished with us and sent us home, it was nearly one o'clock before I pulled into my driveway. In the kitchen, after feeding the vociferous cat, I made a peanut butter and banana sandwich to nibble on as I hit the books. I wasn't doing well in my business statistics class, and the professor had scheduled a test that night. If I didn't make a B on the exam, I needed to drop out before it got too late and a WF went on my record.

I could hardly study because of all the phone calls from people who'd heard about Mr. Jethro. After wasting more than an hour answering nosy questioners, I turned my cell off and let the machine pick up the land line.

Concentration eluded me though. Images of poor Mr. Jethro's bloodied white hair interfered with seeing the words. Finally, about five, I gave up and, after cleaning the litter box of the still whiny cat, microwaved leftover surprise casserole (surprise because Momma wouldn't tell us what was in it). This time I didn't find any strange green things or stringy stuff in it, so I ate and left.

The college was twenty miles away in the next county, and my class started at six. Professor Random was always prompt, and I did not want to be late.

When I parked in front of the building where my class met, Ethan Parters was waiting to pounce. One of Duke Duval's deputies, people assumed he was my boyfriend because we went around together. We didn't have much choice, since we were two of the few unmarried people our age left in town.

Ethan attended college at night, too, but he was in the criminal justice program while I took business courses. When we had time, we went bowling or saw a movie. Mostly we hung out and griped about our dead-end jobs with the county or the unreasonable college professors who knew we had full-time jobs but still assigned too much homework.

Content with the status quo, both of us avoided a more serious step like the plague, despite his momma and mine trying to prod matters along. As it was, our relationship was pretty much platonic. This was partly because of Ethan's changing shift patterns, but mostly because we both lived at home.

Ethan wouldn't dream of moving into a place of his own because he had too good a thing going. His momma didn't go out to work, so she washed and ironed his clothes, shined his boots mirror bright, and made him hot meals every day.

My momma, on the other hand, was a nurse at the hospital with irregular hours. My dad and I pretty much fended for ourselves, which meant I washed my own clothes: I found out young not to throw white things in with red cotton underwear or blue jeans. Daddy and I also ate a lot of fast food, which explained my taste for hamburgers and fries and pizza despite Momma's oft-voiced disapprovals.

Getting back to Ethan, I was surprised to see him at this parking lot since the criminal law class he took on Thursdays met on the other side of campus. Sometimes we got together after class and went to eat, but we hadn't made plans for tonight because I didn't know how long my test would take.

From Ethan's eager face, he had heard about Mr. Jethro.

I blew past his ambush. "I don't have time to talk about it. Yeah, I found Mr. Jethro, and it was awful but I'm okay and I can't talk to you now."

His muscular form trotted along right behind me. "But you must have some theories on why Mr. Jethro was in the office."

"Well, I don't. Delores says he left when she did about one o'clock yesterday."

"Uh-huh. He did. Then he took a woman to church last night. I was with the sheriff when he questioned her."

I stopped abruptly.

Ethan shot past me and had to back up. A whiff of overly sweet aftershave drifted by.

As usual, thanks to his mother, his khaki pants were perfectly pressed, as was the blue oxford shirt beneath his deputy's windbreaker. He'd recently got some sun that made his freckles pop out. His buzz cut was fresh, too, but he still looked like Huckleberry Finn. "So Miss Jeanie did go to church with Mr. Jethro?"

"Yep." Ethan's eyes sparkled. Crime of any sort always revved him up, and this was a biggie. We seldom had murders around here, and when we did they were usually committed by jealous spouses or bar habitués after a night of hard drinking. Once some years back a man ran over another man trying to steal his car. Ran over him, backed up over him, and ran over him again.

Not many crimes like that in the county, though.

I cleared my throat. "I guess Mr. Jethro was alive when he left Miss Jeanie."

"Yep," Ethan said again. "He dropped her off at her house after church and went home. One of his granddaughters saw his car going up his driveway about a half hour after church let out. He lives—lived I should say—alone, but four of his kids built homes right around him."

"I know that," I snapped while digesting Ethan's words. "So he came home after church and then went back to the office. What for?"

"That's what we don't understand." Ethan forgot his new buzz cut and tried to run his fingers through nonexistent locks. "You don't have any ideas? Maybe he left something and had to

30

go back for it. Maybe he remembered the coffeepot was still on. Maybe he was supposed to meet someone. Maybe—"

"Meet someone that late?" I thought about it. "I guess somebody could have needed a paid tax bill to get somebody out of jail."

People often used their homes as bail bond collateral when they or loved ones got arrested for DUI or similar infractions.

"He's gone into the office for that before." Further thought made me shake my head. "But usually he calls—called—Delores or me to meet him and print the tax bill out. Mr. Jethro can't—couldn't—work the printer. He barely knew how to work the computer. He could look up taxpayer names or parcel numbers, but Delores or I had to make sure the screen was on the right menu before he could even do that."

"Maybe he forgot his glasses."

"No way. He couldn't see to drive without them." I looked at my watch. "Uh-oh. I've got to go. I'm late."

"Well, think about it," Ethan called as I strode off. "You know, Corrie, the person who finds the body is always a suspect, so you got a good reason to figure out why Mr. Jethro went back last night."

"What?" I stopped in my tracks. "I'm a suspect?"

"Sure. You and Delores both. That's procedure." He sounded awfully perky for someone giving bad news to a friend.

"God help me." I lifted my eyes to the sky. "That's all I need."

"Listen, I'll see you after class and we'll talk some more."

I started walking. Fast. "Don't wait on me. I've got a test, remember? May take a while. Like all night." I waved over my shoulder and rushed inside.

Obviously, Ethan saw himself personally solving the murder. He was teasing me about being a suspect. I was sure he was teasing. Still, I couldn't help but speculate on what made Mr.

Jethro return to the office last night.

My abstraction with Mr. Jethro's murder, that kept me from my afternoon studies, caught up with me in class.

The professor covered the whiteboard from end to end with problems.

I had no idea how to figure them. One had to do with ships, and Dr. Random, well known for his spelling typos, put down a T instead of a P. There were several grins but few snickers since older people comprised most of the night class.

I, along with everyone else, stared, mesmerized by the board where what should have been "boatyard of ships" loomed prominently as "boatyard of shits."

Dr. Random, busy scribbling, wore a cotton-blend business shirt without a tie. It had been left too long in the dryer and sported a big diagonal crease across the back. Unlike Ethan, he obviously had no mother to pamper him.

Ever since I got put in his class, I'd wondered about his marital status because he was attractive in that bumbling kind of way Jimmy Stewart had in *Harvey*. Seeing that wrinkled shirt made me pretty sure he was single, since a wife would have advised him not to wear it before throwing it back in the dryer for a few minutes.

I waited for someone to tell the poor guy what he'd written on the board but no one did.

Finally, he finished and turned. He really was cute, with spaniel eyes and a lock of hair that kept falling over one eye. "Okay," he said in his Vermont accent. "This shouldn't take long. You can be out in an hour."

Nobody said anything about his T. We kept looking at him.

He must have noticed because his cheerful face clouded. "Is everything all right?" He checked the board and spotted his mistake. "Arghh!"

His neck turned red as he snatched up an eraser and rubbed out the T.

Which he immediately put back.

"Boatyard of ships, I meant to write," he said, turning to address us. "Sorry. Hope nobody was offended."

Nobody set to work. He saw some of us grin so he turned back and gasped again. After repeating the erasure and getting even brighter red, he finally got a P where it belonged.

This time when he turned, he still looked anxious. Only when everyone bent over their desks did he visibly relax.

I started to work grimly. I'd be lucky to get a passing grade, much less the B I needed.

When I did what I could and turned my test in, Dr. Random's complexion was back to normal. I got up the courage to give him a toothy grin that briefly elicited a startled return smile, but then he quickly pretended to be absorbed in reading papers.

I sighed inwardly. His shyness and my natural reticence dampened prospects for any kind of flirtation.

On my way out, I decided to withdraw from statistics and take the course again next semester. Good thing Ethan was still in class, since my depression guaranteed I'd be poor company.

At this rate, I'd be stuck in the tax office for life.

I groaned at the prospect. A couple coming toward me heard and abruptly moved to the far side of the corridor. Guess my sour expression scared them.

CHAPTER 3

Finding Mr. Jethro dead that morning and flunking a test that night, which meant half the semester was shot—I was doing okay in my business accounting class—left me pretty down in the dumps. The deserted roadways allowed me time to think of ways to cheer myself up.

By the time I drove over the high lake bridge—where my former fiancé had become a three-county legend by jumping off it when he was seventeen; his recklessness should have warned me not to get involved with him—that marked the Ocosawnee County line and reached the abandoned railroad overpass half a mile from home, I had a plan. I detoured onto a side road that came out at the busy state highway where the brightly lit local grocery store awaited my patronage.

A half-gallon of Cold Churn Dash Chocolate Covered Cherry ice cream would do wonders for depression.

When a half hour later I reached my parents' modest two-story frame built in the sixties and renovated ten years ago, I almost zipped right past.

This had to be the wrong place. A crowd of strange cars took up half the yard and part of the street. There was barely room to turn into the driveway.

Ever since I'd crashed through the garage door and into the utility room several years back, my Hyundai had been relegated to a little shed on the side that Daddy built specially for it. I negotiated through the unfamiliar cars to my designated parking spot, wondering what the heck what was going on.

At the back door, Daddy's sturdy form blocked the way. "What are you doing home so early? It's not eight o'clock."

I pushed him aside so I could get into the kitchen. "We had a test." No need to tell him I'd flunked it. "The teacher let us go when we finished, and it didn't take me long."

Because I didn't know how to work the problems. Needless to say, I left that part unsaid, too. I put my ice cream in the refrigerator freezer. "Why? You entertaining some of your girlfriends while Momma's out slaving for a dollar?"

He frowned, biting his lip. "Listen, chickadee, I got some people I'm talking to in the living room. Why don't you go over to Ethan's or something?"

"Ethan's?" I swiveled my head. "Are you out of your mind? His mother makes us play chickenfoot dominoes every time I go over there. And she doesn't like to lose. Anyway, he's still at school. Why don't I hide up in my room till your company leaves? I've had a bad day."

Daddy's face softened. He patted my shoulder. "I know, chick. I heard all about you finding Mr. Jethro. I sure am sorry you had to be involved."

"Yeah. Me, too." Not wanting to think about Mr. Jethro's head, I brushed off his consoling hand and headed for the hall. "I gotta pee."

Then I froze.

In the living room open to the hall, all three county commissioners, the county manager, and Judge Hartley turned their faces toward me. The commissioners had been lounging on our new red flowered couch, but as a man, they rose to their feet so that all I saw in the mirror over the sofa were their backs. Their shoulders touched to form a wall of golf shirts. Forest green golf shirts with a pocket emblem of blue sky, black mountain, and red sunset, the county's official tacky logo.

Simultaneous to their rising, the county manager got up from his chair in his own forest green county shirt. Judge Hartley, on the matching flowered loveseat, as befitting his rank, took his time and stood up last.

He had on a yellow golf shirt with an embroidered alligator.

The room tilted a little.

Had they all heard me say I had to pee?

I frequently saw them at work, since the commissioners, like the judge and county manager, had offices in the courthouse, but I didn't know them other than to say hey to in passing. And there they were, all the bigwigs who ran the county. In our living room.

Black spots swirled everywhere. Ethan's warning about me being a suspect in Mr. Jethro's murder came back.

"Am I being arrested?" My voice came from faraway.

Sounds silly, but remember, I had found my boss bludgeoned to death that morning. I had no clue as to what was going on. I mean, hey, I was only twenty-three!

"Br-har har har har har!" The judge brayed as if I'd said something funny. With gray sideburns and mustache and a serious mien, he would have been imposing had he been taller than five foot four. I knew exactly how tall he was because as a tag clerk, I'd had occasion to eyeball his driver's license.

The other men—our county is so far behind the times that it's never had a woman commissioner in its entire history—guffawed along with the judge.

They all stopped abruptly when the judge did. He said, "No, young lady, you are most certainly not being arrested."

My heartbeat slowed to normal.

Daddy, right behind me, put a hand on my shoulder. "Corrie, we'll talk after our visitors leave."

I could tell he was trying to act normal but was excited as all get-out.

What was he up to? No, what were *they* up to?

I drew the only logical conclusion.

Next year was an election year, and gossip said the clerk of court planned to retire. Sam Blanken, the county commissioner who worked with Daddy at the electric cooperative and who'd got me my job with Mr. Jethro, was pestering Daddy to run. This gathering had to be a political powwow.

Nothing to do with me or Mr. Jethro's death. I slumped in relief.

"Now, sugar, don't you bother showing up at the tax office tomorrow morning," said Dick Beaufort, the oily commissioner who built cabins for all the crazy Atlanta people who wanted second homes hanging off the side of a mountain. His smile, probably meant to reassure me, looked more like a leer.

Tiny Garelle, a wizened little man with a huge handlebar mustache who owned the Skyhigh Star Mountain City shopping center outside town, agreed. "That's right. The sheriff says it'll take a day or more to process the crime scene, so the tax office will have to stay closed at least till Monday."

Sam Blanken, with his belly hiding his belt and his bald head perspiring, wouldn't be outtalked by anyone. Especially his fellow commissioners. He quickly rasped out his two cents' worth. "We've had Sheila post some signs letting people know the tax office'll be closed indefinitely." Coming over, he put an arm around my shoulder. "You stay home and rest up, hon. You've had a bad shock."

The county manager didn't say a word but bobbed his head up and down in agreement. All the bobbing made his prominent Adam's apple more noticeable.

"Okay." Sounded good to me. I didn't argue as I slid out from Sam's grasp. The county couldn't dock my pay if the commissioners were the ones telling me to not to go in to work.

"That's all set then." Daddy exchanged glances with Judge

Hartley. "You trot along upstairs, chick, and let us finish up here."

Like an idiot, I went. If I'd had any idea why those men were gathered in my house, I'd have got back in my car and left. I swear I would've.

About half an hour later, when engines cranked up outside my window, I deemed it safe to go downstairs and dish up some ice cream.

"Sure your friends are all gone?" I asked Daddy as he closed the front door.

He didn't notice my sarcasm. "The county has a problem." He'd put on his real solemn face, like when someone he knew died. "With Mr. Jethro dead, we don't have a tax commissioner. The commissioners got to pick one quick so they can get the digest in to the state on time. They want to appoint somebody right away."

Silly me, I still had no idea.

I went on to the kitchen, oblivious. "I bet they *are* in a tizzy. We can't collect taxes till the digest is approved."

The tax digest lists every piece of property in the county, including any acreage that's been divided into separate parcels during the past year, and what it's worth according to the latest appraisal. Each year, the tax commissioner submits it to the state.

Only when the state approves our digest can we calculate tax bills and send them out. Only when tax bills go out, and we start collecting and disbursing the money, can the schools and county and state receive their portion of taxes. The money we pull in for the state is insignificant, but our collections comprise a good part of the school and county budgets.

I chortled, thinking of the county's dilemma. "Guess they do need someone in a hurry if they plan to get their money. They thinking about Delores?" Without waiting for an answer, I headed for the fridge.

Wouldn't make any difference to me. Demon Delores queened it over the office like she was the tax commissioner anyway.

"Delores? Lord ha' mercy, no." Daddy followed me. "Nobody likes her, including the commissioners. She rubs everybody the wrong way."

I opened the freezer. "One of the assessors? Fred Bauers, maybe? He's the logical choice since he's the senior assessor." Fred was on the pedantic side. He wasn't aggressive, but neither was he obnoxious. And he had stood up to Billy Lee Woodhallen. Tried to, anyway. I could work for him.

"Fred is Commissioner Beaufort's son-in-law. And Calvin Dredger," he said as I opened my mouth to suggest the other assessor, "is Commissioner Garelle's first cousin. So both of them are out. The job pays real good, you see. It'd hack off the other commissioners no end if one of them got a relative put in such a plum appointment."

That's when the first suspicion hit me. I pulled my head out of the freezer and fixed a stare on my daddy. "Exactly why were all those people talking to you about this?"

My daddy tried not to beam. "They want to appoint you tax commissioner."

I started to hyperventilate. My appetite fled. I didn't even rail about the fact the commissioners had talked to Daddy behind my back when they should have approached me directly. "I don't want to be tax commissioner."

Daddy put his hand out to soothe me. "Now, chickadee, let's think about this."

I threw the freezer door shut.

Breathe slowly, breathe slowly. "They're crazy. I'll not do it. They can't make me. I wouldn't be a tax commissioner if they paid me a million dollars."

Thoughts of people like Billy Lee Woodhallen and the other weirdoes Mr. Jethro had to deal with in the office—*I'd* have to deal with in the office if I got saddled with the job—swarmed through my mind.

I shuddered like slimy things were crawling all over me.

Breathe, I told myself again. *Breathe. In. Out. In. Out.*

Daddy paid no attention to my shortage of oxygen. "Chick, let's at least discuss it."

I shook my head. "No. No way. Forget it."

I tried to leave. My daddy blocked the way. "You know all about how the office operates."

"So does Delores." I moved to my left; he moved to his right.

"Delores!" He gave a dismissive motion. "She's flat-out crazy, chick. She can't get along with anybody."

"And I'd be flat-out crazy to take the job." I moved right; he moved with me.

All the time of the standoff, he argued, with me shaking my head no and him talking real fast. "Your salary would double, maybe triple. You wouldn't have to be in the office all the time. You could come and go like Mr. Jethro always did."

I stepped to my left.

Daddy mirrored my move. "Your state retirement would be a lot more. You wouldn't have to stay but seven more years and you'd be vested. And the county would put more money into your four-oh-one-kay 'cause they'll match what you put in and you'd make more to put in. Think about it, Corrie. This is a big opportunity for you. It's a cushy job. Real cushy."

"No, no, no! I don't want it! I won't do it!" Ice cream forgotten, I feinted to the right, got around him on the left, and scooted toward the stairs.

Daddy followed me. I couldn't make him shut up.

"But chickadee, you—"

"No! You're out of your mind if you think you can talk me

into being tax commissioner!" I ran up to my room and slammed the door. It took me twenty minutes to calm down.

When Momma came in from her shift at the hospital, she got as excited as I'd ever seen her, which is saying a lot.

My mother has no problems speaking her mind. Some people say I'm just like her, which is the dumbest thing I've ever heard. She's blue-eyed, blond, bubbly, and never meets a stranger.

I, on the other hand, take after my father's side: tallish with nondescript brown hair and eyes. And I don't talk to anybody I don't know.

My mother and I are total opposites.

Propped up in bed with my cat Bill sleeping under my arm, reading a Dorothea Benton Frank novel from the sack my older sister had brought us on her last visit, I could hear Momma squealing downstairs, followed by quick steps pounding upstairs. She practically danced down the hall.

Crud. My father had told her about the county bigwigs wanting me to be tax commissioner. Leaning toward feminism, she's preached for years how much better off the county would be if we would vote some women into office.

Sure enough, she ignored my closed door and burst into my room, a little bouncing ball of pure energy. "What do you mean you won't do it?"

Bill, shocked out of slumber, yowled as if being assaulted and hightailed it into the bathroom to cower in the bathtub.

"Corralie Susanne Caters, you'd be plumb stupid to turn this offer down!" Momma's hands flailed. Still in her scrubs, she broke into a shimmy dance. "With the extra money, you could finish paying off what you owe us for the new kitchen and the garage in no time, not to mention the post at the Tastee Totem Burger you knocked down last September and the Hendleys' fence you ran through this spring. And heaven knows what else you'll do in the future that's going to take a bunch of money to fix."

She stopped to take a breath.

"Most of it wasn't my fault." We'd gone over this so often that the defensive words came out by rote. "I was sick when I left that bacon grease on. And the reason I ran into the garage wall was that my brakes gave out. I admit I didn't see the post at the Tastee Totem when I backed up, but I would never have knocked down Mr. Hendley's fence if that cow hadn't got loose and charged straight across the road at my car."

Daddy had followed Momma and peered over her shoulder. "Well, I got to say that since you and Bodie broke up, you've had an awful lot of accidents. No telling how many more you'll have before it's over." For some reason, Daddy continued to like Bodie Fairhurst, even after he'd jilted me in front of two hundred people. Most of them local.

Mention of Bodie was the last straw. "Don't you talk about *that man* to me. He's got nothing to do with this."

Momma ignored talk of my former fiancé and started on her favorite topic. "You know what? If you take this job, you'll be the only woman who's ever held any kind of management position with the county."

"Momma, they didn't even have the courtesy to ask me if I wanted the job. They asked Daddy. Like he can make up my mind for me! Why would I want to take anything those kinds of people have to offer?"

"Exactly!" She jabbed her finger at me. "Anybody would think we're still living in the nineteenth century, the way the good old boys run our local government. And the city's just as bad. We've never had a woman commissioner, never had a woman mayor, never had a woman county manager, never had a woman in charge of anything. They wouldn't even hire Lavinia Pickardy's granddaughter for county attorney."

My father's eyes popped. "Well, I can see why. That girl's strange. She failed her driving test five times. The driving part, not the written. If I'm not mistaken, she crashed into a brick wall on one try, when the tester told her to turn right and she did, without waiting for a road. I believe she was graduated from college before she finally found somebody who'd pass her."

Momma ignored his reminiscences and shook her finger at me. "They didn't hire her even though she was well qualified, far better qualified than that doofus they finally put in. And if you were tax commissioner," she added craftily, "you'd be over Delores Kineely. Maybe you could do something about her attitude."

That did give me pause. I could crack the whip over Demon Delores.

Reality set in. Delores would make my life a living hell if I took the job. I shook my head. "Don't you talk any more about me being tax commissioner. I won't do it. Close the door behind you."

With a pointed flourish, I opened my book and went back to its lavishly described beachside scenery.

So there.

The next morning Bill woke me up. My twelve-year-old cat looks and acts like his comic strip namesake. Scraggly, with tufts of fur sticking out in all directions, he can unerringly throw out a hairball at the wrong moment.

His hacking this morning was beside my pillow, right under my nose to be exact. Groggily realizing the danger, I put him on the light blanket I kept at the foot of my bed. Bitter experience had taught me the blanket could be thrown into the washer, but cat barf on sheets meant the whole bed had to be changed.

Bill gave one huge last heave and got off the bed, through

with his business. The clock said seven o'clock. Time to get up. Then I remembered what the commissioners had said last night. The office would be closed. No work today.

Checking the foot of the bed, I saw the hairball well over on the other side. It could wait till I got up. I rolled over and closed my eyes, trying not to think of Mr. Jethro and the reason I didn't have to go to work.

My room is the biggest bedroom upstairs and has its own bath. I inherited it when my last brother left home. But it's on the front of the house so I hear whatever traffic comes through our dead-end street. As I began to nod off into peaceful fuzzy realms where I lay on a white sand beach with a cool drink in my hand surrounded by several surfer hotties waiting to give me anything I craved including a neck massage that felt heavenly, a familiar sound broke through my dreams.

It took a few minutes, drowsing on the island of Eden as I was, to figure out where I'd heard that engine before.

My eyes opened. Wide.

Bill slept sideways across my neck, gently kneading me with his claws mostly pulled in. He went flying as I flipped over onto my back. I ignored his indignant yowl.

When Bodie Fairhurst used to pick me up, his motorcycle made noises like those jerking me awake. It couldn't be Bodie, though. He had gone to work in Atlanta after jilting me and didn't come around my neighborhood whenever he visited his parents.

He didn't dare. After what had gone down between us, he was wise to stay far, far away.

"No way that can be Bodie out there." I lay in bed reassuring myself of that fact for several minutes before giving in to curiosity and dragging myself over to peep though the plantation blinds. There, sitting bold as brass by our driveway where he always parked, was Bodie's black Harley ride.

I didn't believe my eyes. "Ooh, that man! That sorry son of a gun! What gall!"

I was so angry that for a moment all I could do was jump up and down.

Bill prudently removed himself to a corner chair.

Grabbing my old pink chenille housecoat that was once white till I'd washed it with red boxers, I rushed downstairs barefoot without makeup and with hair flying in my face. Male bonding-type laughter steered me in the direction if the kitchen.

Sure enough, when I flung myself through the doorway, Bodie Fairhurst sat at the round oak table like he belonged there, reaching out for the cup of steaming coffee Daddy offered. Both men wore big smiles, as lovey-dovey as if they were at a church revival meeting.

Daddy was dressed in his work uniform, navy electric co-operative shirt with navy slacks. Bodie wore a NASCAR t-shirt and jeans, pale blue and frayed from washing. A dark windbreaker hung on his chair back. Reared back with his legs stretched out, he was long and lean and a lot better looking than I remembered.

"You!" I said with all the hate, loathing, and disgust I could summon. "What the hell are you doing here, you lowlife pond scum?"

My daddy's eyes and mouth rounded. He bristled. "You watch your language, miss. Your mother hears you talking like that, she'll throw you out of the house for sure. And this time I'll let her."

"I don't care." I turned on him. "What do you think you're doing, giving that scuzzball coffee? What next? You gonna cook him breakfast?" I gestured toward Bodie. "If you attended to your fatherly duties, you'd run him off with your shotgun after what he did to me."

Daddy sighed. "Corrie, play nice, can't you? This ain't the

time to be rehashing all that old stuff."

Bodie sat there with the same unconcerned air I remembered, looking far too appealing for the no-good dog he was. Laughter flickered in the back of his eyes before he lowered them to the scarlet place mat.

"As I recall," he drawled to his coffee cup, "you were the one who picked the argument at the altar. In fact, it was you getting all hot under the collar that scared Preacher Dempsey so much he stepped back and fell over the baptismal font rail."

He blew on his steaming cup before looking up. "I never heard. Did he get over his broken leg?"

I shifted my anger from Daddy to him. "It wasn't my fault the man was so clumsy. If you hadn't—Oh, I'm not getting sidetracked." I shook my finger at him. "You get out of my house right now, you, you no-good sonofa—"

My daddy gasped and hopped over to clamp a hand over my mouth. Then he caught my arm and shook it hard. "You listen here, miss. That all happened three years ago. Water under the bridge. Bodie's here because he heard some inside information about that offer the commissioners made you. He wants to pass it on. He's trying to be helpful."

"Helpful! He could've been a lot more helpful if he'd never come up to me at that American Legion dance and asked me to go out for ice cream with him."

"Corrie, if you can't be polite, then go back to bed." Daddy took note of my appearance for the first time. "Good grief. You look like something Bill dragged in. Go comb your hair. It's sticking out like a stump full of granddaddy spiders. And wash your face and put on some clothes."

I clenched my fists to keep fingers from raking through my hair and said through gritted teeth, "You're not having a tea party here."

"No, we're not. But this is my house, too, and I invited Bodie in because I want to hear what he has to say. You don't want to hear it, fine." Daddy picked up the bacon tongs and waved them at me. "Go back to bed, if all you can do is pitch temper tantrums."

"Oooh!" I started to stomp out but reconsidered. Why should I be sent packing when Bodie Fairhurst was the one who had no right to be here? I wheeled at the door. "All right, you mangy cur, say what you've got to say quick and get out."

Bodie, calmly sipping coffee throughout the exchange with my father, set his cup down. "All right." He took a deep breath and met my gaze squarely. "I heard the commissioners want you to take Mr. Jethro's place." He showed no trace of his earlier amusement. "It may not be safe, Corrie. I don't think you should take the job."

"Is that so?" I slapped my hands on my hips. What should have been a scornful gesture went awry when my housecoat fell open. I had to grab the lapels and pull them together to cover my boobs hanging out of my brother's old U undershirt I slept in.

Bodie managed to get an eyeful before I covered myself, but except for a little tic at the corner of his mouth, he was smart enough to pretend he didn't notice.

I tightened the belt and tied it before trying another tactic. "So you don't think I should take the job?" I asked sweetly. "Remind me again, Mr. Fairhurst. What right do you have to tell me anything?"

I sniffed the air and smelled bacon sizzling. Six long strips lay browning in the frying pan. Alongside grits simmering in the pot with a big chunk of butter melting in the middle. What's more, Daddy was busy breaking six eggs to scramble and had four slices of bread ready to toast. He actually intended cooking breakfast for the man who'd jilted me!

"What the—" I started, sweetness forgotten.

Bodie cut me off. "I don't have any rights." He loosed the little half-smile that had once made my knees weak.

It still did. I clutched at a chair back.

"I understand that perfectly well, Corrie," he went on, "but that doesn't mean I don't care about you. We didn't part on good terms, but I sure wouldn't want anything bad to happen to you. Talk around town is that whoever takes Mr. Jethro's place may be in danger."

"Is that so?" I thrust out my chin. "I've never been much concerned with gossip."

Bodie's words worried my father. He turned away from the bowl of eggs, whisk in hand. "Are you saying Billy Lee might go after Corrie? Why do you think that? What have you heard?"

Bodie's eyes flicked from me to my father. "Rumor is Billy Lee's sworn he'll keep his liens from getting sold to Arvin Smelting. Delores Kineely told Arvin the paperwork's been started, and if the next tax commissioner does his job like he's bound under oath to do, he'll transfer the liens to Arvin. If Billy Lee did kill Mr. Jethro, he'll be after whoever takes Mr. Jethro's place so his liens won't get sold before he can get up the money to pay his taxes."

Daddy and I digested this in silence. When nobody said anything, Bodie went on. "Now I know a few people who'd be willing to take on the job, and I think—"

A light switched on. "You're jealous. You don't want me to be tax commissioner. You think I'm too dumb to be anything but a tag clerk."

He raised both eyebrows. "I never said you were dumb."

"No?" I went over and leaned into his face, so close our noses almost touched. "What about the time when you said that dumb-blond joke reminded you of something I'd do? Huh? What about that?"

He sat up straight, his head barely missing my nose. "I don't know what you're talking about! I swear to God. Corrie, I'm trying to keep you from getting hurt. I know how you feel about me. Believe me, I'd never have come over here this morning if I weren't afraid something bad might happen to you."

He turned persuasive. "Look, just turn the job down. Let them appoint Don Griggery or Tommy Bullenon or somebody else who can take care of himself."

"Don? Tommy? Oh, I see. You want to slip one of your old buddies in. Hmmm. I wonder why." I snapped my fingers as he clenched his jaw and picked up his coffee. "Oh, I forgot. It's a cushy job. It pays real good. The clerks do all the work while the tax commissioner sits in the office and takes naps. Oh, yeah, I see now. This is a *man*'s job."

Bodie slapped his cup down so hard, coffee sloshed out, and pushed back his chair. When he stood, unfolding his full six foot, two inches, he looked as muscular and impressive as ever.

I remembered why I'd fallen in love with him but thrust the memory away. This man had deliberately jilted me. Left me, dressed up in satin dress and Grandmother's Brussels lace veil, standing like a fool among the flowers at the altar while he, after saying to the preacher, "I don't think we want to do this. Sorry to have called you out," strolled up the aisle by himself while two hundred people goggled.

I fumed.

Bodie scowled. "I don't care who they appoint, so long as it's somebody who can take care of himself. You think I have a buddy I'm trying to get in? Okay, what about this fellow you date? He's a deputy, isn't he? Why can't they appoint him?"

He glared at me.

I glared back. "Aha! You're still mad because Ethan Parters took me to my bridal shower when you wouldn't. Admit it."

"You knew all along I had those Georgia season tickets with my brother that weekend. And it was the Auburn game. There was no call for you to plan your silly shower for that very—"

"Ethan didn't mind missing a stupid football game to take me—"

"Ethan didn't have tickets to the Auburn—"

"Stop squabbling, both of you!" Daddy said sharply.

"But he's—"

"She's—"

"Nank!" Daddy bellowed. At the hush-up-or-else noise, Bodie and I had the good sense to fall silent. Didn't keep us from glowering at each other though.

"That's right, Corrie. Play nice." Daddy frowned. "You, too, Bodie. This isn't the time to revisit old grievances." He gnawed his bottom lip, then said to Bodie, "Do you really think she'll be in danger? If Duke's heard the gossip, he'll probably give her protection till Billy Lee's arrested, don't you guess?"

Bodie calmed himself, sitting back down in his chair and ignoring my taunts about Ethan. "The thing is, Mr. C., they may not arrest Billy Lee. Mr. Jethro was murdered sometime after he left Jean Ogletree's house about ten o'clock Wednesday night, and before eight Thursday morning when Corrie and Delores found him. Duke says Billy Lee's got an alibi for the whole time. He was at home with his wife all evening and all night. She says he didn't leave till after eight thirty Thursday morning when he went to a lower pasture to see about some repairs he was having done on a barn."

I sniffed. My father had forgotten the bacon and it was burning, but I didn't say a word. Served him right, catering to Bodie Fairhurst. "She's his wife. She's lying."

Bodie shrugged. "Maybe so. Duke can't arrest him as long as his alibi holds, though."

That gave me pause. Bodie had got on with the Georgia Bureau of Investigation in Atlanta shortly before he jilted me.

50

Working for the GBI might give him insight into things like alibis.

Then I shook off my doubts. The fact remained that Bodie, the only person against my taking the tax commissioner's job, was somebody whose opinion I didn't value in the slightest. Somebody I despised. Somebody I could never trust.

If he thought he could talk me into turning down a job everybody else wanted me to have, he was out of his mind.

I squared my shoulders and said with as much hauteur as I could muster, "I'm not afraid of Billy Lee Woodhallen. The commissioners offered me the job, and I'm taking it."

Bodie laughed in my face, and hauteur fled.

"I mean it!" I stomped my foot. "Darn it all, I'm going to be tax commissioner! You just watch me, Bodie Fairhurst!"

I stormed out through the bacon smoke curling in the kitchen, leaving Daddy looking worried and Bodie irritated.

Served him right. Served them both right.

Not till I got upstairs and cooled off did I realize what I'd done.

Darn Bodie Fairhurst. I didn't want Mr. Jethro's job. Lord knows I did not want the job. But it'd be hard to back down now.

Bill looked at me from the middle of the disheveled bed and threw up another hairball. This one, a big wet one, landed on the sheets.

CHAPTER 4

The necessity for an autopsy delayed Mr. Jethro's funeral, but the public's outraged demands for tags got to the powers that be. Delores called to tell me Sheriff Duval said we could open up Monday morning and I needed to show up for work.

The county manager had already notified me, but I didn't tell Delores that; she'd have been miffed that she wasn't the only one informed.

First thing I saw when I walked into the office was the three commissioners and Judge Hartley. I had vacillated back and forth all weekend, not wanting the job but not willing to let Bodie Fairhurst talk me into turning it down. I still wasn't sure what to do. Seeing them lined up waiting for the coffee to finish dripping—Delores had bestirred herself to put a pot on, surprise, surprise—made my knees shake.

They absentmindedly returned my reluctant greeting and fought for the finished pot.

Tiny Garelle, using his slight size to advantage, slid in and filled his cup first. Looking around, he pointed to the yellow tape across Mr. Jethro's office door. "Guess Jethro's office is still off limits."

"How 'bout the vault room?" Sam Blanken rasped, busy dumping several packets of sugar into his coffee. "It's big enough to hold us all."

After the judge and Dick Beaufort got their coffee, they herded me into the secure room where we stored our tag plates

52

and kept our fireproof safe.

A suspicious Demon Delores watched us go. She would have it in for me if I let myself be appointed tax commissioner. That was almost enough to make me not take the job, but the thought of Bodie thinking he could boss me around still had me hopping mad.

Judge Sutherhold Hartley, that silver-tongued devil, made it seem like the whole county was dependent on me.

After a rousing pep talk, he finished up. "You're the only one the commissioners can appoint that everyone will accept and trust. Think of the good of the county," he admonished when I stuttered a half-hearted dissent. "I mean it. All our citizens who live here are counting on you, Corrie. You're the only one who can do it."

I hemmed and hawed. "That's the problem. I don't know that I *can* do it. I've only been here three years. I don't even know what Mr. Jethro actually did." *Besides nap and read the paper,* the evil side of my mind suggested. Time for the truth. "I don't have enough experience, Judge Hartley. You need someone who knows more about the work."

Exasperation crossed the judge's noble features. "Don't let your modesty keep the best person from taking on the job. We've talked to the Georgia Department of Revenue. They'll be sending someone out as soon as they can to give you a crash course on how to run the office."

I dithered. "I don't know." I still had big reservations. Real big ones. "I'm kind of scared of Billy Lee Woodhallen," I blurted.

Judge Hartley threw back his head. "Br-har har har har har! No need to be. Sheriff Duval will see to Billy Lee. He's already on it." He patted my arm. "Yessirree, don't you worry about that old boy. You just take care of running the tax office and let Duke worry about Billy Lee."

"Do you really think I'm up to the job?"

He turned the full force of his personality on me. "Of course you are, Corrie. We all agreed you're perfect for it. Besides, it'll only be for a little while. The election's next year, and we can get somebody qualified then."

My back stiffened. Oh, they could, could they? I reckoned I was as qualified as the next person. Just because I wasn't a man . . .

I took a deep breath and, being a proper southern girl brought up to be pleasant and agreeable, smiled as I meekly accepted the position of tax commissioner.

That'll show Bodie Fairhurst he can't tell me what to do, I thought with no little satisfaction.

While I was busy with the judge and commissioners, Delores had opened up the office and started waiting on the line of customers. There were a lot since we'd been closed the past Thursday and Friday. She finished up with one as we filed out of the vault room, and turned around to see what was going on.

I admit I enjoyed watching her face change when the judge told her I was to be tax commissioner. That lasted about two seconds, till she hopped down from her stool and turned ugly.

"I've been here thirty-four years working with Mr. Jethro!" She put both hands on her hips and glowered at Judge Hartley and the commissioners. "I know everything there is to know about this office. I keep current on all the laws. I handle all the deposits and the disbursements and refunds. I balance the bank accounts. I fix the errors. I do more in this office than Mr. Jethro ever thought about doing. Now you're appointing this little flibbertigibbet to finish out his term instead of me?"

With her eyes narrowed and nostrils distended, she looked like an old bull that had once chased me out of his pasture.

Across the counter, the packed lobby of customers looked on with interest.

Their elected officials put themselves behind the judge's commanding figure.

I tried to get back there, too, but there wasn't room for all of us. He was too darned small.

I ended up to the right of Sam Blanken, unprotected when Delores's bony finger jabbed the middle of my chest. "She doesn't know the first thing about how this office runs. She'll be breaking the law inside a week and not even know it."

"It's only an interim appointment," Judge Hartley soothed. "Next year's an election year, Delores. Nothing to keep you from running then if you want the job."

The three commissioners slunk around me toward the door leading out front, but Delores didn't notice. She seethed at the judge. "You know doggone well the incumbent always has the best chance of winning. If she"—another jab of the pointy finger—"runs, nobody'll realize she's an incompetent little twit, just that she's the incumbent."

I had to defend myself. "I've been here three years, Delores. I do know a few things."

She made a rude sound. "Puhleeze!"

This did not bode well. Maybe I wouldn't take the job.

I was opening my mouth to say I'd changed my mind when the judge took me by the arm. "Come on upstairs, sugar," he said, pulling me past Delores and through the door leading to the front. "We'll get this all settled in a few minutes. Delores, you look after all these people, you hear? Can't have our constituents put out by everything that's happened, no matter how tragic it is."

Helpless, I let myself be towed in Judge Hartley's majestic wake.

"Excuse us." He elbowed his way past a stout man in overalls clutching a mobile home bill.

"Pardon me, ma'am." He pulled me around a matron in a business suit with new car paperwork.

"Excuse us, folks." He threaded us right through the public line slick as glass. "Delores'll be right with y'all," he called back over his shoulder as we headed for the elevator in the hall. "Sorry for the inconvenience."

Not only was that devil persuasive, he was also efficient. Turned out he had all the papers ready and waiting.

Upstairs in his office lined with legal books, he appointed me and swore me in that same morning with all the commissioners signing my appointment and their secretary as witness. He'd even arranged to have the county manager on hand to take the signed paperwork wherever it needed to go to get filed.

No ceremony, no parents and relatives beaming, no reporter from the local paper with a camera, no friends offering congratulations and support. The judge simply administered the oath while the county manager, the commissioners, and Sheila, their secretary, looked on. I signed, the commissioners signed, the judge signed, and Sheila signed. The deed was done.

My mother was mad as fire when she heard how they'd rushed up my appointment without the normal pomp, but my daddy took it in stride, telling her, "They needed to get it done right away, darling. They didn't have time to make a big hoop-ti-do of it."

Momma sulked. "If she'd been a man, they would have. I don't even have a picture of her with her hand on the Bible."

She griped every day for a week. Good thing none of the commissioners or Judge Hartley had to be hospitalized under her care. They might have died.

But that day, after the few attendees congratulated me and the commissioners got through patting themselves on the back for picking me and I was left alone to go back downstairs and face Delores, I realized I had outsmarted myself. I had let my anger with Bodie Fairhurst make me do something I never intended to do.

I was the tax commissioner.
I was doomed.

Chapter 5

When I returned to work from my swearing in, chaos reigned. We had been closed for two days and a weekend, so umpteen tag and mobile home tax customers spilled out into the outer hallway. Inside our small lobby, the pews Mr. Jethro had salvaged from the old Methodist church when it was torn down to make way for a new office building, were stuffed with more people.

Waiting patiently.

Uh-oh. Trouble. Only problems sat down and waited.

Sure enough, all the people seated wanted their tag late fees waived. Delores, still seething from my appointment, had informed them that she had no authority to waive penalties, and that they'd have to talk to the tax commissioner.

"These folks need to see you," she barked from her post at the counter. "And the phones been ringing so much I put them on night service till I can get time to answer them. I need help." She didn't turn around to look at me.

Help from where? I bit my tongue and smiled at the seated customers. Delores knew quite well she could have waived any fees for tags expiring on one of the days we'd been involuntarily closed. But that was Delores for you. Making everything as hard as possible.

Sliding in beside her at the counter, I opened my computer and beckoned to the first seated customer. "Come on up." The older man looked professional in his dark suit with the yellow power tie.

"Hello, young lady." He exuded confidence as he slapped down a pre-bill and a check already made out. "The only thing I need is a new decal for my tag plate. There was really no need for your clerk to make me wait for you."

My clerk.

Delores threw a knife-edged glance at him.

I hastily pulled his tag up in the computer. My smile faded. "Mr. Johnsfield, your birthday was two weeks ago. I hate it, but you're going to have to pay interest and penalties."

He donned a guileless face. "I was out of town till Thursday. Important business. My company's buying a company in California and I had to be available on site."

I looked at the check. "This amount is what you would have paid if you'd come in Monday before last. Late fees were due last Thursday, too."

He radiated innocence. "As I explained, I couldn't get my tag before then. I was out of town."

I outwaited him, never saying a word, never looking away, never typing on my computer.

He heaved an impatient sigh. "I'm an attorney. I had to be out there to go over all the paperwork before everyone signed off on it," he explained as if to a kindergartener. "My job was to make sure everything was legal."

Like waiving his late fees was legal?

Any attorney worth his salt wouldn't urge a tag clerk to break the law to save a few dollars. I gave him my sympathetic smile. "Yes, sir. I understand perfectly. I wish I could do something for you. But I can't."

His good humor vanished.

I continued to smile, never moving.

Once he saw I wouldn't budge, he wrote out a new check,

still fuming. "See if I vote for you come election time."

See if I care. "Next!"

After I got the people seated in the lobby taken care of, I helped Delores with the others. Mobile home taxes were due May first, which meant we were busier than normal and would be for the next few weeks. Only then would things slack off until the fall tax season began.

When we got down to two people in line, Delores put up her closed sign and went back to her desk in the back where she immersed herself in her computer.

She didn't tell me directly, but she did mutter something to empty air about the bank accounts not balancing. I suspected she was pretending to be busy with her accounting so she wouldn't have to work the counter or talk to me. She'd always hated working the counter. I guess now she hated talking to me, too.

Since she turned the phones back on and started answering them, I didn't ask for help with the walk-ins. After her little tantrum that morning, I was afraid to. I could see that until I hired another person, I'd have to keep doing my normal duties in addition to worrying about Mr. Jethro's. That meant dealing with the loopy tag buyers myself.

When Sheriff Duval and one of his deputies came in before lunch, things had slowed down. The sheriff motioned me to follow him to Mr. Jethro's office. "Got a minute?"

"Sure." I trusted Delores would bestir herself if a customer came in, but didn't say so. I was too intimidated to ask her anything outright.

The sheriff jerked the yellow tape down, and we stepped inside the room that still smelled like Mr. Jethro's cigars (that he continued to light up, even after smoking was forbidden in the courthouse) mingled with all the dusty old books and papers he'd left strewn around.

Mr. Jethro cleaned up once a year when the county held an open house for school kids in the spring before graduation. Being as this was April, it would be coming up soon. When it dawned on me I'd be the one to do the housekeeping this year, I groaned inwardly. I'd never get all his papers sorted.

Added to the mess was some kind of powder sprinkled all over everything. Fingerprint? I wondered if the cleaning service would take care of getting it up or if I'd have to. I tried to blow it off my desk.

The sheriff, in a matter-of-fact manner, dusted off the side chair with his bare hand. I followed his example with Mr. Jethro's upholstered tilt desk chair, using some tissues I had in my pants pocket.

"Didn't have a chance to ask about your dad the other day," Sheriff Duval began as he sat down.

In our part of the country, we usually preface business with polite inquiries regarding family and work.

He went on. "Hope he's doing all right."

"Dad's great, thanks." I tried to remember if the sheriff was still married to his last wife or not. He didn't wear a wedding ring, but that didn't mean anything.

As I sat down in Mr. Jethro's chair, I had to grip the desk to keep from rolling back.

Of the many deficiencies of the courthouse built in 1904, which included inefficient design, slow-draining bathroom sinks, running toilets, and rickety stairs, the one most noticeable to county workers was the heart of pine floors. They were darkened by age and no longer level, but sloping toward the inner walls. This defect was particularly obvious in Mr. Jethro's office.

Whenever a bond issue for a new courthouse made it onto the ballot, we employees crossed our fingers. So far the voters had shot down higher taxes for courthouse renovation eight times.

The sheriff unconsciously patted his foot. "Saw your mother at the hospital last night. She's proud as can be about your taking the tax commissioner's job. She's a real pistol." He grinned, remembering the encounter. My mother has that effect on people. "Says exactly what she thinks, doesn't she?"

"That she does." I grimly held onto the desk. Sheriff Duval might be divorced again by now, but I was pretty sure he had kids. I chose the safe path and didn't mention a wife. "How's your family?"

"The boys are fine. The youngest one's busy with ball and the oldest is a freshman at the University. The middle one's got a job bagging groceries. Paying for his own car."

Pleasantries over, he pulled his chair close to the desk and got down to business. He laid a square hand on Mr. Jethro's desk and tapped his signet ring on the scarred honey maple top. "I wanted you to be aware that Billy Lee Woodhallen claims he was at home when Mr. Jethro was killed, and his wife confirms it. We're checking their story, but looks like they may be telling the truth."

Ack! I couldn't breathe.

Bodie had been right about the alibi. "Then who killed Mr. Jethro?"

"Don't know. Just thought you ought to be aware it might not have been Billy Lee."

"It had to be him." I didn't want to call Billy Lee's wife a liar, but she was his wife, after all. Though I'd never met her, I could picture her: sloppy-fat and ignorant, with a whiny voice from yelling at Billy Lee and getting no response but Neanderthal grunts. Definitely under Billy Lee's thumb. He probably bullied her. Maybe even beat her. I repeated with more assurance, "It had to be Billy Lee."

The sheriff shrugged his shoulders.

"Nobody else would hurt Mr. Jethro," I argued. "Everybody

loved him. He was the nicest, sweetest—" Tears ambushed me as I remembered how Mr. Jethro patted my back when I aced a test. Or the way he rushed out to confront a particularly nasty customer who threw a pen at me. And his pride when he showed me pictures of his newest great-grandchild.

I sniffled and fumbled in my pocket. Luckily, I had another tissue tucked away.

Sheriff Duval sat there silently while I blew my nose and composed myself. "You may be right," he finally said, "but unless we break his alibi, we can't arrest Billy Lee. What worries me is that maybe whoever killed Mr. Jethro, whether it was Billy Lee or somebody else, didn't intend to murder Mr. Jethro, *per se.*"

I didn't understand. "Excuse me?"

He was patient. "It may be that someone intended to kill the tax commissioner."

Forgetting the sloping floor, I let go the desk and rolled back. My chair hit the wall before I could stop. Out of habit, it tried to tip back against the wall where Mr. Jethro had indulged in his catnaps. I nearly fell out.

I straightened myself and pushed the chair back up to the desk. "Mr. Jethro and the tax commissioner are—were—one and the same. If you kill one, you kill the other."

He cleared his throat. "Not now. Now you're the tax commissioner."

I still didn't comprehend. "But Mr. Jethro's already dead."

Then, what the sheriff was tiptoeing around to keep from spelling out, soaked in. I let go the desk and the chair rolled back and hit the wall again. Hard.

This time I did fall out.

Sheriff Duval's mouth dropped open. He got up to help.

I waved him off and picked myself up. "You're saying somebody may try to kill me?"

Heaven help me, Bodie had been telling the truth about everything. I collapsed into Mr. Jethro's chair.

"Not necessarily." Sheriff Duval sat back down. "But I do think at this point in the investigation we need to take that into consideration as a possibility. Now the commissioners think, and I agree, that you need protection. So I'm assigning a deputy to you. One of my people will hang around for the next few days till we make sure it was Mr. Jethro and not the tax commissioner somebody wants dead."

My hands shook. "Oooooh. This isn't good."

The sheriff gave me a John Wayne look of exasperation. "No, it isn't. But it's not necessarily that bad either. I brought James Cleuny with me. He'll stay here today and when his shift's done, I'll have another deputy for you, I'm not sure who yet. But somebody'll be with you at all times. Here and at your house. I don't want you to worry your pretty little head about a thing."

I barely noticed his condescension, that's how upset I was.

Don't worry. Easy for him to say. He wasn't the one Billy Lee would be gunning for. I felt dizzy, like the time I'd fainted in church. Black spots flickered before my eyes.

The sheriff noticed. "Hey, you're white as a sheet. Roll your chair up here and put your head down on the desk. I'll get you some water."

I was not only going to have to deal with rude people and Demon Delores. I was going to be murdered.

I cursed Daddy and Bodie Fairhurst.

Sam Blanken, the county commissioner who worked with my daddy, caught me when Sheriff Duval left.

Sam didn't waste time with polite patter. His belly bounced as he rasped, "You need a tag clerk to take your place out front, and I got somebody for you. Lucy Coffee, used to be Monrove.

64

She's real good with people. Right now, we got her at the landfill as the gopher, but she's not happy with all the driving around she's got to do. She's too good an employee to lose, so maybe we could switch her to you?"

Took me a moment to wrest my mind away from the fact that I was liable to be killed.

Sam was right. I did need help.

My oldest brother had dated Lucy when he was in college and I knew she was bubbly and good-tempered, but not extra bright. However . . .

What would Mr. Jethro do? "I'll think about it," I said.

Sam Blanken was the first of a tidal wave of drop-ins and phone calls.

Ten minutes after the commissioner left, one of my neighbors came by. He nudged his candidate for the vacant position into the office before him.

"She's a real hard worker." His enthusiasm bubbled over as he nodded toward the bucktoothed woman who looked at the floor and never said a word. "Little rough around the edges, but needs a job bad. Dependable, too, once she gets her car out of the garage and lines up somebody to sit with her mamma, who's bedridden and can't stay by herself."

"I'll think about it," I said.

Then came my mother's supervisor, my daddy's cousin on his father's side and another cousin on his mother's side. The next few hours brought in our assessor Calvin Dredger, the county manager's niece, a sister of Judge Hartley, our family doctor's nurse, two lawyers, a banker's secretary, one of Sheriff Duval's office clerks, and a bunch of other people I didn't know from Adam.

All of them had a candidate for my clerk's job.

I gave up trying to figure out who anybody knew or was related to, kept trotting out the stock reply. "I'll think about it."

Never in my life had I realized how many people coveted jobs with the county. Personnel hadn't advertised the opening yet, but it seemed like every unemployed and a lot of employed persons were sending emissaries to intercede for them.

"I can't believe this," I said to Demon Delores. "It's a tag clerk job, for pity's sake."

Delores didn't answer because she still wasn't talking to me.

About that time, Sherry Nuckles Lowman Bartovich, who's been my best friend since preschool, came in, oozing Coco Mademoiselle and swishing her little spandexed behind.

"Corrie!" she squealed and made for me.

I hugged her back. "I thought you and Caleb were in Panama City for two weeks."

She flapped a hand, made a moue. "He had a load of cars coming in so we had to cut our trip short. But what's all this I hear about Mr. Jethro getting killed and your getting his job?"

I filled her in as my stomach rumbled. I had forgotten to bring my lunch, and it was one o'clock. Catching her up on events, I ended, "So now I'm the tax commissioner."

She clapped her hands. "I can't believe it!"

"Me either."

She looked around. "Listen, I need to talk to you a minute."

"It's lunchtime and I'm starving. Why don't you come eat with me?"

"No, gal, I've already eaten. Since we had to leave the Redneck Riviera early, I went on in to the cleaners this morning and now I've got to get back." Sherry worked the counter for the dry cleaning and laundry two blocks over. "Let's talk back here. Won't take a sec."

She pulled me into the office, where she plopped down in the guest chair without noticing the powder remnants left after the sheriff's lick-and-promise cleaning. I didn't see fit to tell her she'd have it all over her. Her skirt was black, so maybe it wouldn't show.

She put both elbows on the desk to prop up her chin. Her perfect lips curled in a wide red smile.

Sherry wears her hair big and her sweaters tight. She's a free spirit who always looks like she expects something wonderful to happen any time. After five minutes of her sunny disposition, everyone perks up. I was no different, but after twenty years I knew her.

Sherry wanted something.

Sure enough: "You need a clerk and I'm available."

The nagging headache I'd nursed all day burst into full-fledged pain. I could see all kinds of problems. Sherry and Delores would never get along. Much as I loved her, Sherry was not detail oriented which, as a tag clerk, you had to be.

Get a title VIN wrong and hello! It took forever to get the ensuing tangle straightened out. Especially when the car owner was breathing fire down your neck every day while you wrangled with the state bureaucracy trying to convince them it was a real snafu and not the customer's fault.

On top of that, Sherry had recently remarried, and her new husband was a used car lot owner.

No need for tact with Sherry. "I can't hire you."

"Why not?" She didn't lose her expectant look.

"Think, Sherry. Caleb deals in automobiles. You'd be doing auto titles in here. Conflict of interest big-time."

She pouted. "Well, darn. You know how long I've been trying to get on with the county? Two years. They got a lot better benefits and hours than the dry cleaners. I thought sure you'd hire me."

I spread my hands wide. "Sorry."

She left resigned rather than angry, but I felt bad. I didn't like turning down all these people, especially my best friend, but my goodness! Everyone and his brother had someone they wanted me to hire, and I needed a warm body right away. I could see a lot of people were going to be mad no matter who got picked.

My first big decision as tax commissioner.

I took a deep breath, picked up the phone and called Sam Blanken. Naturally, I got his voicemail since all the commissioners were part-time. They seldom visited their offices, but they checked in occasionally for messages. Elected officials can't afford to ignore constituents for too long.

I waited for the beep and said, "I have a friend who wants to work for the county. I'll take Lucy if you'll get my friend hired in Lucy's place and if I can get Lucy immediately. Like tomorrow. Let me know."

There. Maybe I could help Sherry out and still get a tag clerk right away.

CHAPTER 6

After I left my message for Sam Blanken, I headed toward Joanie's Vittles in the next block. The place looked like a greasy spoon with its booths needing new upholstery and the tables needing leveling, but Joanie Stevensen was the best country cook in town. My stomach growled with anticipation: Monday was chicken-and-dressing day.

James Cleuny, the deputy assigned as my bodyguard, sauntered along. Fortyish and oft-divorced like so many in law enforcement, he had jowls and wore a morose expression like a sad basset hound. I suspected he drank.

Adept at turning the conversation to himself, he talked about his romantic difficulties as we faced each other over the red checkered tablecloth. "Can't stay married because of my profession." He unfolded the napkin around his fork when our food came. "Can't find a woman who'll put up with the crazy hours and worrying about me getting killed and all that stuff."

I happened to know from one of my brothers that he'd run around on all four of his wives, so I gave a sympathetic *um* wherever it was appropriate and dug into the homemade cranberry sauce.

This security stuff wasn't going to work out, not if I got stuck with deputies like James to guard me. I'd be too tempted to throttle them.

After lunch, we walked back toward the office, him still rattling on about how he desperately wanted to get married again but couldn't find anyone interested in taking him on.

Enough was enough. "Don't talk about it so much. Women don't like needy men." I had read that in a magazine somewhere, and it sounded like good advice. It shut him up for a few minutes, too.

As we reached the courthouse, ninety-year-old Lavinia Pickardy came mincing up on her three-inch heels. Lipsticked and powdered, she wore a spring-like lavender dress and a hat that was big, floppy, and fire-engine red. Two big purple hydrangeas dangled precariously off one side.

"Corrie!" she cried, wafting a rose scent toward us when she lifted her arm in greeting. "Just the person I was coming to see."

"Miss Lavinia, how are you?"

She caught me staring at her hat and preened. "My Red Hat club met today, dahlin'. I dug this out of a closet where I kept some things from when I was young. Do you like it?"

"Are those hydrangeas real?"

"From my early blooming bush, dahlin'. The one by the back trellis. Don't they give the hat some real pizzazz?"

I tore my eyes away. "Oh, they definitely add pizzazz. And they go so well with your dress. What can I help you with, Miss Lavinia?"

The corners of her cherry red mouth drooped. "My daughter says I need a lawyer to sell my car. Is that right?"

I laughed. "Oh, I don't think you have to go that far. Come inside the office and we'll talk about it."

Once in Mr. Jethro's—my!—office, Miss Lavinia commiserated about Mr. Jethro as I wiped the customer chair down with some damp paper towels. Then she settled herself. "My daughter Laurie—she lives in Macon, you know—is selling my old car for me down there to a friend of hers. But she called last night and says there's a problem, that I need to get her a lawyer."

"Get her a lawyer?" I sat down in Mr. Jethro's chair. "Did she say why she needed a lawyer?"

Miss Lavinia shook her head and the hydrangeas jiggled. "No, dahlin', Laurie didn't say much. She was in a hurry. Just that she needed an attorney and that I'd have to get her one. A . . ." Her forehead wrinkled as she tried to remember. "An attorney with clout."

Clout? Could Miss Lavinia be getting a little dotty? Daddy had said for years that she was too old to be driving. Letting go the desk, I promptly rolled back.

This darned old courthouse with its slanting floors. I hate it. Why can't they build us a new one?

I hauled the chair back up and clung to the desk's edge. "Why do you have to get him? Why can't your daughter find one in Macon? And why does he have to have clout?"

Miss Lavinia drew an exasperated breath. "I told you, Corrie," she said with exaggerated patience. "I don't know. That's the reason I'm here."

"I don't see why you'd need an attorney to start with. Not for selling a car. What kind of car is it?"

"It's my old car."

"Yes, but what kind? A Ford? Buick? Chevrolet?"

She *tsk*ed. "Now, Corrie, you know Mr. Pickardy always insisted we buy Cadillacs."

"So it's a Cadillac." Forgetting, I relaxed my grip and the chair rolled back. I scooted it up again, still mentally abusing those skinflint voters who didn't want to put out money to build a decent place for us to work.

Miss Lavinia nodded complacently. "A Cadillac. Seven years old. With five thousand miles on it. Excellent condition. I hated to replace it because I really like it, but Mr. Pickardy always said to keep cars at least five years but not over eight so I decided it was time to—"

"Yes. Well. Let's think about this." I tried to figure out what Miss Lavinia's daughter meant when she told her mother to get an attorney with clout. "Did your daughter say anything else? Like what she needed the attorney for?"

Miss Lavinia looked at me hopefully. "No. Laurie did say he had to be a Republican, though."

"A Republican," I repeated, clinging by my fingertips to the desk.

Miss Lavinia's emphatic nod sent the red hat bobbing and the hydrangeas wriggling. "Laurie said to make a special note. That he had to be a Republican."

Ah, a glimmer of light. "Could your daughter have said you need a notary public?"

"Yes!" She clapped her hands in delight. "That's exactly what she said, that I need a noted Republican attorney. Do you know one?"

I took a deep breath and let go the desk. My chair rolled back, but it didn't matter because I needed to stand up. "Okay. I think what your daughter was saying is that you need to get her a power of attorney—"

"Powerful attorney! That's it! That's it!"

"—because she'll need it to sign the title for you."

"You're so clever. I knew you'd know what she meant." Her mouth pursed before she confided, "I hate to say it, but Laurie isn't the smartest person when it comes to everyday living. I know she's a big wheel in that architectural firm and all, but when it comes to ordinary decisions, she doesn't have a lick of sense. You're so much better off than these people with book learning, Corrie, inheriting your daddy's common sense like you did."

My daddy's common sense? His common sense that got me in this whole mess where I was liable to be murdered?

I did not scream.

I may have even managed a tight smile.

Going out front to the computer, I found the car she was selling and filled out the power of attorney form. By then I was calm again.

"Okay, Miss Lavinia." I brandished the form at her. "What you need to do is sign here and get the document notarized. In fact, if you want to go ahead and sign it right now, I'll notarize it for you. Then you can mail it to your daughter."

She signed and I notarized. As she tottered out to the front on her high heels, she thanked me profusely. "You've been so good to me, Corrie, getting all this straightened out. You know what I'm going to do this afternoon? I'm going to bake y'all a big ol' batch of my lemon-lime bars. I'll come by in the morning when I go to my reading group and drop them off, so don't you bring any dessert for lunch tomorrow, you hear?"

"No, ma'am, you'd better believe I won't. Not if you're baking us your famous lemon-lime bars."

Bearing her paperwork triumphantly, she gave one last wave.

Powerful attorney indeed!

I turned grinning, to find Delores still sulled up. Ill-tempered old hag.

Maybe Lucy could start soon. I needed someone to laugh with at moments like this.

Lucy showed up Tuesday. She wasn't exactly pretty, but she was good-natured. And she exuded cheap sex appeal. I hemmed and hawed and finally told her the low-cut tank top and tight jeans she wore at the dump weren't suitable for the office. "I know we're casual, Lucy, but we still have to seem like we know what we're doing."

Lucy puffed up like an angry hen. "My husband likes me to dress like this." She looked down at her cleavage. "Are you saying people'll think I'm stupid because I've got on a tank top?"

"No, no. It's just easier to handle customers when you wear more . . . um, when you wear clothes that cover you up. The thing is, in tight jeans and little bitty tops, men'll enjoy the view while women'll think you're a slut. Neither one will listen to what you're telling them about their tags."

"You don't say."

I could tell she was miffed and trotted out some diplomacy. "Face it, you're just too sexy in those clothes to sell tags. You've got to tone it down."

Slightly mollified, she looked unconvinced but gave in with a shrug. "Okay. I'll look and see if I've got something else I can wear tomorrow."

"That's the spirit. Save your sexy stuff for parties or your husband."

Whew. Now to start her on tag renewals.

Miss Lavinia, true to her word, brought in a huge platter of her famous lemon-lime bars the middle of the morning. Lucy and I both ate one between customers. James Cleuny, back as my protector this morning, gobbled up two. Delores nibbled on one at her desk, still working on the bank accounts, she said, though I passed by once to get a University of Georgia tag plate out of the vault and saw she had a computer game up on the internet.

I didn't say anything. I was scared to, especially since she seemed to be thawing a bit. She went so far as to advise Lucy and me to put aside a lemon-lime bar for later. "To take home with you. If you don't hide you one now, you know good and well they'll be gone once the rest of the courthouse finds out Miss Lavinia brought us a batch."

We both took her advice, Lucy wrapping up two and me one. Lucy stashed hers away in what was formerly my counter drawer, while I laid mine back on what had been Mr. Jethro's desk that I had scrubbed inside and out but still felt funny using.

At lunch, Lucy and I, accompanied by James, went over to Joanie's Vittles. They were slower than usual that day, and we were gone an extra ten minutes. I stewed a bit, but it worked out okay because when we finally got back to work, Delores said, "Billy Lee Woodhallen came in asking for you. I let him wait a while in Mr. Jethro's office, but he had to leave."

"Good."

Delores looked smug. "He said he'd be back later. Ate three of Miss Lavinia's lemon-lime bars, too. And when the assessors came in from the field, they found 'em. Still about half the platter left, but I bet not for long."

Sure enough, word spread quickly. The horde descended five minutes later. After our IT guy, the registrar, Judge Hartley's secretary, the clerk, and the entire zoning department made their inroads, only a few crumbs remained.

Good thing I'd saved one to take home.

At the counter Lucy and I stayed busy. She learned how to do simple mail renewals on the computer while I supervised her and waited on customers. All afternoon I watched the clock, hoping against hope that Billy Lee would put off coming by till another day.

As per my usual bad luck, he appeared about four thirty. He strolled in, looked down his nose at James Cleuny sitting at his post by the door, and made a contemptuous noise in his throat. Then he came over to the counter where I sat and lowered his voice. "Need to talk to you in private."

"Oh." After escorting several people with problems to the office that day, I couldn't think of any excuse not to take him back there, too. "Um, okay."

To my relief, James Cleuny slipped in behind Billy Lee when I opened the door to the reception area. Then he stood directly outside the office when Billy Lee and I went inside, his hand resting on his unsnapped holster.

Billy Lee looked him up and down in disbelief, snorted, then ignored the suggestive pose.

I sat down behind the desk, pulling myself up on the uneven floor. Billy Lee already had his chair right at the other side of the desk. He planted one big elbow on its surface and leaned over so that our faces were only a few inches apart. "What you plan to do with them tax liens?"

"I, um, I don't know yet. I've got someone coming from the state this week to help me out here. I'll know more when I talk to them."

"The state, eh?" His face darkened. "Ol' Jethro said he was gonna sell 'em to Arvin Smelting."

"So I understand."

"I want to set up a payment plan."

"A payment plan?" A glimmer of hope kindled. Hadn't I heard something about Mr. Jethro putting a few people on payment plans before? I jumped up. "Let me go check something."

I went out to Delores's desk where she sat filing her nails. "Don't we do payment plans?"

The emery board continued its work uninterrupted. "Sometimes."

"Can we do one for Billy Lee?"

She curled a lip, still not looking at me. "He already tried that." She jerked her head toward her filing cabinet in the corner. "His payment plan file's in there. Mr. Jethro put him on one a couple of years ago when he first got delinquent. He made a few payments and then let it slide. That's another reason Mr. Jethro was so riled with him."

Demon Delores didn't offer to pull the file for me. After letting me fumble around in the wrong drawer for several minutes, she finally deigned to direct me to the right one. I found the hanging folder with Billy Lee's paperwork and took it back into the office.

Sitting down, I cleared my throat. "It looks like you had a payment plan two years ago, Billy Lee. I have the paperwork with your signature on the agreement right here. But the last payment you made was on . . ." I turned the sheet. "My goodness, Billy Lee. You only made four payments and then stopped." I closed the folder. "I don't think we can go that route again."

"You won't set me up on a payment plan?" Billy Lee took umbrage. "I'm offering to pay you cash money!"

My legs shook but my voice remained steady. "Looks like Mr. Jethro tried taking payments from you and it didn't work. I'm pretty sure the state won't let us do it again." Nice to be able to blame the state. Besides, it was the truth, wasn't it?

"Listen, I can't afford to have them liens sold to Smelting."

"Well. Then I guess you need to pay your taxes," I said in as nice a way as I could.

He glared before donning a meek expression. One ham fist opened in supplication. "I ain't got the money at the moment. I'm financhally stressed, you might say."

"I'm sorry. I don't know what else to tell you." Again speaking as nicely as I could, while hoping he didn't jump up and go for my throat. Would James Cleuny be quick enough to stop him before he killed me?

After a moment apparently spent waiting for me to take back my words and tell him not to be concerned, Billy Lee stood up so abruptly he propelled his chair backward. His meek expression fled. "Well. You better not sell 'em, that's all I got to say. If you do, you'll be sorry."

He swept his bulk out, scowling and muttering under his breath. When he threw open the door to the outer lobby, he dented the wallboard.

"You want me to go bring him in and cite him?" James Cleuny asked in a manner that said he hoped I didn't.

What, bring Billy Lee back in the office and really make him mad? "Nah. That wall needs painting anyway. In fact, the whole courthouse needs painting, inside and out."

"It needs tearing down and rebuilding," Lucy said. "The ladies' bathroom is the pits. I don't want to even imagine what the men's looks like."

"Want me to escort you in and show you?" James Cleuny leered. He and Lucy had hit it off.

She giggled and flapped a hand at him. "Oh, you."

Then it was five o'clock. I gave the last customer his mobile home decal and got up. Lucy vanished before I got my purse from the desk. Delores and I followed her example soon after, both clutching our wrapped goodies from Miss Lavinia. James Cleuny tagged along behind.

Delores was back to her ill-tempered self, but at least she mumbled a half-hearted goodbye. Maybe things would work out once she got used to the idea of me being tax commissioner.

"Are you going home with me again tonight?" I asked James while searching for my car key.

"Sure am. Just like yesterday. I'm on duty till six, then somebody else'll babysit you."

We waved at Delores as she drove out of the parking lot. "That might not work," I told him. "I'm going straight to my night class tonight and won't get out till nine."

"Oh." He knit his brow. "I guess I haveta go with you. Oh, well, I can use the overtime. The other guard can take over when I get you home. I think it's Rayla Cothrew tonight."

I stopped short. "Rayla Cothrew? I thought she worked in the office."

"She's been after the sheriff ever since she took her POST

training to let her do real deputy work. He's started giving her some other duties."

Rayla Cothrew stood about five feet two and weighed maybe a hundred pounds. I might as well have my momma for a bodyguard. "Do you really think Billy Lee will try to hurt me?"

He shrugged. "Sheriff thinks somebody might."

"I feel kind of silly, like I'm taking up your time for nothing."

"No sense taking chances. I get paid regardless."

We started out, James's patrol car following close behind mine. He'd explained the day before that he might need his wheels in case of emergency, which made no sense to me but I went along with it. However, I refused to ride in his patrol car like a criminal. So we comprised a two-car motorcade everywhere I went.

Before I could pull into the street, Lucy's old rattletrap wheeled back into the parking lot. She braked at my window with hers rolled down.

I let mine down, too. "What do you need, Lucy?"

"I forgot my lemon-lime bars. Can you let me borrow your key so I can get back in?"

"I don't have a key. They haven't got me one yet." Sam Blanken had told me they wanted to see if the sheriff would release Mr. Jethro's set to save making another. The commissioners were chintzy about anything that didn't concern them. "And Delores is already gone with hers. Can you wait till tomorrow?"

"Aw, heck." She puckered up like a little girl about to cry. "I've already told Briant I was bringing him one of Miss Lavinia's lemon-lime bars. He got so excited. He really loves them."

"Doesn't everybody?" I picked up my bar on the seat next to me. "Here. Take this one to him. I'll get one of yours tomorrow."

She demurred half-heartedly but was already reaching for it.

"I hate to do that, Corrie. You'll want to eat it tonight yourself."

"I have Cold Churn Dash ice cream at home. Go on, take it. But remember, I get yours tomorrow."

With her profuse thanks, we all went on our way, me with that rosy glow you get when you do something good for somebody and James Cleuny impatient because we'd held him up.

CHAPTER 7

Going to my business accounting class, I ran into my former statistics professor. Literally. I went reeling one way, he went another.

"I'm so sorry!"

"No, no, quite all right," Professor Random said, unpeeling himself from the wall. "Oh, hello there. Cora, isn't it?"

I was surprised he remembered me and more surprised that he spoke to me. He always ignored me in class. Then again, he's so shy, he pretty much ignores everybody. "Um, yes. Actually Corrie. Corralie Caters, Professor Random. Hi."

"This is a stroke of luck." He dusted himself off. "I hoped I'd see you this week."

"You did?" Could he be annoyed that I'd dropped his statistics class without talking to him?

He nodded shyly before picking up a book he'd dropped. "Someone told me you work in the tag office in Ocosawnee County."

"That's true." No point in mentioning my unwanted elevation.

Professor Random threw a puzzled glance at James Cleuny, standing nearby watching us, but decided to overlook him. "I bought a house over there recently and moved in. My birthday's coming up, so someone told me I need to renew my tag there. Is that true?"

I should have known. From the time I started work in the tax commissioner's office, people stopped me to ask questions about their tags or titles or property taxes or mobile home decals. In church, on the street, even in the ladies' room at the movie theater.

"That's right. Come down to the office and we'll be glad to help you." I told him what he needed to bring and let him thank me before going on to my business accounting class.

That professor droned on and on, nearly putting me in a coma as I took notes. James Cleuny fell asleep in his seat at the rear, but woke up from his own snores before he actually fell over. He did make some noise before he realized where he was though, and the professor didn't look pleased. That's probably why he rushed through his lecture and let us out early.

"That guy's got a monotone, don't he?" James asked as he loped to keep up with me.

Hoping no one would realize the snorer was with me, I grunted and hustled to my car.

My mind wandered as I drove home. While the office was closed Friday, I had gone over to the college and dropped the statistics course. Maybe I should drop the business accounting class, too. However, the previous tests in that class had gone pretty well, so maybe I could keep up even with my new duties.

Unfortunately, those duties might include selling Billy Lee Woodhallen's liens as Mr. Jethro had intended, but could I, should I do it? I didn't want to take anyone's property away from him, not even an unpleasant person like Billy Lee.

Especially an unpleasant person like Billy Lee who held grudges, and who beat up people and burnt down buildings.

Oh, well, the state auditor was coming up to see me soon. I'd ask her about my options.

Yes, I confess my mind wasn't on driving because I had so much to worry about. But I was minding my own business, not doing anything out of the ordinary, going home from school on the same roads I drove every week, slowing down when I went over the high lake bridge as I always did, speeding up on the straightaway.

Thus I was totally unprepared when my windshield shattered.

Something smashed through the glass and slammed me in the head.

My feet automatically hit the brakes.

Raw pain stung my forehead. Dark spots sprang up and massed but I didn't black out.

I've been shot! Someone shot me!

James was obviously following too closely because he rammed me in the rear and knocked my little Hyundai off the road and through some trees, where it came to rest in some scrub brush. Shocked, I put my hand to my head.

I thought, even after the car stopped, that someone had shot me. There was no other explanation for the pain in my forehead. I touched it gingerly with the tips of my fingers and looked at them.

Even in the moonlight I could see the dark wetness.

That was *blood* trickling down beside my eye. I had definitely been shot.

Then I realized a huge bird lay on my lap, cradled between me and the steering wheel and the console.

I squealed while I pushed at it. I finally threw/shoved it over to the other side of the car, then squealed some more.

There I was, trying to get my seatbelt loose, blood oozing down into my eye, a dead bird on the seat beside me, safety glass crystals all over the place, and the deputy assigned to protect me puffing over, saying, "Are you all right? Are you all right? What happened? Are you all right?"

"You hit me in the rear!"

"You braked!"

My fumbling hands finally freed the seatbelt. "I thought someone shot at me."

"Someone shot at you?" James made as if to draw his gun and quickly looked around to search for the unknown assailant.

"No. Can you open the door?" I reached around behind my seat where I kept a tissue box handy and miraculously found it still there. As I blotted my bloody head and wiped my eye, James tried to get the door open. He talked into the little radio he wore on his lapel the whole time he worked on the door. "—Bobolink Crossing Road west of the bridge—subject was shot at—"

My hysteria calmed enough to take in what he was saying. "I wasn't shot at. I said I *thought* I'd been shot at. It was a bird."

He wrenched the door open. "What?"

"A bird. A big one. There." I pointed.

He goggled. His mouth gaped. He leaned over me for a closer look. "That's a bald eagle. You've killed a bald eagle. How'd you kill a bald eagle?"

"I didn't kill it. It committed suicide."

He shook his head doubtfully. "Killing a bald eagle is a federal offense. You hadn't ought to of done it."

Tissues in hand, I put my head on the steering wheel.

At least the air bag hadn't deployed.

"My mom can tend to my head." I objected as the EMTs put me in the back of their vehicle and turned on the flashing lights. "There's no need to go to the emergency room."

I didn't want to go to the hospital. On my last visit to the emergency room, a doctor who looked like a certain popular movie star had bandaged up my arm that I'd cut on some glass when I ran over the Hendleys' fence earlier this year. Unfortunately, he was the same doctor who had sewn up my toe the month before that, when it got caught in the refrigerator grate.

I most certainly did not want to see him in the emergency room again under these circumstances.

The EMTs, busy debating how I'd managed to kill a bald eagle when everyone knew bald eagles didn't hunt at night, paid no attention. After a wild ride with siren blaring, I was ceremoniously unloaded, forced into a waiting wheelchair despite my vehement protests that I was perfectly capable of walking, and whisked into the ER lobby.

From my VIP treatment, this was obviously a slow night in Medder Rose for emergencies.

"It's the Caters girl again," I heard one of the EMTs tell the receptionist.

I caught her rolling her eyes as she reached for the phone.

Great. Now my mother would get involved.

Once I gave them all the required information, they put me in a cubicle to wait for the doctor. Maybe Momma would come down first and get me out before the doctor showed up. Maybe the cute one wouldn't be on duty tonight. Maybe . . .

Tall, dark and handsome, Dr. Bennigan strode in with my paperwork in his hand. "Ms. Caters," he greeted me, then took a second look at me. "Have you been here before?"

"Um." I clapped a hand to my head, half hiding my face. Maybe he'd think I couldn't speak.

He came up to the examining table and nudged my hand aside. After he moved the gauze and pushed the hair back, he peered at my forehead. "Nasty gash. We're going to have to shave a patch of hair off before I can clean you up. Be right back."

Shave my hair? I was off the table and halfway to the door when he came back. A nurse trotted after him with a tray of ominous metal things.

He blocked the exit. "Now, now. Don't be worried. Won't take a minute, then we'll see what we've got, whether we need stitches. Hop back up here."

"Oh, I hardly think I need stitches," I said, forced back against the examining table by his entrance. "Ha, ha, ha. It's barely bleeding now. See?" I pushed my forehead at him.

He paused, frowning as if my voice jogged some chord. "Caters. Now I remember. Jenny Caters' daughter. You had a run-in with a refrigerator didn't you? Was that before or after you hit the cow? And now a bird?" He wagged his brows. "Pugnacious, are we?"

Would I never live those incidents down? "I did not run over a cow. The cow ran out in front of my car and made me veer off the road into a fence."

"Okay." He was grinning. "But you hit a bird tonight?"

"The bird hit me! I was just driving home and it came through the windshield."

"Broke right in, eh? He must have been a big one. And coming at you hard enough to break a windshield . . . My, my, must have wanted you bad." He looked at the chart. "Ooh! Bald eagle. Are they still considered endangered? Going to be in trouble big time for that."

"I can't help it that he ran into my car. I had nothing to do with—"

"I'm sure." He pushed me back onto the table and looked at my head.

A nurse fiddled with the tray of things I didn't recognize and didn't want to. She wheeled it over and he got busy. When he brought out a needle, I closed my eyes. I felt something scraping my forehead before the anesthetic took effect.

The razor. I would look like one of those cult members who ran around airports selling flowers.

They were still working on me when my mother burst in.

"What in heaven's name happened?" she asked me. "Is she all right, Dr. Bennigan?" she asked him. Then back to me without waiting for an answer, "Baby, I'm here. What on earth happened to you?"

I was the youngest. I would always be her baby. Never mind how humiliating the nickname.

"I'm fine," I mumbled as best I could from behind the hands holding my face sideways.

"Hello, Jenny. No sign of concussion, nothing broken, but she did need a few stitches," the doctor said cheerfully as he finished up and surveyed his handiwork.

My mother calmed down and came over to look at me. "Oh, my. That's a nice job you did there, Dr. Bennigan. How many stitches?"

"Just five."

She sighed, still staring at my forehead. "Well, at least they're under the hairline. And hair'll grow back."

About that time, a different nurse bustled in. "Doctor, we need you right away. Room three. May be food poisoning but . . . The patient's unconscious."

Dr. Bennigan's smile glinted. "Your mother's right. Hair'll grow back," he said and was gone.

Before the door closed, I heard the nurse say, "A detective's on his way."

To check on me?

Momma clicked her teeth. "Well, miss. What's this about a bird?"

I told her and she closed her eyes. "What next, oh Lord?"

"It wasn't my fault."

"Never is." She scanned me up and down, making sure I was okay. "I have to go back to work, but I've already called your father. He'll be here to get you soon as he can. I'll walk you to the front so you can meet him there."

As we reached the waiting room, Sheriff Duval strode in. James Cleuny intercepted him, talking in a low voice and waving his hands around. I couldn't hear anything of the conversation except "her fault" and "couldn't stop" that James kept repeating.

If Momma hadn't been beside me, I'd have damned him out loud. As it was, I had to do it mentally.

Sheriff Duval looked confused. When he started toward Momma and me, I silently cursed again. He was going to arrest me because of that stupid bald eagle.

"Am I going to get cited or hauled off to jail?" I asked him directly.

"Don't be silly, chickie," Momma muttered. Her hand clutched my arm. "You couldn't help it."

Sheriff Duval looked surprised. "Cite you for what?"

"For killing a bald eagle."

"You killed a bald eagle?" He pondered this information, eyes fixed on my bandage.

James hadn't told him about the eagle. I damned my big mouth.

"That's a federal offense." The sheriff shifted his gaze to my eyes. "Did you have a reason or did you just feel like killing it?"

"It hit my windshield and died."

"Oh." He pondered some more. "In that case, you're probably in the clear."

My mother's hand on my arm relaxed. "Of course she is. It wasn't her fault." Repeating my mantra, I noticed. I love my momma.

Sheriff Duval nodded toward the bandage on my forehead. "Who did that?"

"The bird. Can I sue him?"

He laughed. "See an attorney. I thought you might be here because of your new clerk's husband. But it was a bird, eh?"

The bald eagle was forgotten. "Lucy's husband?"

He nodded. "They brought him in having trouble breathing.

Thought it was an overdose, but Lucy says no, he doesn't do drugs. Now they think food poisoning."

"That's awful. Is Lucy here now?"

Momma touched my arm and stood on tiptoe to kiss my cheek. "I've got to get back to work. Your daddy'll be here in a few minutes. You just sit still and wait for him. Duke!" She shook her finger at Sheriff Duval. "You better watch over my girl or you'll answer to me."

Sheriff Duval assured my mother that I'd be safe as in my cradle, that another deputy was on his way who'd stay with me the rest of the night.

I barely heard him and didn't even notice Momma leave.

I pulled at the sheriff's sleeve. "Is Lucy back there with her husband?" I gestured toward the doors leading to the ER rooms. I didn't want to go see what was going on, but since I'd hired her, Lucy was kind of my responsibility.

He looked around. "I don't know where she is. I just got here."

A nurse came out about that time and saw him. "Sheriff Duval. You came in person. Good. Let me take you back."

I trailed along but she stopped me at the door. "Sorry. No visitors back here."

"I have a friend in there with her husband."

"Mrs. Coffee?"

My traumatic evening drove Lucy's married name out of my head, but Coffee sounded right. "Yes."

"Oh. Well." You could see thoughts spinning behind her snooty expression. "Wait here. Her minister's on his way. She may want you afterward." She glided away on her rubber-soled shoes.

Her minister! Why'd they need her minister?

Not long after they disappeared, a plump man in dress slacks and clutching a Bible rushed in and spoke to the desk clerk. I heard Lucy's name so I figured he must be her pastor. The clerk hustled him to the back, too.

This boded no good. What should I do? I wished Daddy would hurry up and get here.

Then the most unearthly scream I'd ever heard in my life came from the ER rooms, a sound like an animal caught in a claw trap. The hair rose on my arms while chills ran down my back.

Daddy came in about that time, clucking over my bandage. He wanted to take me right home, but I told him about Lucy, and we waited together.

Ten or fifteen minutes later, the nurse and pastor came out, supporting a half-fainting, weeping Lucy. She saw me and broke loose to throw her arms around me.

"Bri's dead," she said between her sobs. "He's *dead*. He got sick right after supper and started throwing up. I should have called for help, but he didn't want me to, said it was just indigestion and it'd go away. Finally I called anyway. I didn't know what else to do."

She held on to me as if I was her sister, and I comforted her as best I could.

When she got over that round of tears, she pulled back and wiped her eyes with a sodden tissue. "They say it was food poisoning, but I ate everything he did. We had spaghetti and a salad. He used French dressing and I used Ranch, but they were the same bottles we've had all along. Do you think that was it, maybe his dressing went bad?"

I patted her back. "I don't know, Lucy. It could be."

Still dazed, she fumbled in her purse and came up with another tissue that looked used. She blew her nose. "I can't believe he's gone. He got home while I was draining the spaghetti and started teasing me. He asked me if I didn't know how to cook anything else, so I threw a big handful at him."

Her voice broke and she sniffled. "He laughed. He never gets mad about anything."

I didn't know what to say. "He didn't eat or drink anything else? You didn't have anything with mayonnaise in it or something else that might have spoiled?"

She shook her head. "No. The only other thing he had was his lemon-lime bar. But I ate one at work and I didn't get sick. That couldn't have been it."

His lemon-lime bar? No, it had been *my* lemon-lime bar.

And Billy Lee Woodhallen had been in the office alone with it while I dug up information about payment plans.

No way Billy Lee could have put anything in the bar though. That was reaching into left field. What could he have done in the few minutes I'd been out of the office?

I swallowed. Face it, there was time to do anything. Like put in some poison or something else he meant for me to eat.

I would have to tell the sheriff.

CHAPTER 8

In light of the new death linked to the tax commissioner's office, the county commissioners decreed we should close the
next day, which was Wednesday. I slept late and nursed my head
all day while a monosyllabic deputy with shaved head watched
daytime TV on Daddy's big thin screen.

Sam Blanken came by the house that night after he got off
work. Giving a sidelong glance at the impassive skinhead in
front of the TV, he drew Daddy and me aside.

"This is getting serious." His raspy voice sounded more than
ever like a frog, even when he was trying to speak softly. With
his jowls and bulging belly, he kind of looked like one, too.
"First somebody murders Mr. Jethro, and now Lucy's husband
is dead."

Was he accusing me of something? I cleared my throat. "What
do they think killed Briant?"

"Don't know. Duke thinks poison of some kind, but he won't
know for sure till the autopsy. Says it'll take a while."

Daddy had been upset since picking me up from the hospital
the night before. "Bodie was right," he kept repeating. "You're
in danger. I hadn't ought to of made you take the job."

I kept reassuring him, "You didn't make me take the job. I
chose to do it."

"You need to quit. Now."

He repeated this opinion in front of Sam Blanken.

His vehemence took Sam Blanken off guard. "Now, Keith,

hold on here. Things aren't that desperate. Duke's on top of things. I don't see as how Corrie needs to throw in the towel yet."

I wanted to. I was really tempted. But when I'd talked to our personnel manager about my new salary, I'd widened my eyes. Visions of a new car and my own place to live danced within reach. Besides, if I quit, that would give Bodie something else to smirk about. Not to mention I was starting to get the hang of being the boss. The worst part had been breaking the news of my appointment to Demon Delores, and that was over and finished. She was even beginning to thaw.

Well, at least she was talking to me again.

Besides, I had twenty-four-hour protection.

That didn't help Briant Coffee, my timid side said.

On the other hand, if it was my fault Lucy's husband had died, I needed to help get Billy Lee convicted. That would be the only way I could make up for causing a man's death.

I put up my chin. "I took the job and I'm not going to back down. I'll simply have to be extra careful."

"Atta girl," Sam said.

Daddy threw up his hands. "All right. But you're going to take a gun to work with you."

"Daddy!"

"You know how to shoot." He stuck out his jaw. "You were runner-up in the northeast regional shooting tournament your junior year in high school. If it hadn't been for that ROTC gal who—"

I fell back on the law. "It's not that, Daddy. I can't legally take a gun to work. Weapons aren't allowed in the courthouse."

Sam Blanken had to butt his big mouth in. "The tax commissioner can be an ex-officio deputy, sugar. Did Duke swear you in yet?"

"The sheriff?" Swear me in to what? "No."

"I'll get him to do it, and I'll talk to the other commissioners too," Sam rasped. "Fix it so's it's okay for you to tote. That's a real good idea, Keith. Good thing you thought of it. You can load you a pistol, sugar, and keep it in your desk so's if you need it, you'll have it handy. That way you'll feel better."

"What? With a loaded pistol in my desk drawer for the cleaners or anyone else to find or steal? I don't think so."

"A revolver would be better," my father mused to his crony, ignoring me. "I got that three fifty-seven in the gun safe she nearly won that contest with."

"Good thinking. She'll be used to it." Sam waxed enthusiastic. "I'll talk to the other commissioners and Duke about an exception. They won't have a problem."

"I don't think we should be hasty about this." I wasted my breath. The two men walked off without listening, heading toward the basement and Daddy's gun safe.

From past experience, I knew when to cut my losses. There would be bigger battles, I felt sure, and my desk had a key.

The skinhead deputy had heard everything. He looked at me with open disapproval.

"What's the matter?" I snapped. "Don't you think I can handle a gun?"

How long could I take this? Sheriff Duval needed to get his act together and put Billy Lee in jail.

We would have reopened the tax office Thursday, but Mr. Jethro's funeral finally got scheduled for Friday, so the commissioners told me to close up the office for the rest of the week.

Guilt over her husband's death led me to go over to Lucy's house and tell her so in person. She was apathetic, but I could imagine what our customers would have to say Monday morning about idle county employees.

Oh, well. I had insurance to file on the wrecked Hyundai

languishing in the repair shop, and maybe some car rental places to visit. Momma said she would let me use her Focus whenever she could, but I needed a car of my own.

Everywhere I went, thank goodness, I had a deputy tagging along.

Not James Cleuny. I hadn't seen him since he bashed into my rear end with his patrol car and came with me to the hospital. Some older guy who needed conditioning took his place Thursday, while Rayla Cothrew, an airhead who was not too many years older than me, continued to stay with us nights.

"I declare, you make me feel lots better about Corrie," my momma told her. "Don't you feel lots safer, Corrie, having a woman guarding you instead of those dimwitted men?"

Sure.

Friday at the funeral, however, James was back on duty, somewhat subdued and acting as if he didn't want to be around me. I figured he'd been chastised for wrecking his patrol car and seized the opportunity when he followed my parents and me into the church to ask, "Did you get in trouble for bashing my car?"

He gave me a dirty look. "The car was totaled. I'm driving an old clunker the department was using for mail pick-up. I got written up. I'm on probation. I had to go take a drug test. My personal auto insurance is bound to go up, too. I guess you could say I got in trouble."

That seemed like some harsh consequences for a fender bender. On the other hand, he shouldn't have been following my car so closely. "Gosh, that's too bad," I cooed.

Inside, the Mirror Creek Baptist Church overflowed with way more than its two-hundred-and-forty-person capacity. Mr. Jethro had six children, twenty-one grandchildren, twenty-eight great-grandchildren and three great-great grandbabies. With two surviving sisters and all his nephews and nieces in attendance, anyone not related to him could barely squeeze in.

Our little group arrived late, as the local gospel quartet commenced singing, "How Great Thou Art."

Someone was slightly off key.

Fortunately, Sam Blanken had saved us seats at the back. Delores, I saw when I slipped into the pew after Momma, had snagged a prime seat right behind the family and four rows up from us.

Kind of pushy. Then again, she had worked for Mr. Jethro for over thirty years.

After a scripture reading, another hymn, poems from four young grandchildren, and fiery sermons from two preachers who tried to outdo each other with hellfire warnings for the unbaptized and unsaved—and who, incidentally, gave maybe four sentences between them to Mr. Jethro's life and character— the casket departed.

Daddy and I climbed into his truck and joined the cortege to the church cemetery a mile away on the other side of the road up on a hill, while Momma drove her car back to the hospital.

So far, so good. The funeral service had been nice and normal. Sad, but nothing out of the ordinary if you didn't count Mr. Jethro's youngest daughter running up to the closed coffin and flinging herself, sobbing, on it while her exasperated sons hissed at her not to make a spectacle of herself as they tried to pry her off.

The problem occurred at the hillside cemetery. Daddy, James Cleuny, and I stood at the edge of the mourners, halfway up the hill but well below the family tent situated at the burial plot on top.

We didn't miss out on anything though, not even the view. Off to the side we could gaze across the county road to the little white frame church where Mr. Jethro's funeral had taken place. The steeple rose like a needle against a sliver of azure sky. Plump cotton clouds floated dreamily overhead. To the side of the church lay the Appalachian foothills all rounded and verdant with spring buds.

Too pretty a day for a funeral.

As the service began, Daddy, James, and I moved into the scant shade of a large white oak sheltering a mausoleum, to escape the afternoon sun.

The first preacher talked about Mr. Jethro's salvation in a voice so booming that even we stragglers on the lower outskirts could hear.

"He was saved, yessir, praise the Lord!" the preacher shouted. He threw up his arms as if daring God to say different. "A man can profess to believe and be baptized so often the fishes know his face, but that don't mean he's been saved. But Mr. Jethro was saved, yessiree. We know he believed in Jesus Christ and believed in God and heaven. And we know Mr. Jethro's gone up yonder to that place where he'll wear fine robes and sit on a golden throne. But friends, are you sure you'll be joining Mr. Jethro in heaven one of these days?"

Sad to confess, while I had my head tipped back so I could keep polite eyes on the preacher, I wasn't listening very closely. I stood and thought not of Mr. Jethro, but of the big mess he'd left in his office. I wondered when the state auditor would arrive, and if Lucy would be able to come back to work soon, and how I would ever learn all I needed to know to be tax commissioner.

One thing I didn't wonder about was Billy Lee Woodhallen's whereabouts. He hadn't been at the church and wouldn't dare show his face here either. Besides, I had a bodyguard. I felt pretty confident I was safe here in the cemetery.

James Cleuny must have thought the same thing as he rocked back and forth on his heels and toes and watched a dog meander down the hill on the far side of the grave. As he swayed, he occasionally popped a breath mint into his mouth.

No, James was caught as unawares as Daddy and me. The first hint was someone huffing and puffing behind us. As I was registering the fact a latecomer was joining us, the latecomer tapped on my shoulder.

I turned and nearly wet my pants. "Billy Lee! What are you doing here?"

Daddy looked aghast.

James stiffened and slid a hand down toward his gun.

Billy Lee, winded from climbing halfway up the hill, ignored them both. "Come to pay my respects to ol' Jethro and . . ." He gasped for breath. "And to ask you if . . ." puff, puff, ". . . you heard from the state auditor yet about my liens."

The words popped right out. "I thought you hated Mr. Jethro."

Billy Lee tucked his thumbs through the belt loops on his worn jeans. Since he didn't wear a belt, there was room for his thick fingers. He caught his breath before answering. "Naw. He warn't a bad fellow." He sniffed. "Stubborn, maybe. Tried to do his job right, though. Gotta respect a fella for trying to do his job, even if you don't agree with him."

I looked around, perversely hoping someone had noticed Billy Lee so he couldn't kill us, but at the same time hoping no one was watching who would take offense at his presence.

Everybody's eyes were trained on the coffin and on the second haranguing preacher up front, who began wildly shaking his Bible at the crowd and threatening to break into some kind of frenzied dance. Good thing, too, since Billy Lee seemed harmless for the moment. Still, this was not a good situation.

Daddy tried to pretend everything was fine and kept his mouth closed, but he stood on the balls of his feet as if ready for action. James Cleuny, looking like a deer caught in headlights, slowly unsnapped his gun flap and put his hand on the gun handle.

Thank goodness he had enough sense not to pull his pistol out. I didn't think Billy Lee would do anything to me at Mr. Jethro's funeral, not in front of all these witnesses. He was taking a big risk just being here. If any of Mr. Jethro's relatives noticed him, he'd be dead meat. Mr. Jethro's family had adored the old man. And like everyone else, they were sure Billy Lee had killed him.

"I don't know whether you ought to be here," I told Billy Lee in a low voice, looking up where the relatives clustered in and around the tent. "Mr. Jethro's kin might not take kindly to your showing up."

"I know what people's saying, but I didn't have nothing to do with Mr. Jethro's murder," he growled. "That's what else I come up to tell you. I was mad, sure, but I wouldn't have hit old Jethro. I ain't never hurt an old person in my life."

"Well. Ahem. That's, um, good to know."

Already nervous, I got plumb antsy when one of Mr. Jethro's grandsons, who stood outside the tent, turned to blow his nose. The movement pointed his face in our direction. He did a double take as he spotted Billy Lee. "Er, Billy Lee, I think you'd better leave."

"I know what everyone's thinking, but I didn't kill ol' Jethro." Billy Lee's rising voice attracted more unwanted attention. "I didn't have anything to do with whatever happened to that little gal's husband, either."

"James, maybe you better escort Billy Lee out before something gets started," Daddy said as the muttering from Jethro's family started to drown out the shouting preacher. "I don't like the way people are vacating that tarpaulin."

The tent sheltering Mr. Jethro's nearest and dearest began wobbling. Word of Billy Lee's presence must have passed to some of Mr. Jethro's sons and grandsons under it, because I could see them climbing over their relatives' laps as if they couldn't wait to pee.

"What?" James gawked at the crowd trying to head our way. "Oh. Yeah. Right. Come on, Billy Lee."

Billy Lee shook off James's tentative attempt to take his arm.

"Listen," he told me, "I ain't killed nobody. And if you'll hold off on them liens a few more weeks, I'll have the money I—"

The tent by the grave collapsed. Amid the screams and groans, a mob emerged and surged down the hill toward us.

"Good godamighty!" Daddy grabbed my arm. "You look after Billy Lee, James. I'll take care of Corrie."

We ran one way, Billy Lee and James Cleuny another.

I looked back. Billy Lee, for all his bulk, could move fast, and he'd had sense enough to double-park nearby. He reached his Ford F-450 crew cab pickup well ahead of James Cleuny, got in and fired the engine as Mr. Jethro's relatives swarmed over the graves separating them from their prey.

A few hot-blooded young people scrambled for their rides to give chase, but Billy Lee's souped-up truck peeled out through the lower section of the cemetery. Long before any other vehicle reached the gate, it had vanished down the main highway.

"Sheriff figured he wouldn't dare show up here," James panted as he escaped the crowd and met up with us. "Boy, was he wrong."

I looked up the hill toward the abandoned coffin, saw the forlorn preachers standing over the fallen tent. They limply clutched their Bibles. A few elderly relatives of Mr. Jethro remained sprinkled around the gravesite. They gawked at everyone milling around at the bottom of the hill and swelled with righteous indignation at such goings-on.

Mr. Jethro wouldn't have cared for all the Bible-thumping histrionics anyway.

★ ★ ★ ★ ★

Ethan Parters, my kinda sorta boyfriend, played night bodyguard over the weekend.

Clean-cut and freckled, a regular Huck Finn lookalike, he wore his uniform with pride. He loved being a deputy, but his driving ambition was to join the FBI. He lacked about twenty hours getting his bachelor's degree in criminal justice, after which he planned to apply for his dream job.

That was another reason we weren't serious. I didn't want to have a boyfriend in Washington or Texas or anywhere else I might have to move if we decided to get married. In fact, I didn't much want a boyfriend with law enforcement ambitions at all. I'd gone through that with Bodie, and look how we turned out.

Ethan was a pretty good guy, though, and someone to hang out with. Since he was on duty that weekend, we stayed at my house and watched TV and talked.

He'd heard about the bird and disapproved.

"A bald eagle, at that. I don't understand why this stuff keeps happening to you, Corrie. In school you were fine. You didn't ever do weird things like get hit by a bird or nearly cut your toe off in the refrigerator."

"You don't think I'm asking for them to happen on purpose, do you?" I shot back.

He quickly retreated. "No, of course not."

I could see he did. Why the heck did I put up with him? Why couldn't I attract men like the statistics professor or the ER doctor? Was a momma's boy FBI wannabe the best I could do?

My future looked dull.

Assuming I had a future.

Momma worked the weekend shift, so Daddy went grocery shopping and fed us off the grill. Stuff she'd disapprove of, like hamburgers, barbecued ribs, and on Sunday, steak.

After helping clean up Sunday night, Ethan and I went out to the front porch swing. The warm April evening brought out the tree frog chorus. The moon stared down through the greening oak, an imperfect orb making the light pearly gray.

"Have you heard any more about Briant Coffee, Ethan? About how he died?"

The porch swing creaked. "The sheriff hasn't said anything to me, but I overheard him talking to somebody on the phone when I ran by the office today to straighten out my time. He thinks it's some kind of poison, but he won't know for sure till the results come back from the state lab. Could take weeks."

"Poison." My hand tightened on the wooden swing handle. "Do they know how Briant got it?"

He cleared his throat and avoided my eye. "Well, I think the sheriff might have an idea."

"Was it my lemon-lime bar?"

"I can't tell you that," he said loftily.

"You don't know."

"I do, too. Lucy told him how she took yours Friday, so Sheriff Duval thinks the poison was meant for you."

I hadn't wanted to believe it. I balled my hands into fists, feeling as sick as if I had killed Briant myself. If I hadn't offered Lucy my cookie bar for him, if I'd let her go home without it, Briant would be alive today.

You didn't know, I tried to excuse myself. *You couldn't have known.*

It wasn't my fault.

The usual mantra didn't help, but I unclenched my hands. "Did Lucy tell the sheriff Billy Lee was in the office that day?"

"Darlene did. Believe you me, the sheriff's looking real close at Billy Lee. We found something else out, too."

I waited while I willed the nausea from my part in Briant's death down. "Well? What did you find out?"

"I don't know if I ought to tell you."

"Ethan!"

He didn't need further urging but put his head close to mine like he didn't want anybody else to hear him blab. "There was a light blue pickup truck parked back behind the courthouse, beside Mr. Jethro's car the night he died."

Mr. Jethro always parked at the lot in back behind the shrubbery where passers-by couldn't see his car. That way, nobody riding by the courthouse would know if he was at work or not. The wily old politician had managed to avoid a lot of disgruntled constituents with that little trick. I probably ought to start following his example.

Ethan's words sank in. "Wait a minute. How'd anybody see the truck if it was parked behind the courthouse?"

"One of the cleaners. They do the courthouse first and then the jail and the other county offices right beside it. She was bringing the trash from the buildings and maintenance office to the dumpster back there behind the courthouse when she noticed the vehicles. She was running late, but she thinks it was about ten o'clock. Right in the time range of Mr. Jethro's death."

"So the sheriff's looking for a light blue pickup?"

"That's part of it." Ethan looked around to make sure nobody was around. "This woman says it was an old pickup. A real old, old pickup. And you know who collects all those antique cars and trucks."

"Billy Lee Woodhallen." The knowledge seemed anticlimactic. "Does he have an old blue pickup in his collection?"

"No, but he's got an old silver one. At night and under those sodium dioxide parking lights and all, she might of thought it was blue."

"So when's the sheriff going to arrest him?"

Ethan pulled away, looking at me in disgust. "Soon as he has a case. Can't arrest a man without a case. Right now, Billy Lee's alibi looks good."

"Geez, you think if I'm murdered, the sheriff'll have a case?"

"That's why I'm here." Ethan put a reassuring arm around my shoulder. "Don't worry. We'll take care of you."

Why did I not feel comforted?

CHAPTER 9

Over the weekend, I had a brainstorm and called both our part-time people to see if they could come in to help us out. One declined since she was about to leave for an extended visit with her daughter in California, but the other said she could and would come in, and showed up Monday, raring to go.

Ruby Fay Bromfield, or Miss Ruby as everyone called her, enjoyed working in the tax office. She knew everyone and used our office as a gathering place for information to keep up with whatever was going on in the county. At seventy-four, she had been Mr. Jethro's seasonal employee for a decade before I went to work for him. She wore her snow-white hair in a bun wrapped in lace like the Amish and took no guff from anyone. Even Demon Delores. Her plump little body might be slow, but her mind was sharp as a tack.

Since she could sell tags as well as take taxes, Miss Ruby hoisted herself onto her usual stool at eight o'clock. Delores unlocked the door, then jumped back so the tag and mobile home customers didn't run her down as they charged into the office. We'd been closed nearly a week, so the small reception area was full. The line extended well into the courthouse hall.

Delores hurried behind the counter and locked the inner door. Without offering to help, she went straight to her desk at the back of our area. She, of course, hadn't got her accounting straightened out.

Supposedly.

And she still wasn't too friendly.

Which was fine with me. I could ignore Demon Delores as well as she could ignore me.

Especially since Miss Ruby was around. She and I would whittle down this crowd of customers and later, she could do mailed-in tag renewals while I did dealer titles between walk-ins.

Miss Ruby had the most infectious laugh I've ever heard. If she got tickled, her shoulders and little round body shook all over while that laugh boomed out. When I told her about the bird attack, she whooped so hard she started crying. She made the whole day brighter.

With Miss Ruby around, even the line of crazy tag customers seemed endurable.

I put the tag fees in my cash drawer. "All right, Mrs. Drostowski, here's your tag plate and registration on your new Mercedes convertible." I held them out to the older woman across the counter. "You're good to go."

With her chic hairstyle and bored expression, I could tell she was one of the retirees from out of the state. None of our local people came to town in athletic capris and workout bra barely covered by a bicycling jacket. At least, no one over fifty did.

The woman's boredom changed to horror as she viewed the plate. "This says FAT."

"Yes, ma'am, but it doesn't mean anything. That's the letter series we're issuing now."

She pushed the plate back at me. "I don't want a tag that says FAT. Give me another plate."

"They all say FAT. The state sent us ten boxes of that series, a hundred tags in each box, and they all have FAT on them along with the numbers. Our county just happened to end up with this particular series."

She slapped the plate down. "Well, you can just *happen* to

find me some other tag. I'm not going to take this one."

Hey, the letters on my tag spelled BAH, but did I pitch a fit? Nevertheless, I took the plate and put on a soothing smile. "Okay, we can do that. You can get a specialty plate for fifty dollars."

"Fifty dollars!"

"Yes, ma'am. But afterward, it's just twenty-five a year extra to keep it," I added enticingly.

After some muttering and head-tossing, she chose the wildflower plate. I had to back out the previous transaction, void the payment, give her back her cash, and start the process all over again. She fumed as she waited and was still hot under the collar when she left. "You bureaucrats know how to squeeze every dollar out of us, don't you? One of these days, people are going to revolt."

"Yes, ma'am. Next, please."

The state auditor called mid-morning and made an appointment to come by Wednesday to audit the books and go over a few things with me about running a tax commissioner's office. "Mr. Jethro's final report's due, too," she added. "I don't know if he'd worked it up or not, but I'll help you with it while I'm there if you want me to."

I had no idea what a final report entailed, so I meekly agreed. Despondent, I wondered how I'd ever manage to do the job. I didn't know anything about any of the responsibilities Mr. Jethro had, and with a murderer loose after me, how could I concentrate enough to learn?

Rayla Cothrew stood guard that day. Actually, she sat on a pew in the front lobby and read some of Delores's magazines most of the morning. Lunching with me at Joanie's Vittles, she discussed hair color. She didn't know if she wanted to go red or lighten up to ash blond. "I'm pretty sick of this dishwater blond shade," she complained over her corned beef and cabbage.

I myself had the Monday special: chicken and dressing. "At least you've got hair. I just hope mine grows back pretty quick once I get these stitches out." I self-consciously touched the shaved spot with its small bandage hiding the stitches.

"Oh, that little place they shaved is hardly noticeable," Rayla lied before prattling on. "I want to keep the color professional looking though, you know? I don't want Duke to think I can't handle a regular field job. Ash blond might make me come across as a ditzy airhead. What do you think?"

"You're guarding me. The sheriff must trust you." Although I wasn't sure what a barely five-foot-two woman weighing maybe a hundred pounds soaking wet could do to keep The Hulk from killing me.

"Yeah, but this isn't real deputy work."

"Excuse me?" My fork of dressing dripping giblet gravy stopped in midair. "Your job's pretty important to me!"

"Well, sure." She shrugged. "But I don't think Billy Lee's dumb enough to try to kill you with everybody already suspecting him of murdering Mr. Jethro. What I mean is, guarding you is not like patrolling and answering burglary calls and all the exciting stuff. I've been nagging Duke for a year, trying to move up. If this gig with you works out, I'm hoping to go the full route."

"I think guarding me is pretty exciting. Especially since it looks like Billy Lee may have got Lucy's husband instead of me," I said with remorse. "Even with everyone knowing he killed Mr. Jethro."

"Aw, who knows? I bet the test'll come back food poisoning. Lucy's aunt told my mother that she never could cook worth a darn."

Great. I had a pint-sized bodyguard who didn't believe I needed guarding or that Briant Coffee was murdered. If Billy Lee killed me, would she finally realize I was in danger or would she put it down to a freak accident?

Murdered. Unexpected terror sent a frisson down my spine. I pushed my plate away half uneaten.

On Tuesday after lunch, during a lull in customers, my cute ex–statistics professor came in to get his tags. He tiptoed in and peered over the counter where Miss Ruby sat.

When I noticed him from my office, I abandoned my stance at a tall filing cabinet. Unfortunately, I turned too quickly and swished the monthly county-memo-re-tardiness-no-one-ever-bothered-to-read that I was filing against my nose. The sting automatically brought my hand up.

Blood. Oh, crap. I'd given myself a paper cut on my nose.

I pressed hard, trying to get the bleeding to stop.

Luckily, Miss Ruby didn't like to be disturbed when she was on the computer. It took her several minutes to notice the professor. "Well?" she barked in her nasal voice. "What do you need?"

He stepped back in alarm.

Miss Ruby could be intimidating to someone not acquainted with her. Especially when she glared and said, "Speak up, mister. I don't hear good."

"I, ah, I need to get a tag. I understand this is the place."

On the other side of the lobby, Rayla abandoned her magazine to give him the once-over.

I searched feverishly for my lip gloss, one hand still pressing my nose.

Miss Ruby scowled. "I can't do one for you now. I got something working in my machine. You stay right where you are. I'll get to you quick as I can."

I found a brush in my purse and ran it through my hair. When the bristles hit the scalped part, I winced.

Great. Shaved head and stitches. Now a bleeding nose. This

was not the best day for Professor Random to show up.

Out front, he shifted his weight from one foot to another. His stance revealed panic. He was ready to flee.

Rayla, divorced and looking, evinced her interest by getting up and strolling toward him on the pretense of selecting another magazine from a corner table. "Nice weather we're having, isn't it?"

He responded politely but didn't invite further advances.

She walked back, still ogling him.

His rocking back and forth got on Miss Ruby's nerves. "Stop that fidgeting, man, for God's sake. Well, shee-it!" She scowled at him. "I hit the wrong key. You distracted me with all that jumping and wiggling around you were doing. Now I'll have to start all over."

He backed away as if having second thoughts about getting a tag.

I'd done all I could for my appearance so I hurried out. "Professor Random. You made it in, I see."

His face lightened. "I did." He flicked a wary glance at Miss Ruby.

Oblivious of her frightening impression, she leaned back on her stool. "Come here, Corrie." A wide arm wave beckoned me to her side. "This dad-gum machine is messing up again. You're gonna have to fix it before I can finish up this tag renewal."

I reached over her to the keyboard, got her out of the forms screen she'd somehow managed to pull up, and brought up the decal renewal screen. "Okay. Computer's ready to go, Miss Ruby."

Ignoring her under-breath mumbling about people not being able to stand still, I slipped onto my stool. "All right, Professor. I can help you over here. What do you need?"

With a tentative smile, he pulled out his pre-bill on a vintage yellow Mustang coupe. The title was in his name, and insurance information showed on the computer. All I had to do was change the address, take payment, issue the decal, and give him a county sticker. We were through in ten minutes.

He took his paperwork and hesitated. "Um, one of my students gave me this old pickup I'm restoring. Do I have to get a tag for it? It won't be drivable for several years."

"How old is it?"

He looked blank. "Pretty old. It's a Chevrolet from like the early seventies."

"It doesn't need a title then. Personally, I wouldn't worry about tagging it. Once you get ready to put the truck on the road, come back to see us." Technically, he was supposed to pay ad valorem taxes even if he didn't tag the truck, but something that old in the process of restoration wasn't worth anything. We'd catch him when he tagged it.

"Okay." He continued to linger. "I'm, um, sorry you dropped my class."

"I hated to drop it," I lied. "It was something I had to do though."

"I hope it wasn't because of my teaching." Sincerity shone out of his brown eyes.

"Heavens no. I enjoyed your class." Lie, lie, lie! I hoped my nose didn't grow. "It's just that I have a lot going on now. And statistics take a lot of work."

"You should have come by and talked to me if you needed help. I'm always glad to help interested students." He glanced at me and looked quickly away.

Stupid bandage. I must look like a dork with it stuck over the stitches. "I'll remember next time."

He kept glancing at me and away, and I noticed Miss Ruby unobtrusively trying to catch my attention. She patted her nose.

Not the bandage. Lower. Oh, no. "Is my nose bleeding?"

He nodded, avoiding my eyes.

"Paper cut," I muttered, looking for a tissue.

Miss Ruby handed me one. "Paper cut? On your nose?" Now that my problem was out in the open, she had no compunction talking about it. "How in God's name did you manage to get a paper cut on your nose?"

I waggled my fingers. "It happens."

She went back to her work, shaking her head in disbelief.

Once I stanched the bleeding, Professor Random cleared his throat a couple of times. "I don't suppose you want to eat lunch with me?"

Think I wouldn't jump at the chance? Bloody nose and all.

Then I remembered. "Oh. I've already eaten."

He looked so downcast, I said without thinking, "But I'd love to go drink some iced tea with you if you're eating somewhere close."

He brightened. I had second thoughts about taking another lunch break. Then again, who would fuss if I took extra time?

I was the tax commissioner, wasn't I?

Ignoring Delores's frigid disapproval, I got my purse and we left. With Rayla, naturally.

Despite my telling her we were just going down the street and I'd be fine, she gave a sidelong glance at Professor Random and smiled like a cat licking cream. "It's my job, sweetie. So do I call you 'professor' or what?"

"Um, Jeffrey. Jeff."

"Great, Jeff. Let's go."

She recommended Joanie's Vittles to him, and we started back down the street. Professor Random wasn't much of a talker, but Rayla was. With a few helpful comments from me, she carried the conversation. At the restaurant, once we touched on his classic Mustang that he'd restored himself and the college and his classes and the weather, even Rayla ran out of topics.

After a short silence while he tackled his food, he cleared his throat and made an effort. "I, ah, I'm thinking of doing some work to my house. I wondered if you might know anything about a Friendly Houzer."

"Is that like one of those portable potties?" Rayla asked.

He blinked.

She pressed on. "My uncle works for a rental company and they rent them, I think. If you need one . . ."

"Oh, um, actually, Mr. Houzer's a building contractor," Professor Random said with a pink face. "He gave me a quote on some things I needed done. I don't know anybody here, so I hoped you could tell me if he was reasonable and reliable. Or not."

My face heated in sympathy.

"Oh." Rayla, unfazed, didn't notice his complexion. "No. Never heard of him, Jeff. Sorry. You ought to check with the planning department and see if he's got a business license. I bet he's one of those Houzers living out in the County Line community."

Time to change the subject. I asked, "Where did you buy a house, Professor?"

He gave all his attention to piercing a green bean. "Down at the bottom of Goat Ridge."

"Really?" Billy Lee Woodhallen lived on top of the ridge. Rayla and I exchanged glances. Should we warn the professor? I tiptoed around a decision. "What made you decide to buy over there instead of closer to the college?"

He gathered up some sweet potato soufflé. "It isn't that far from the school. And the lot is quite pretty. There are some big trees and a little brook running down the back of it. My, um, my—some of my relatives used to live near the ridge a few generations back. When I was looking for the area where they were located, I saw this house for sale and thought, why not?"

"Are you interested in genealogy?" I asked.

He swallowed his soufflé. "I do research whenever I can. Um, I've been wondering how Goat Ridge got its name. Do you know?"

I nodded. "My father said there used to be bunches of goats there a long time ago. In his grandfather's time, I think. Not any now, so far as I know."

Rayla choked on her tea so I knew she was thinking the same thing I was.

Except for Billy Lee.

As she coughed, I pounded her back. "What was the name of your relatives, Professor?"

He picked up another bean, avoided my eye. "They've all died out."

"The only people I know ever actually lived on top of the ridge were the Woodhallens. Your relatives didn't live up there, did they?"

"Um, I don't really know at this point. I'm still researching."

Surely to goodness the professor wasn't related to Billy Lee. I looked at his guileless, sweet face and thought of Billy Lee's scowl. No way. "Well, Billy Lee and his momma are the only Woodhallens left who still live up that way. The big house on top of the ridge is his."

"Oh?" Professor Random picked up a homemade roll and broke it in two. "Do you know Billy Lee?"

Do I know Billy Lee! "I've met him."

"Do you suppose he could fill me in on some history about the community?"

Rayla sputtered tea again.

I ignored her. "Billy Lee's not what you call real sociable. He probably could help you if he wanted to because his family's been there forever. Thing is, he's not too keen on helping people."

"You might be better off going to somebody like Delores or Miss Ruby," Rayla put in, using a napkin to wipe up the tea she'd splattered. "They live up that way, too."

"The old lady in your office?" Dismayed, the professor shook his head. "I'd rather not bother her. Maybe I'll take my chances with this Billy Lee."

Miss Ruby did sometimes frighten people, with her blunt speech and forthright manner hiding her heart of gold. But if he asked Billy Lee, he'd think Miss Ruby was the good fairy.

No, the professor didn't need to approach Billy Lee. I said, "Maybe Delores in our office could tell you something. Like Rayla said, she and Miss Ruby both live over in that area. Billy Lee's not the best person to ask though. He's kind of known as a—" Murderer? Arsonist? Drug runner? "He kind of has a bad reputation."

"Really?" Half a roll remained suspended. Professor Random blushed. "You mean like—Women? That kind of reputation?"

Rayla tried not to snigger. She was enjoying this, darn her.

I frowned at her. "Uh, no, I haven't heard that about him." The thought of Billy Lee as a ladies' man made me want to throw up. "More like the local hoodlum bit. I'd guess he doesn't take kindly to strangers coming up to his house. He keeps guns, I'm pretty sure."

"Oh." Professor Random blinked and put his roll in his mouth while I debated telling him about Billy Lee and his unsavory past, including his suspicious present. In the end, neither Rayla nor I said anything because Professor Random asked for the check right after that.

Kind of a bust, but he did insist on paying for our teas.

CHAPTER 10

To save me rental fees, Momma had decided she and I could share her sedan, so it was her Ford Focus I took to school that night.

Since my homework for Tuesday's business accounting class was done, I was set to leave at five when Rayla mentioned we needed to wait for James Cleuny. "Since he's on duty with you tonight, he's coming in a little early."

"Aw, no, don't tell me that. He snored last time he went to class with me and embarrassed me no end. When I woke him up, he nearly fell out of his seat. Can't you extend your shift till after I get out of class?"

James showed up in time to hear. "I need the overtime to pay my alimony. I'm behind."

"And I've got some paperwork to catch up on," said Rayla, though I knew from a chance remark by Sherry that she was actually meeting some friends for happy hour at the disreputable Old Dixie Bar and Grill outside town that Daddy had absolutely forbidden me and all my siblings to go near from the time we could drive.

Miracle of miracles, James did manage to control himself and not go to sleep during class. I'm pretty sure he was either playing games or surfing on his county cell phone, but at least he had the tones silenced, so it didn't matter.

Afterward, headed home with his headlights right behind me, I couldn't help but think of the last time he'd followed me on the way home from class. The other evening's skies had been as peaceful as tonight's. Then the bird fell out of the blue and the pleasant drive had turned into a nightmare.

Well, it fell out of the dark, I amended. Anyway, the attack was a total surprise, no matter where it came from.

The slumbering, lonely countryside made me apprehensive.

"Don't be silly," I said out loud. "How many times can a bird break your windshield?"

The night was beautiful, warm and clear with an almost full moon that lit up fields and shrubbery like a dim sun. After we passed the lake marking the county line, I turned onto my regular route. The short county road linked the road coming from the school to the road leading home.

James stayed right behind me.

Coming out of a curve, the sedan drifted into the middle of the road.

Yeah, maybe I was going a little fast, but this was a deserted country road. In three years traveling on it this time of night, I could count on one hand the number of cars I'd seen.

Maybe James won't notice my veering out of my lane, I thought as I approached the old railroad overpass. Still blaming me for his probation, he probably wouldn't hesitate to write me a ticket for driving over the centerline.

When the windshield on Momma's car shattered, my first thought was, *No, not again!*

James didn't ram me from the rear as before, but the force of the impact caused me to jerk the wheel to the right.

The car hit the concrete pillars supporting the bridge head-on.

The airbag deployed.

James's siren went off as I gasped for air. My ribs and shoulder hurt from the seat belt. Worse, my face was smashed against the airbag so that I couldn't breathe.

When I finally got my nose to the side, the air smelled funny, like the bag had puffed rubbery talcum powder out.

"I don't believe this!" I croaked to nobody in particular. "I frigging don't believe this!"

The sound of my own voice reassured me I was alive.

My shoulders, still sore from my first accident, hurt like anything. The talc smell was suffocating. I had to gasp to breathe.

This couldn't be doing my lungs any good.

James came running up, yelling, "I saw it! I saw it all! There was a truck up on the old railroad bridge and somebody hefted something over at you! Don't know what it was! I saw it falling though! I saw it hit! I saw—"

I was beginning to see red. "Why the heck are you here then? Why aren't you going after the bozo who threw it?"

He calmed a bit. "Don't get your bowels in an uproar. No way to get up there from here. I already put in a call to throw up a blockade to catch that truck. We got him this time!" He started talking into the radio on his shoulder.

I managed to push aside the airbag enough to brush little pebbles of safety glass off my lap and arms. This was beginning to seem real familiar.

My fingers scraped something hard on the seat beside me. I shoved back the airbag so I could see.

"It was a concrete block," I told James.

To myself, my voice sounded strangely calm, but there must have been something disturbed in my tone because he stopped talking to his radio. "What?" He sounded like he thought I'd lost my mind.

"The thing you saw fall." I worked with the airbag, wrestling it back enough to show James the cinder block sitting on the seat beside me.

The block had smashed through the middle of the windshield,

barely missing me. Had I not been driving over the centerline, it would have come through my side of the windshield and hit me smack in the face. A foot more in my direction and I'd have been hurt bad.

No. I'd have been dead.

Miracle of miracles, Dr. Bennigan was not on duty that night. My mother was, but finding me relatively unscathed except for the bruises from the seat belt, she turned her attention toward her car.

"Is it hurt bad?" she asked, wringing her hands. "Was there much damage? Which side hit the barrier?"

I avoided answering her anxious queries about her car's condition. With liquids dripping from the engine, the Focus had looked pretty much totaled, but I didn't want to tell her that.

Besides, someone might be able to repair it. Wilder things had happened.

Sheriff Duval came over to see me after Daddy brought me home. He listened to my story, then admitted under Daddy's questioning that they hadn't been able to catch the truck James saw. "We threw up a roadblock within minutes, but the truck had vanished. We figure it's someone who lives in the vicinity of that overpass, so we're going to canvass the area. We'll look in every garage and shed we can find as soon as it gets to be daylight."

Daddy watched him coldly. "You better check out Billy Lee Woodhallen first. He lives not too far from that overpass. If you go the back roads."

The sheriff stood up, picked up his hat. "About five miles away as the crow flies. But he—"

"Has an alibi," I finished.

He gave a reluctant grin. "His wife says—"

"You know what? I'd like to meet his wife, tell her a thing or two!"

"Now, Corrie." He shook his head. "You can be sure we'll check it out."

Some kid I'd seen only once before, another Huck Finn type with shaggy hair and big excited eyes, was assigned to play guardian that night. After Sheriff Duval left, we stared at each other for a while. He perched on the edge of his seat as if expecting something to happen.

"I'm going to bed," I told him finally.

"Don't be afraid. I'll be right here if you need me," he assured me earnestly. "You just holler. I'm gonna sit up all night so I'll hear you if you call."

This was beginning to get on my nerves.

Wednesday morning at work, even though I figured the sheriff had already thought of it, I began looking up owners of old trucks. The state computer held every currently tagged and titled vehicle in Georgia. Since I worked here, I had access to the data. I wasn't supposed to use it for personal reasons but hey, this was in search of a killer. Besides, Sheriff Duval had sworn me in as ex-officio sheriff. The reasoning behind a tax commissioner being an ex-officio was so he, or in my case, she, could sell property for overdue taxes without the sheriff's help. I figured being an ex-officio should let me get by with doing other things a tag clerk couldn't do.

Georgia didn't start issuing titles till the mid-1960s, so there might not be a title on the truck if it dated back far enough. But if anyone had driven it on the road, there would have to be a tag listed.

Probably with Billy Lee's name on it.

I looked him up first. Along with eleven cars, most of them vintage collector types, I found three trucks. One was a big flatbed, one was the new F-450 crew cab pickup he normally drove, and one was an old truck with a Hobby Antique tag. This last, a '58 Ford, was the silver pickup Ethan had mentioned he owned.

Maybe I should talk to the courthouse cleaner on the chance she'd noticed anything else about the truck besides its color. Maybe she could remember some detail she'd forgotten to tell the sheriff.

Like its tag number.

"Looking for trucks?" Delores said from behind my back.

I jumped a foot. "Geez, Delores! You scared the pee turk out of me."

"Miss Ruby told me about what happened to you last night. Sheriff's crazy if he doesn't arrest Billy Lee." She didn't sound especially friendly, but at least she was talking to me again.

"He's got an alibi."

She snorted.

I laughed. "Yeah, that's what I think, too."

Rayla Cothrew, today's bodyguard, overheard. "Last night he's alibied for sure. He was at Sylvia Smythe-Ramali's dance studio. Ballet practice."

In unison, Delores and I swung shocked faces toward her.

Even Miss Ruby, from her stool at the counter, turned her back on her mobile home customer to stare. Her mouth sagged.

Rayla bristled at our disbelief. "Well, he was. Everybody there saw him."

This boggled the mind.

Miss Ruby put a hand on her heart and leaned forward conspiratorially. "Billy Lee takes ballet?"

Rayla huffed. "Are you crazy? His daughters do."

I took this news in. Girls who looked like Billy Lee in tutus.

More than mindboggling.

Miss Ruby and I locked eyes. She was imagining the same images I was. She started to laugh, tried to stop, couldn't, and had to excuse herself to her customer. "Be right back, miss. Heh heh."

As fast as her stubby little legs would carry her, she made her way into the vault, where we soon heard her whoops floating out to us and the customers.

I asked Rayla, "Do you think Billy Lee could have hired somebody to throw that cinder block through my car?"

"I wouldn't put it past him," Delores piped up. "Everybody knows he set that fire at the nuns' place and is probably dealing drugs on the side." She frowned toward the vault. "Hadn't you better make that old biddy get back out here and finish up her customer?"

I disregarded the last comment.

"Aw, who knows what happened?" Rayla said. "A concrete block. Kids out playing pranks. They do awful things like that all the time 'cause their parents let 'em run wild. Might not have been meant for you in particular at all."

Delores snorted again. "You ask me, the bird gave him the idea for throwing that block." She went back to her accounting.

I felt like snorting, too, as I headed to my office. Next to Rayla, James Cleuny was beginning to look like a pretty decent bodyguard. At least, he believed somebody was out to get me.

Miss Ruby came out of the vault, wiping her eyes after getting her mirth under control. Five minutes after she went back to her customer, she called in her penetrating voice, "Corr-reee! I can't find this mobile home on this blooming computer."

I sighed and went out to help her look. After searching several ways, I couldn't find it either.

The hard-featured woman waiting grew impatient. "Hey, what's the problem? Cedric Jessop signed the title over to me all legal. I got it right here. See? But she—" She jerked her head in Miss Ruby's direction. The big hoop earrings wobbled in front of her pulled-back hair. "She won't let me change the title till I pay the taxes. Now she won't let me pay the taxes 'cause she says the doublewide isn't in her computer. I got somebody lined up to move it, and they're coming this afternoon. I got to get a decal before they show up or they won't move it."

I looked at the title. "I can't find any record taxes were ever paid. Mr. Jessop's name isn't coming up as owner, and the VIN isn't coming up either." I didn't mention that sometimes mobile home VINs get confused because of the hyphens or slash marks and we couldn't pull them up on the computer. "Where's the mobile home located?"

She told me, but she was vague in her directions.

I still couldn't find any record. "Is there a decal on it?"

She shrugged. Movement under the knit top revealed she didn't wear a bra. "How should I know?"

The scandalized Miss Ruby saw the bobbing breasts, gasped, and pursed her mouth.

"Look. I just bought it." The woman leaned an elbow and a breast on the counter. She put her chin in her hand. "Tell me the tax amount and I'll pay it, okay?"

I studied the title. The mobile home was a four-year-old doublewide. The seller didn't own property in the county, which meant he couldn't claim homestead. If I had to charge taxes for four years, this woman was not going to be a happy camper.

I got her name from the title. "Ms. Pendervil, you might be better off to go out and check for a decal on the mobile home. If there's a decal to show taxes are already paid, you won't have to—"

She jerked upright and slapped the counter. "Listen to me, dammit! Figure the taxes and let me pay! I've got to have a current decal before that mover comes, or he won't move it and I'll be out a bunch of money!"

She was going to be sorry. I put on a fake smile. "Okay. I'll be happy to do that."

I typed in the mobile home information, looking up each year's assessments for that particular model in the manual issued by the state. It took about twenty minutes.

"Looks like it's going to be two thousand six hundred eighty—"

She hit the roof. "Two thousand dollars! Are you crazy? That's nearly what they're charging me to move it! This is a mobile home we're talking about! A trailer!"

"Yes, ma'am. But if no taxes have been paid for four years, then I have to charge you for the back years, too."

Turning her back to me, she made as if to leave. Then her skinny blue-jeaned rear stopped its swinging. She raised her face and both fists to the ceiling as if threatening God, then turned back. "This is the most—" She leaned on the counter in front of me. "Listen, taxes must have been paid. It's been right there on the river the whole time."

"Whereabouts on the river?"

She got a little more particular about its whereabouts, but I still couldn't find anything. "Okay," I finally said. "Why don't you ride out there and see if it has a decal on it. If you can find one, jot down the year and the number and we'll go from there. Maybe taxes were paid under somebody else's name or something. That does happen occasionally."

She clumped out, muttering.

"We close at twelve thirty," Miss Ruby squawked after her. "You need to get back here by then or you'll have to wait till tomorrow."

The woman flapped a hand behind her. "Yeah, yeah."

At least I think she flapped a hand. She may have done something else with her fingers, but if so, I didn't want to know.

About midmorning, the state auditor showed up. "I'm Jerri Sinclare. I've met you before when I audited Mr. Jethro." She looked askance at my head bandage.

"Little accident," I mumbled.

She waited for me to say more.

I didn't.

She smiled at me, inviting my confidences.

I looked out the window.

She gave up. "Oh-kay, let's get started then. I usually work in Mr. Jethro's office."

"Right." I led the way, glad I'd managed to clean it up before she came.

In dress slacks and pale pink shirt that flattered her milk-chocolate complexion, Jerri spent half the day going over the legalities of running a tax office. I heard and understood the first part of what she said without a problem, but after thirty minutes, my mind couldn't help wandering no matter how hard I tried to keep it on track.

The phone rang constantly, and Miss Ruby's nasal voice answering callers distracted me. Especially when I heard her saying, "No, I can't tell you. I'm just part-time. You gotta talk to somebody who knows something about salvage. Delores!"—and then mutter—"What the Sam hill? I hit the transfer button like I was s'posed to. Hello? Hello? You still there?"

Besides worrying about what the phone callers would think, I also worried about the mobile home customer. I should have told the skinny witch to go back to whoever she bought it from and find out . . .

The words *hefty fine* suddenly penetrated. "Um, Jerri. Excuse me? Can you repeat that? The part about the hefty fine? Now what's that for again?"

"If your tax digest isn't submitted to the state on time," the auditor repeated patiently, "the county will have to pay a hefty fine."

"A fine? Er, how much?"

She told me. My hair stood on end. "Let me get this straight.

The assessors have to get the tax digest together. But getting it in to the state on time and swearing that it's accurate is *my* responsibility?"

"Yep. As tax commissioner. By law. Of course," she went on cheerfully, "this year will be different. Mr. Jethro's death can be considered mitigating circumstances. We'll be more forgiving if you're a little late. But you still need to ask for an extension in writing if you see you can't make the deadline."

"Aiiigh," I said weakly. I vaguely remembered Mr. Jethro complaining about the countywide reassessment the assessors had embarked on and how much work it was and how worried he was about how long it was taking. I'd have to talk to Fred Bauers and find out how close he and Calvin were to finishing. No way would a late digest and hefty county fine be pinned on me.

The auditor planned to work all day, but this was Wednesday, our half day.

I told her so.

The auditor didn't care. "Miss Ruby can go, but I need you and Delores to stay. I already have to spend one night up here, but I am not coming back." She might as well have added, "Back to this godforsaken place out in the boondocks where there isn't even a coffee house or yuppie restaurant," because that's sure what it sounded like she meant.

When I told Demon Delores we'd be working late that afternoon, she looked up over her bifocals at me as if I were clueless. "Duh. I figured that. We always work late when the state auditors come."

The impatient mobile home buyer returned right before lunch with a decal number from the previous year.

I looked it up on the computer. "Um, this decal was issued to a nineteen ninety-two single-wide mobile home."

"What?"

I didn't like the fire in Ms. Pendervil's eyes. "Er, yes, and the name's different, too. This decal was issued to a mobile home owned by a J. Hoffman Browmeyer."

My customer calmed down when she recognized the name. "Jay? That's Ceddie's ex-father-in-law."

"Ceddie? The seller?"

"Yeah. Ceddie lived in Jay's old trailer till he bought this new one a few years back."

"I see here that Mr. Jessop is the one who actually paid taxes on it."

She smirked. "I told you so."

I gave her the bad news. "Looks like he paid taxes and got a decal for the single-wide. In fact, he's paid taxes on the single-wide for the past four years. Up till this year."

"Fine." All she heard was paid taxes. "So can I pay this year's taxes and get my decal?"

Boy, was she naïve. "I'm afraid it's not that simple."

When I explained all four years' taxes on the double-wide would have to be paid, I thought she'd have a hissy fit.

I moved back slightly on my stool so she couldn't reach me across the counter. "If the old trailer is gone, Mr. Jessop may have kept paying taxes on it because he didn't realize the tax bill was for a different mobile home. However, if the old trailer's gone, he can come in and we'll talk about refunding what he paid on it for those years when it wasn't here."

All the while knowing the truth.

This Cedric Jessop character knew darned well what he was doing. Taxes on an old single-wide trailer were lots cheaper than taxes on a brand new double-wide.

The woman seethed as she wrote out a check. "He's going to pay me back every cent of this," she vowed as she handed it over the counter.

I gave her a current decal. "I hope it works out for you. At least you can get the mobile home moved."

She left muttering. I didn't blame her.

Mobile homes were impossible to keep straight. This Jessop fellow had more than likely moved the old one out and the new one in without telling anyone. Most mobile home owners knew that as long as they had a decal displayed, even if it was for a different mobile home, the sheriff's department would think taxes were paid and leave them alone.

There were too many shifty people like this Ceddie fellow.

The clock said twelve fifteen. Before closing the office and breaking for lunch, I asked the auditor about selling tax liens.

"When people don't pay taxes, you are bound by your oath to do what you have to do to collect," she said sternly. "You can either sell the property yourself or transfer the liens."

"I don't know how to do either."

"Use your delinquent tax manual to guide you."

What delinquent tax manual?

Seeing my face, Jerri relented. "Or you can contract with one of the delinquent agencies. There are several good ones in the state. In fact, they'll be at Athens next month. You *are* coming to Athens for the state meeting, aren't you?"

"I don't know if I'll be able to leave the office, since we're shorthanded. Mr. Jethro and Delores always went to Athens, but I stayed here to help customers. I usually went to a seminar in Dalton or Blairsville or somewhere closer to home."

She sighed. "You're the tax commissioner now. If you don't go to any other conference all year, you go to Athens." She shook a finger at me. "That's where you learn about all the new rules and regulations the legislature has saddled us with. It's *the* conference for tax commissioners. Even if you have to close the office for a couple of days, you go. Plus it gives you your mandatory fifteen hours of continuing tax education every year."

I gulped. "I guess I'll be there, then."

"I guess you better."

After twelve thirty that Wednesday, the office turned surprisingly peaceful, with no customers tramping in. Delores had brought her lunch, but the auditor, Rayla, and I headed down to MoJo's Magic Eatery for sandwiches. I needed to be at home working on my accounting homework, but resigned myself to hanging around as long as it took to get rid of the state auditor.

Jerri had fast turned from a life preserver to a pain in the butt.

After lunch, sitting beside me at Mr. Jethro's desk in the visitor's chair that didn't roll, she went over the collection and disbursement procedures of which, surprise surprise, I knew exactly nothing.

"You really need to deposit daily," she said, studying some reports Delores had given her. "I know in the off season you don't have that much property tax money coming in to deposit, but still. One deposit a month won't cut it."

"Delores always handles the deposits and disbursements. You ought to tell her." I sure wasn't going to. Delores was still pretty cool toward me, and my head was beginning to hurt from all the dos and don'ts the auditor kept throwing at me. "She keeps the books, too. I don't have anything to do with that stuff."

Jerri clucked. "That's fine, but ultimately you're the one responsible if the disbursements are off."

I hadn't realized what a smug smile the woman possessed. "Which means exactly what?"

"If your final report is off, or if you turn it in late for that matter, then you, and not the county, will be personally liable for fines. Or sitting in jail, as the case may be."

My eyes bulged as I tried not to hyperventilate.

She laughed. "I don't think you need worry. Delores has always been dependable. I'm sure after all these years she's trustworthy, although there have been cases . . ." She cleared her throat. "Anyway, I'm going to help you this year because of all the circumstances involved. Now," she said briskly, "on to the final reporting."

I had found some papers on Mr. Jethro's credenza that said "Final Accounting" at the top. She took them between her thumb and one finger, and shook her head in disapproval. "Mr. Jethro always did it by hand the old way, even though we've had a computer program set up for years. He could have worked his whole report up in a couple of hours if he'd let us give it to him. Never mind. I'll install the program so you can use it in the future. Right now I'm going to plug these figures he's written down into my laptop and see where we stand."

She worked all afternoon, occasionally getting Delores to run different reports or asking her questions about something or other. I guess the answers were satisfactory, because around five thirty, when we prepared to knock off for the day, she said, "Everything looks good. We'll send you an official notice saying so, but you don't have anything to worry about moneywise. Looks like you've overpaid us by about two hundred dollars, so the county'll be getting a refund. Otherwise, everything's in order. I'll drop by in the morning to finish up. Shouldn't take long."

I breathed a huge sigh of relief. I didn't have extra cash to pay any fines the state might have slapped me with.

CHAPTER 11

Thursday morning, I talked to Fred Bauers, the chief assessor, about the digest.

"Right on schedule," he assured me proudly. He slicked his thinning hair back and straightened his glasses in evident satisfaction. "Took us all year working a lot of weekends, but the last reassessment notices went out Monday." He leaned over to peer at me earnestly. "Of course the taxpayers have forty-five days to appeal their new assessments, you understand."

I nodded as if knowledgeable about what he meant.

"However," he went on, as exacting as ever, "the percentage won't be big enough to hold up the digest, not even if all of this last batch appeals, and I doubt they will."

Not having the slightest idea what he was talking about, I didn't know whether to congratulate him or agree with him. I compromised. "Um, fine. Good job. So we can count on the digest being ready to go to the state on time?"

"Oh, heck, yeah." He beamed. "We'll be ready to hand it off to you July first, so you can start working on your part. No problem."

My part? My part? This called for some research to see exactly what my part was.

Ask state about what to do with digest once assessors finish their part, I wrote down on a note pad I'd started keeping.

After talking with the auditor when she showed up about nine, I found that, upon receiving the digest, I was expected to reconcile the assessments and other data from the assessors' computer system with our own collection system. I had to make sure no assessment amounts had been dropped or changed during the transition, and that every taxpayer got all the exemptions due him or her.

I also had to make sure nobody got extra exemptions they weren't entitled to.

"You don't want anyone getting more benefits than they deserve." Jerri laughed like the whole idea was hilarious. "Cuts down on your tax money coming in."

I laughed, too, but my laughter was hollow. How in the world would I know the difference?

The auditor went on, "Once you're satisfied the data is accurate, that everything the assessors have has been transferred to your computer system, you can calculate tax bills."

Once calculations were done, I would fill in forms required by the state, sign off on them, and submit them. The state could either accept or reject the digest.

"After all the trouble we've gone through, why would you reject it?" My voice rose as I listened to the list of what I was expected to do.

"Normally we don't," Jerri soothed. "As long as you've done your advertising correctly and your figures are within a certain percentage of what they should be and everything's signed off on. There are several things we'll be checking on, but I'm sure you'll be fine."

My eyes glazed over as I looked at the fistful of forms she handed me. "All these have to be filled out? I don't even know what they mean."

"Not all of them are yours. Your assessors will do some, and your board of commissioners will do some. One in there is for the city to sign off on, too. Just be sure you have them all finished before you submit the digest."

Sure I would.

The bottom line was, once the state okayed the digest as accurate, I could actually generate tax bills and mail them out.

"Assume we get that far." My head hurt in earnest. "All this calculating and generating tax bills entails . . . Exactly what?"

The auditor gathered up her laptop and purse. "I suggest you talk to your IT guy. He's been here a while. He should be up on that part." She held out a hand, shook mine firmly. "I put a card there on your desk with my cell number on it. Call if you have questions. I try to return calls. Usually."

Too dazed to protest, I watched her blithely leave me to my fate. It was an hour before I could summon the energy to look for the IT guy.

"Oh, yeah," he said when I chased him down and cornered him at the computer room door. "I know all about it."

Dressed in jeans and t-shirt, he looked younger than me, like maybe sixteen. And what was that sweetish smell hanging around him? "Um, this is real important, Dyson."

"Yeah, I know." He rubbed something clinging to the front of his shirt.

Tobacco or—were those weed particles he was brushing off?

He took advantage of my distraction to slide around me. "I've done the digest for five years now, Corrie. Don't sweat it."

I watched him weave down the hall. Yep, that whiff I caught was definitely pot. His brain was probably soft, but what choice did I have except to trust he could do his job?

After recovering, I called one of the delinquent tax companies the state auditor had mentioned. The lady I spoke with seemed knowledgeable, so I made an appointment for her to come talk to me the next week. Then I called two of the others and made appointments with them, too. I didn't want to be accused of favoritism.

Much as I dreaded it, I was going to have to do something

about Billy Lee's liens. My stomach got butterflies as I thought about his reaction. So I tried not to think about it.

When I started to leave work that evening, the battery on my rental car (actually Momma's rental car, since her insurance paid more toward one than mine) was dead, probably because I'd left the lights on that morning. The bodyguard of the day, the snotty skinhead, didn't carry jumper cables, nor did he seem interested in rounding any up. Daddy was at a Rotary dinner, so that left a tow truck demanding cash on the barrel or . . .

"Shoot. Guess it'll have to be Ethan." I pulled out my cell.

He showed up in twenty minutes and waved at my bodyguard. "Yo, Tim. How's it going, man?" They chatted a moment, then he approached the rental car. "Hey, Corrie, what'd you do? Leave your lights on again?" He stared. "What happened to your nose? Did that concrete block hit you when it came through your windshield?"

I gritted my teeth. "No. Paper cut got a little infected."

"Paper cut? On your nose? You beat all."

"Don't start on me."

He wisely backed off. While he put cables on batteries, the skinhead leaned against his car and watched. Lazy bum.

"Heard you had a date with the statistics professor Tuesday," Ethan called from under the hood.

"It wasn't a date. He came to get a tag, and Rayla and I walked over and had iced tea with him while he ate lunch."

"That so? Okay, get in and try it."

I got in, turned the key, and the rental car started right up. Tim the Skinhead ambled toward his car. Ethan waited a minute, took off the cables, and closed the hood. Curling the cables up, he poked his head in my window. "Did you know he had a trespassing charge filed against him?"

"Who did?"

"Professor Random."

"You're kidding!"

"Nope. And guess who filed it?" Ethan's eyes danced.

"How would I know?"

Ethan gave a quick glance to make sure Tim was out of earshot. "Billy Lee Woodhallen."

My mouth dropped. "What . . . how . . . ?"

"Said he saw the professor skulking. That was the word he used. Yep, said the professor was skulking around his ten-acre pasture and earlier, he saw him sneaking round his—Billy Lee's—woods."

"Oh, come on. That doesn't mean Professor Random's trespassing. He lives over that way, and he was probably out walking. Lots of people like to walk nowadays."

"That's what Duke told Billy Lee, but Billy Lee still insisted on filing a complaint. Duke's going over today to talk to the professor."

Guilt overwhelmed me. I should have warned the professor about Billy Lee when I found out he'd bought a house in the vicinity of our local criminal.

Ethan didn't notice. "Oh, and something else. I got to take his class next term, and everybody says how hard it is. You think you could put in a good word for me?"

"With Professor Random? Hey, I had iced tea with the man. That's all I did. Why the heck do you think I can finagle you a passing grade if I had to drop his course myself before I flunked it?"

He held up the cables, crossed as if to ward off a demon. "Don't get your panties in a wad. Just thought I'd see if you could do anything for me."

Mollified, I asked, "What's happening on the big case?"

He shrugged. "Billy Lee's alibi is tight. For the murder and for the block someone threw at you. Sheriff's thinking of looking elsewhere. Doesn't want to, but says he may have to call in the GBI."

"Where else can he look? Nobody else has anything vaguely resembling a motive." I tried not to think of Lucy's poor husband killed by mistake. "The state auditor was here yesterday. She suggested I use a tax service to help with those liens. I think the best thing to do is to go ahead and sell them. Once they're gone, Billy Lee won't have any reason to come after me."

And maybe nobody else will get hurt.

Ethan cocked his head knowingly. "Appears to me Billy Lee might be pretty p.o.'ed if you sell his liens. May come after you out of spite. Everybody knows how he is."

"You make me feel so much better."

He didn't recognize sarcasm and waved his hand as he left to put the jumper cables back in his car. "Any time."

Briant's body hadn't been released, but Lucy came back to work on Friday anyway. She was quiet and red-eyed in a button-up blouse similar to the ones Delores habitually wore. Without makeup and with her hair carelessly pulled back in a pony-tail, she didn't look like the perky Lucy I remembered.

Her wooden demeanor worried me. "Should you be at work so soon after . . . ?" I couldn't say the words.

On her work desk, she had lit a vanilla-scented candle, one of the big heavy ones enclosed in a pint-sized canning jar. Maybe in memory of her husband. I didn't ask. I didn't tell her candles weren't allowed either. Delores had put the kibosh on them a long time ago, ruling they could set the office on fire.

Demon Delores didn't like perfumes or strong scents.

But I was the one in charge now. If a candle made Lucy feel better, let her burn one.

Lucy studied its flame while a tiny muscle in her jaw worked.

"I can't stay home. All I see there is Bri. At least here I can keep busy and take my mind off what happened."

I made Miss Ruby, protesting volubly, wait on walk-ins and gave Lucy the mail to process, since she was still learning. That worked well except for Miss Ruby's way of avoiding controversy with argumentative customers.

"I'm just part-time," her nasal voice could be heard whenever a tag buyer took exception to the cost of the tag or to penalties due. "If you've got a problem, you need to take it up with the tax commissioner." Then she'd bellow, "Corr-reee! Come on out here and talk to this man!" Or *woman.* Or an occasional muttered *idjit.* Miss Ruby wasn't particular.

Much as I loved her, she did keep me hopping.

At lunch Lucy and I, accompanied by Rayla, walked to Joanie's Vittles. A man stopped us on the sidewalk in front of the restaurant, offering earnest condolences to Lucy. Rayla knew him, too, and joined in the conversation. Reluctant to witness the stiff demeanor that hid Lucy's grief whenever her husband was mentioned, I went inside and found a table.

Despite telling myself Briant's death wasn't my fault, I knew the truth. I was the one who'd given Lucy the cookie bar that killed him. After I picked up the tattered menu and focused on my choices, a soft voice from behind made me jump.

"You did it anyway, didn't you? You took the job after I told you Billy Lee had an alibi. When I warned you he'd be out to get the new tax commissioner."

Slim hips in faded jeans came into view. Bodie Fairhurst.

I kept my eyes on the menu. "I hope you're not talking to me."

The snake in the grass put his hands on the table and bent toward me so other diners wouldn't hear. "Tell me this. Did you do it because I told you not to?"

He wore a University hat on his dark hair and a pastel check button-up shirt with the collar open. Its short sleeves revealed a sprinkling of hair on muscled arms and a mole on his wrist that I'd once known intimately. The expression currently on his face was an unfamiliar one. Bodie had always been laid back, but today he looked ready to explode.

My temper rose, but I heard my daddy's voice saying, *play nice, play nice.* So I stared up at the ceiling. Looked like a fly or something had got in and was hanging up there. "Strange how some people seem to think they have so much influence over other people. They even believe their opinions might make someone do something she didn't want to do," I mused. No, maybe that spot was a spider up there. "Those kinds of people must have really big egos."

His hands made fists. "You did. You let yourself get talked into being tax commissioner just to spite me. You put yourself in danger because I told you not to."

"Really big egos," I repeated. "And I'm very well protected, thank you very much." I didn't want to know what the spot was, so I ostentatiously held up the menu. "You're blocking my light."

About that time, Rayla and Lucy came in.

Bodie, who had been a year behind Lucy in high school, immediately softened his stance. He hugged her with genuine concern. "I sure am sorry, Luce. How are you holding up, hon?"

Lucy managed a mechanical smile. "Thanks, Bodie. I'm doing fine. I came back to work today."

"Hi, Bodie," Rayla said, switching on the flirtatious aura that any attractive male brought out.

White teeth flashed. Black lashes narrowed. "Hey, Rayla. Are you the guard today?"

Rayla squared her shoulders, a movement that accentuated her breasts. "Yeah. Duke's letting me do some field work."

Bodie raised an ironic brow at me. "Well protected, I see," he murmured.

I flushed.

About that time a striking redhead entered, and called Bodie's name. The modest charcoal suit and heels didn't hide her attributes but rather emphasized them.

He waved at her before turning back to us. "Good to see you out again, Lucy." His features formed into the calm ones I remembered from before the disastrous wedding that wasn't. "Take care, Corrie, Rayla." Another minute found him across the room pulling out a chair for the redhead.

I turned my back on them as the waitress rushed up.

"That's Maura Czerny with Bodie," Rayla volunteered after she ordered a grilled chicken sandwich with fries. "She's the new editor of the paper."

"Is that right." I allowed my disinterest in anything concerning *that man* to show.

Lucy said, "I wouldn't of thought she'd been here long enough to be latching onto Bodie that way. Reckon they already knew each other?"

"They could have," Rayla said. "She came up here from Marietta, I believe. They could of met in Atlanta."

"I'm sure I don't know," I said coldly. "Nor do I care. Did I hear Miss Ruby tell that last customer he needed to see a shrink, or did I imagine it?"

That effectively changed the subject until our food came. I didn't notice how my roast beef and creamed potatoes and fried okra tasted. I was too anxious to finish and get out of Bodie's vicinity.

I gulped my food down but still had to wait. Lucy picked at her vegetables. Rayla, after daintily cutting her sandwich in half, took her time eating it.

After patting my foot a few minutes, I got impatient and took advantage of Rayla laying down her sandwich to wipe her fingers. "Y'all through eating?"

"Give me a minute." Rayla hastily stuffed another bite into her mouth.

"Yeah, I'm done." Lucy pushed away from the table, leaving her roast beef half finished and the sweet potatoes and corn barely touched. She noticed me checking out her plate. "I'm not hungry. Want me to get a to-go box for you? You might want some of this later."

"No, thanks." All I wanted was to leave.

Rayla stood, grabbing one last fry to nibble on, and we went up front to pay. I was careful to keep my back toward Bodie and his friend.

As we walked back to the office, Lucy said, "I heard Bodie's gonna be in town a few weeks."

"Is that right," I said between clenched teeth.

Lucy either didn't catch my warning tone or was naturally foolhardy. "He's on admin leave or something. My cousin, who cleans house for his aunt on his daddy's side, told me that the aunt told her that Bodie's brother's wife says the GBI's doing some kind of internal investigation on him."

That stopped me in my tracks. Rayla, walking behind me too closely, stumbled into me. I caught her arm so she wouldn't fall.

"An internal investigation on Bodie?" I asked. "Someone's gotten confused in all this he-said, she-said stuff."

Rayla got her balance. "Investigating him for what?"

Lucy shrugged. "My cousin said there were rumors about him being mixed up in drugs or something."

"That's ridiculous. Bodie thinks drugs are stupid. He'd never be involved with drugs!" I was furious that anything like that was being said about him. I might despise and detest the dirty dog, but he didn't deserve blatant lies being circulated about

140

his character.

Lucy shrugged listlessly. "Not that Bodie was doing drugs. I think he was maybe taking bribes or something to overlook some trafficking or something. I don't know anything but what my cousin heard. Oh, she did say the GBI is looking into whether they should bring charges of corruption or something. One thing for sure is that Bodie's on admin leave while they look at the evidence."

Bodie was as straight as they came. His ethics, in fact, were probably better than mine. He'd no more take a bribe than shoot his favorite hound. I felt sick at my stomach, so sick I almost turned and went back to talk to him, tell him . . .

What? That I believed in him, that I knew the rumors were untrue?

He's not my concern any more, I reminded myself.

I could hate the man and still feel bad for him.

At five, my mother, being off for the day and the rest of the weekend, picked me up in her rental car to go tire kicking.

"You don't need me," I had protested that morning when she outlined her plans for my weekend. "I can't spare the time to go with you."

"I can't spare the time either, but you totaled my car. The least you can do is help me pick out another one. You know your father won't."

Daddy quit auto shopping with Momma years ago, after she dragged him to fifteen car lots in one day and then, after two more weeks of like shopping, went back to the first dealer to buy the one car he'd advised against.

So Momma and I had to inspect automobiles with a body-guard dogging us all weekend. Friday night, when we started at Caleb Bartovich's lot, we had an older, out of shape deputy who'd guarded me once before. He didn't say much but ate a lot of salted peanuts while we inspected cars.

After Momma spent an hour yearning after a year-old BMW red convertible with a black top, we took a test drive with the deputy crammed into the back seat. "You can only have the top off in nice weather, and it'd probably be drafty in the winter," Momma muttered as she bobbed its nose at a four-way stop and whipped through.

I held onto the dash. "I bet it gets good gas mileage since it's small."

"Insurance is probably high, too." She may have had two wheels on the ground when we turned a corner, but I couldn't swear to it.

I said between gritted teeth, "It only has eight thousand miles on it."

She shook her head gloomily. "Red convertible and speeding tickets go hand in hand."

"Keep your eyes on the road, Momma."

She sighed. "I don't think it's for me."

I felt knees pushing against the back of my seat. A quick glance revealed the deputy braced for an accident, forgotten peanut pack gripped tightly in the hand pushing against the side.

By the time we got the convertible back to the lot, the deputy had lost his appetite, and Momma had managed to talk herself out of buying the Beemer. We went to four other dealerships that night and test-drove five more cars.

The ashen deputy threw his peanuts away.

Saturday wouldn't have been much better except we had Rayla Cothrew trailing us. She didn't take long to get fed up with Momma's vacillations.

"What's wrong with this one?" she asked at the fourth place, after we spent thirty minutes inspecting a black Solstice convertible. "It looks just like you."

Momma dithered. "I don't know. It's more than I wanted to spend. I don't really like the color either. Black's so sober, don't you think? I'd feel like I was going to a funeral every day. Besides, it's a two-seater. There's barely room for me and groceries."

Rayla didn't give up. "Look, you've been checking out convertibles at every one of the places we've been this morning. We've tried out six of them already. Obviously you want one. All we need to decide is what color you want. What color do you like?"

Momma's spine stiffened. Her eyes narrowed. "I don't know, Rayla. If I knew, I'd be looking for that color, wouldn't I? And I don't necessarily want a convertible."

Rayla didn't pay attention to the gathering storm clouds. "You've complained about the blue one, the gray one, the green one, the white one, the maroon one, the orange one, and now this one. What does that leave? Red or yellow. Great. So we've narrowed it down now."

"I do not want a yellow car!"

"Okay, you want a red one. A red convertible."

Rayla's assertiveness spooked Momma. "That is most certainly not true. I wouldn't say I've decided anything. Simply because we're standing in front of a—"

"Sure you have. You're not looking at anything but convertibles, and you've ruled out every color but red," Rayla insisted.

Could Rayla be on to something? Crossing my fingers, I chimed in, "Ahem. We saw a red convertible at Sherry's husband's lot yesterday."

"There you go." Rayla turned to leave. "Come on, Jenny, we'll go over to Caleb's lot and you can get it."

Momma balked. "I don't really think—"

"Sherry ought to be able to swing you a discount," Rayla flung back over her shoulder. "After all, she owes Corrie for getting her that job with the county."

I stopped in my tracks. "How do you know about that?"

Rayla gave an insouciant shrug. "Come on, girl. Not much gets past our department. That's our job, to keep up with what goes on around here."

Momma set her chin and stood firm. "I'm not going back there."

Hope fled. Poor Rayla. Poor me. I'd known Momma's car-buying wouldn't be that simple.

Momma went on, "Your daddy needs to go check that car out before I make an offer on it."

Once I picked myself up off the ground, we went home, sent Daddy and his cousin who worked in a garage back to Caleb's lot, and that night a red BMW convertible stood in our garage.

I did a Snoopy dance.

Sunday would be free for homework. Maybe Rayla wasn't the airhead I thought.

CHAPTER 12

Monday, it was back to the office with Demon Delores and Miss Ruby for an uneventful day. Delores was never going to be my friend, but at least she shared my conviction that Billy Lee needed to be arrested. Miss Ruby was loyal as always, even if she did occasionally look at me doubtfully, mumble to herself, and shake her head in amazement.

On Tuesday, my school day, I had a late customer. When I finally got my drawer counted and stashed in the safe, it was well after five thirty. Lucy and Miss Ruby had long since gone, but Delores, whose purse had been hanging on her arm for twenty minutes, waited with tapping foot to lock the safe. Possessive about the accuracy of her deposits and accounting, Demon Delores still didn't trust me to do the simplest task concerning money. Even though I was now her boss.

Anxious to stay on her good side, I kept my mouth shut and let her do what she wanted. Peace at any price. That wasn't a bad motto.

"We're going to have to head straight for the college to make my class," I told Rayla, tonight's guard, as the three of us walked out into the courthouse hallway. "We'll have to eat supper later."

As Delores flipped the office door lock and pulled it shut, a group of people milled around. Overheard snippets of conversation reminded me that tonight was the commissioners' monthly meeting, during which they were considering a bond referendum to build a new courthouse. Most of the people in the hallway wore red as a sign of their opposition.

"Remember, people, be courteous!" one red-shirted opponent admonished the others. "No need for heated words. We just want to make it plain that we won't stand for them raising our taxes to build some big ol' Taj Mahal to rule the county from. There's nothing wrong with the courthouse we got."

"Amen," several voices chorused.

"No Taj Mahal!" someone started chanting. "No Taj Mahal!" Soon others picked up the refrain.

Hah. Too bad they couldn't be forced to work in our outmoded and rickety offices, using the unseemly and stained bathrooms for a month. Even a week.

Naturally, being a politician now, I kept such sentiments to myself and managed to smile blandly while greeting several red shirts I recognized.

Beside me, Rayla grumbled. "I'm starved. Can we stop on the way to the school and get something to eat?"

"No time." I dug in my purse. "Here. Try these." The cheese crackers I kept for emergencies should tide her over.

She turned up her nose. "At least let's whip through the Tastee Totem so I can get me a slaw dog."

And go five miles out of our way and back? I thought not. Bribery was called for. "Once I'm through with class, we'll stop by Georgia Scallops on the way home for a late supper. My treat."

"Scallops!" she squealed. The local seafood place served three counties, boasted a pricey menu, and was always crowded. But the food, including fresh seafood trucked in from the Georgia coast, was worth the wait and the cost. Rayla grabbed the crackers. "Okay, you got yourself a deal, girl."

Rayla, Delores, and I wove through the crowd toward the outside doors. I saw a commissioner, Tiny Garelle, stick his head in a fire exit door and quickly withdraw when he saw the militant red shirts. Judge Hartley, taking the other tack, strutted through the lobby, smiling and greeting the anti–new courthouse group as if he were behind them 100 percent and wasn't the driving force behind the referendum. He'd long campaigned for new courtrooms and judge's chambers.

Someone else was in the crowd, too.

As we reached the outside doors, Billy Lee Woodhallen pushed in front of me with a grunted, "Get outta my way."

I hadn't noticed him among the red shirts. He must have come out from one of the departments around the tax office, like zoning or the assessors. Not that it mattered. All I cared about was that he had skipped the tax office.

"That Billy Lee's like a bad penny." Delores led us outside. "Always shows up whenever you think you're rid of him. You mark my words, Corrie. He'll get you yet if the sheriff doesn't do something about him."

She didn't have to sound so satisfied about it, the old witch.

Rayla and I made it to class on time. She didn't embarrass me like James Cleuny, but on break, she cornered a reluctant Professor Random. I turned after getting a root beer from the vending machine to find her batting her lashes and inviting him to join us at Scallops for a late supper. "We'd love to have you, Jeff," she cooed.

The professor turned bright red as he mumbled what sounded like a refusal and made his getaway.

Unfazed, she watched his hasty departure. "Shy, isn't he? The shy ones always take a little patience, but they're usually worth it."

"Um." She did not seem like the professor's type to me, but I didn't say that.

After class was over, as I'd promised Rayla, I detoured to Georgia Scallops, the seafood place right before our county line. Though it was after nine, the front lot was full when I cruised through, so I went across a side road and entered a dirt lot used for auxiliary parking.

Rayla pulled in behind me and hopped out of her patrol car. "I'm starving, aren't you? I thought that old goat would go on lecturing all night. My eyelids kept trying to droop while he droned on and on and on. How the heck do you stand it every week?"

I didn't have an answer, but she didn't expect one.

She smoothed her pants and made sure her gun was straight before poking out her chest, which—she'd confided the first day she babysat me—was enhanced by plastic surgery. "Does my hair look okay?"

"Lovely." I was grateful she hadn't fallen asleep in class and snored as James Cleuny had done. The professor wasn't real thrilled with me anyway. How would I ever find time to do the homework he'd piled on? I should have dropped the class. The withdrawal date had passed, but maybe I could plead extenuating circumstances.

Rayla fell into step with me, babbling all the while and fussing with her hair. "I like this new honey color Evie tried on me. Don't you think it looks more professional? You know, you'd look good with a few blond streaks in your hair."

"You think?"

Headlights approached. We stopped at the roadside to wait for the vehicle to pass.

"Oh, yeah. A nice streaking would really bring out your nice brown eyes. Evie says—Whoa!"

As headlights swerved toward us, she shoved me back. Hard.

What the heck?

My left knee hit the ground before I fell and rolled. Dirt and gravel scuffed my face. I ended up sprawled on my back, gasping for air and watching taillights recede.

That car could have hit us! The driver must have been drinking. Maybe he didn't see us in the dark. He could have . . .

Then the outline of the vehicle showed when it spun around. Not a car. A truck. A pickup truck.

My thumping heart froze. *What's Rayla doing?*

"Shit shit shit shit shit!" Rayla was snarling somewhere to the side. I rolled my head, saw her scramble up from the ground. Beyond her, under Scallops' dim outside lights, the truck headed back.

Holy crap, it's coming straight at us!

"Rayla!" My warning yell was more of a croak.

Rayla wrestled with her gun holster and ran toward the road. Just as she freed her weapon and pulled it out, the truck roared up, so close I thought it would run over her.

She jumped back and fired, screaming imprecations.

I couldn't move.

Her shot didn't make any impression on the truck. It kept moving. Rayla stopped screaming. She bent in half.

The truck's hit her!

The pickup rushed on, its driver an indistinct featureless form in the shadowed innards. When it passed, I could see light numbers on the tag plate flash from a dark background. F411—

"Sumbitch." Rayla dropped down on one knee and held her pistol up with both hands.

She fired again. This time glass tinkled from a back window. The truck didn't slow.

Scallops had bright lights in front. They illuminated the speeding truck body. Light gray or pale blue maybe. Or silver. The wheel covers were prominent, and it had running boards.

An old truck. A really old truck.

It disappeared into the night.

Rayla was struggling to her feet. She was all right.

I saw the tag. I saw it!

What was the number? F41 something something? F411

something? Close enough. I could get on the state computer and . . .

Reality cut in.

What the heck kind of tag number is that? Forestry truck tags start with FA to FZ, but nothing starts with an F. And those white letters on dark isn't like any Georgia tag I've ever seen. I don't even remember a special tag with those colors.

Rayla was limping toward me and screaming at the top of her lungs. "Dammitall to pieces! Shit shit shit!"

I managed to clamber up on both knees. "Ouch!" My left one stung something awful.

As I stood shakily, Rayla sank down on the gravel in despair. Her gun hung limply from one hand. She wouldn't stop wailing.

Geez, she thought she'd failed.

"It's all right. I'm all right," I assured her, ignoring my burning knee. "You got me out of the way and scared him off. You did good."

Her fury spilled out at me. "No I didn't! That sumbitch ran over my foot. I think it's broken. I wish I'd a killed him! I can't believe—I should of killed him!" She fumbled for her radio and started talking.

Some of Scallops' departing customers began crowding around us. I told them what happened while Rayla talked between angry hiccups to the dispatcher.

Then the aftermath hit me. Someone had tried to run us down.

I began trembling so much, my legs would hardly hold me upright. My speech wasn't much better.

Before anyone from the sheriff's department had time to arrive, a motorcycle with a familiar sound pulled up. "Having a party out here?"

Bodie Fairhurst. This was all I needed. I dropped down on

the ground beside Rayla, and put my head between my knees.

In two steps, he was beside me and bending down. "Fluffball, are you okay?" That was the pet name he used to tease me with. The first time he heard Daddy call me chickadee, he said I looked more like an Easter marshmallow chicken to him, one of the fluffy kind that tasted . . .

I rallied enough to raise my head. "Don't call me that. Don't you ever call me that again. I'm fine. Leave me alone."

He turned his attention to Rayla. While he got the story from her, a deputy I didn't know showed up. A few minutes later, the sheriff himself pulled in, followed by the emergency crew.

The EMTs spilled out. From habit, they rushed to me.

"Sorry. Not this time." I motioned toward Rayla. "I'm fine. Rayla saved me. Go do CPR or something on her."

After some soft exchanges between Bodie and the sheriff and the deputy, Duke came over to me and squatted down. "Close call, eh?"

"You could say so."

"We've locked down the area. Rayla says it's gotta be the same truck we've been looking for. Can you describe it?"

I told him what I'd seen. He frowned when I told him about the tag colors and its strange numbers. "Out of state, most likely. I'll have some people start checking. Sounds like our man, though."

He stood up, heaving a sigh. "You might want to go in to the ER with Rayla, get checked out." He offered me a hand.

I took it and got up. My legs wobbled, but were no longer like jelly. My stomach gnawed at me, reminding me I hadn't eaten since lunch. "I'm fine. Except I'm hungry. I'm going to eat some dinner and go home."

His gaze flitted around, not meeting mine. People do that when they don't want to tell you something. He looked as uncomfortable as I'd ever seen him. "Ahem. Uh . . ."

I went on full alert. "What?"

"I'm kind of shorthanded right now," he said apologetically. "I don't have that many people, to start with. And two of them are out sick. I'm calling some off-duty officers in, but they'll be working the roadblocks like the regular patrol crew. We'll all be manning the roadblocks for the next few hours, I'm pretty sure. For the moment, I can't spare a deputy to stay with you."

That didn't sound good. I shivered. "So I'm on my own?"

"Why don't you ride with Rayla to the hospital, like I suggested?" He took off his Smoky-type hat and smoothed the brim. "You'll be safe enough with the medics."

"I don't want to go with Rayla." I could imagine the ER people gawking at me if I came in. And Momma would get called and come rushing down to see about me. Again. And the sexy Dr. Bennigan would probably be on duty. Again.

I jutted my chin. No way was I going to the hospital. "The truck's long gone. I expect its driver is, too. I should be all right." Not that I wanted to drive home alone, but for sure I didn't want to go to the ER.

"There's another option." Sheriff Duval eyed me measuringly. "Bodie's volunteered to stick around until I can free up someone for you."

The breath rushed out of me. "I don't want Bodie Fairhurst anywhere near me, thank you very much."

"Won't be for long. Just till—"

"No thank you," I said in my most frigid tone.

"Okay. Then you go with Rayla."

I opened my mouth, took a breath to argue.

"One or the other." His tone said there was no debate. He put his hat back on for emphasis. "You're a bright girl, Corrie. You know you're in danger. Tonight surely proved that to you."

I mulled over the choices, and let my breath out in a gush. "I don't appreciate this, Sheriff Duval. You know Bodie jilted me at the altar."

"Years ago. Got nothing to do with this."

He stared at me.

I stared at him.

"Make up your mind," he said. "You go to the hospital or let Bodie stay with you till I can turn somebody loose to look after you."

I fumed before capitulating. "He better keep well away from me."

"Work that out with him," Sheriff Duval said. He added approvingly, "You got good sense like your daddy. Suck it up, and in a couple of hours I'll send James or Ethan over."

He nodded toward Bodie, who waved back from his cell phone conversation, and went over to where the EMTs were loading Rayla. When Bodie closed his cell and strolled over to me, I pointed at him. "Don't talk to me, don't stand close to me, don't even look at me."

He smiled the slow grin that narrowed his eyes and drew his thick lashes close together. "Duke says you're hungry. Let's go inside and get something to eat while we wait for another deputy to show up."

"I am not hungry."

"You're always hungry."

"I mean it. I'm not hungry." My stomach growled. Loudly.

He glanced down at it. "Uh-huh. Well, I'm starved. Been waiting all day for some of the cheese biscuits they fix here."

My stomach growled again at the mention of Scallops' biscuits. I stood indecisively.

He took my arm.

I jerked away and stalked toward the restaurant entrance.

Inside, I visited the ladies' room first thing to wash my hands and face. Back in the lobby, despite the late hour on a Tuesday, several people still waited for tables. The hostess greeted Bodie like a long-lost friend, but looked me up and down as if wondering why in the world a hunk like him would take up with the likes of me.

To be fair, I was dirty and disheveled from my roll in the dirt. Still, she had no call to turn up her nose the way she did.

"Got a table by the water?" Bodie asked as she pulled out silverware and menus from the greeter's lectern.

She winked. "For you, doll, sure."

Ignoring two couples ahead of us, she led the way back to a crowded porch overlooking the big catfish pond. The white moon reflected in the dark water while dim hurricane lamps on the tables didn't keep us from seeing the stars. Low voices conversed around us. An occasional burst of laughter broke the intimacy.

The table hadn't been cleared and wiped, but the hostess took care of that herself. Bodie's influence again, 'cause it sure wasn't mine. After spreading a new white tablecloth, she seated us and batted her eyelashes at him. "Sweet tea like usual?"

So he came here often. After I ordered water, I opened the menu. Sea bass, orange roughie, tilapia grill . . .

My stomach gave a long howl.

The waitress, a fashion doll look-alike, brought our sweet tea and water, then hovered at Bodie's elbow while reciting the specials. "—and salmon steak with dill sauce. If you don't like those, the shrimp came in this afternoon, caught on the Georgia coast this morning and trucked straight in to us. Real fresh." She ogled him and lowered her voice. "I bet you like 'em fresh."

With his signature smile, Bodie handed her his menu. "You sold me, Ava. I do like 'em fresh. Broiled shrimp with hushpuppies, slaw, and the veggie medley. Also, can we get some biscuits?"

My mouth watered at the thought of fresh shrimp but I chose the salmon steak special. Bodie wasn't going to decide anything for me, even when it came to food.

"So you come here a lot?" I asked after surrendering my menu and watching Ava strut away. Okay, so Bodie had an effect on women. So what? I had no reason to care if they acted all giddy-headed when he smiled at them. Wasn't any of my business if they got sucked in by that face and body and ended up like me.

He rested his elbows on the table. "Not too much."

I raised a brow. "Enough to call the waitress by name."

Almond-shaped eyes crinkled. "Name tag."

As always, he had an answer for everything. I looked away first. "So if you don't come here that often, what were you doing over this way tonight?"

"Riding the Harley."

"Way over here? You live on the other side of the county."

He grinned at me, but didn't answer. The waitress hustled over with a big basket of cheese biscuits and hushpuppies.

I reached for one before the answer hit me and made me draw back. Hadn't I heard the new newspaper editor owned a condo somewhere over this way on the lake? Why this explanation of his presence would make my heart drop, I was sure I didn't know. Bodie's private life didn't concern me. "Never mind, I can guess where you were going. I'll be fine if you want to keep your date with Maura."

"Thought you went over all that with Duke," he drawled, still seeming to laugh at me. "I promised him I wouldn't leave till he can get you a deputy, and I'm not going to break my promise. Besides, I already talked to Maura."

I tried to fan up the old anger. "And she's okay with your being here? With the person you jilted?"

"Why not? It's not like we were ever married. Or still seeing each other."

His blasé attitude started a slow burn.

When his capable hands broke apart one of the cheese biscuits, I averted my eyes. I didn't want to remember how often those hands . . .

This was unproductive. *Get back on track,* I told myself.

I wanted to ask him about the rumors I'd heard about him being on admin leave but wasn't brave enough. Instead I picked a safe subject. "Do you think the road blocks will catch that pickup truck?"

"Hope so." He took a big bite. "Man, I love Scallops' biscuits."

Me, too. Why should I let Bodie Fairhurst dictate what I would or wouldn't eat? I snatched one defiantly.

Bodie raised his brows. "Ava can always bring more if we eat all these." He paused. "Duke said the truck might be from out of state."

I nodded, mouth full of feathery cheese-flavored bread. "Because of the tag." I hadn't eaten since lunch, and it was nearly ten. No wonder I was starving. Ooh, that biscuit was good. Light and fluffy with cheese and a little garlic . . .

I reached for a second, wavered between another biscuit or a hushpuppy.

"Don't even think about it." When Bodie moved to protect his side of the basket, lean fingers touched my hovering ones.

I jerked away, but not before the heat from his hand ran up my arm and through my body, raking up old memories normally kept locked away.

His mouth curved, first one side going up and then the other in his trademark smile, as if he knew the effect on my insides of the accidental caress. "The hushpuppies are for me. They came with my shrimp, remember? I don't take kindly to losing what's mine."

I grabbed another biscuit. "I don't want your old hushpuppies."

Ice clinked as he took a long swallow of tea. "Rayla said the truck was light colored, maybe blue. With fenders. She right?"

I refused to let the ripple of his throat muscles affect me. "The color was hard to see at night. It could have been gray or silver. Or light blue."

"But it had fenders?"

"Yeah. And running boards. The wheel wells were round on the outside, you know?"

"Like a step-back."

I shrugged, not sure what a step-back was. "I guess."

"Fifty-seven or older, I'd bet. The wheel wells were absorbed about then."

"Older than nineteen fifty-seven?" The water glass stopped on its way to my mouth. "Wow, that's a real antique."

"Yeah."

I set the glass down carefully. "Billy Lee's old truck is a fifty-something. I think maybe it's listed as a fifty-eight?" There were a few biscuit crumbs left to pick at. "Of course, sometimes registrations on untitled vehicles get year models wrong."

He didn't say anything. The waitress brought our plates out. We ate for a few minutes in a comfortable silence.

This was too much like old times. Before he'd jilted me. I ought to stand up and throw my water in his face and run away.

Play nice, I heard my daddy's voice say. Okay, I could be polite. "How's the job?"

He was being investigated for corruption, idiot. I could have kicked myself.

His expression didn't change. "It's okay."

Change the subject. Think of something else quick. "Do you like living in Atlanta?"

He cut off a shrimp tail, lifted meditative eyes to mine. "That was the whole problem, wasn't it?"

Mystified, I took the bait. "What whole problem?"

His blue gaze didn't waver. "With you and me. You were fine after we got engaged. Happy as a lark. You were busy making wedding plans, picking out bridesmaids' dresses, choosing flowers and all that stuff. Then when I got the job with the GBI, you realized you'd actually have to move away from here. Go all the way down to Atlanta. Scared the stuffing out of you, didn't it? Leaving your folks, your friends, your home. Made you want not to get married." He popped the shrimp into his mouth.

"It did no such thing. I did want to get married. *You* jilted *me!*"

"You're raising your voice." He broke eye contact to cut the tail off another shrimp. "I've mulled it over for three years, and you know what? Maybe I didn't want to get married either."

I snapped, "Obviously not." For good measure, I added, "Your mother for sure didn't want you to marry me. She was overjoyed after you walked out and didn't bother to hide it."

"She and Dad would have preferred me to wait a while before settling down. It wasn't like she didn't want me to marry you in particular."

"Hmph. She never liked me. She never thought I was good enough for you."

He finished chewing. "I don't know why you think that. But it didn't matter then, doesn't matter now."

I wanted to say a lot more about his mother, the stereotypical southern belle who thought only a debutante from a distinguished family with deep roots was good enough for her oldest son, but restrained myself. Bodie was right. His mother was no concern of mine any longer.

And Daddy was right, too. I needed to play nice. Giving in to my emotions made Bodie assume a more prominent place in my life than he deserved.

So I kept my mouth shut except to swallow a bite of salmon covered in dill sauce.

"Nope." Body speared another shrimp, chewed and swallowed. "My mother was never the problem."

That was too much. I opened my mouth, but he went on. "When right before the wedding, you started nagging like a wife, maybe I should have said something then. But I figured once we were married, you'd get back to normal."

"So now your jilting me is all my fault." Incensed, I half stood up.

"Afraid to face the truth?"

"I'm not afraid of anything you have to say."

My father's voice whispered, *Play nice. Play nice.*

I took deep breaths and sat back down. I stayed calm. "For your information, I did not act like a nagging wife. If you recall, I never got the chance to be a nagging wife."

He shrugged. "Don't know what else you'd call it. One day you're all lovey-dovey, excited about the decorations for the church and the presents we were getting. The next day I couldn't do anything right. The day after I told you I got the job where we'd have to live in Atlanta."

All breath left me.

He shot me a shrewd glance. "I think you wanted out of it, Corrie, but you were like me. Didn't know how to say so."

My dry swallow was painful. "You jilted me."

"After we got in front of the preacher and you started carping about my tie being tied all crooked and my hair being cut too long to suit you."

"It looked terrible. I only wanted you to straighten—"

He reached over and got my hand. His clear eyes caught mine and wouldn't let them go.

I'd forgotten how his black eyelashes emphasized their blueness. Something heavy pressed against my heart, traveling all the way up to my throat.

"You wanted out, Corrie. You gave me all the signs but I'm a guy. I don't know what women mean whenever they say and do things that don't make sense. So I couldn't read all your signals till the last. When you snapped at me so hard you scared Preacher Dempsey into stumbling backward into the baptismal pool, I figured we'd be better off calling it quits right then and there rather than going through a divorce later."

My chest hurt. I couldn't speak. I couldn't remove my hand from his.

"It's okay," he said gently, letting go my cold fingers. "We really were too young. Took me a while to admit it, but we were. I'd like us to be friends though. Do you think that's possible?"

Willing the tears back, I sat like a statue. After a while I could speak. "I'm not hungry any more. I want to go home now."

Facing the truth about yourself and your motives, conscious and unconscious, is sometimes not pleasant.

CHAPTER 13

Bodie trailed me home on his motorcycle and came inside uninvited. I didn't have any gumption left to protest. Maybe I didn't want to.

Daddy and Momma were up, sitting in the den and watching the late news. Momma still wore her scrubs, while Daddy had on his flannels and house shoes.

Their mouths fell open when Bodie followed me in, but they quickly recovered. As they popped up out of their his-and-her recliners, I said quickly, "Don't get yourselves in an uproar. He's only here till Sheriff Duval can get me a bodyguard."

Momma enveloped Bodie in one of her bear hugs before releasing him. "I'm tickled to death to see you, Bodie. You just sit down here. What happened to the bodyguard you had, Corrie?"

I told them about the incident at Scallops.

"Dadgummit, I knew it!" Daddy hit his thigh. "I was scared something like this would happen. I never should of made you take this job to start with. You've got to quit, Corrie."

Momma was almost as upset. "Your daddy's right. This is getting too dangerous. You can't go on like this. If Duke Duval won't arrest that Billy Lee Woodhallen, you need to resign. Lord knows I don't want you to let our ladies voting league down, but this is too much. Maybe once that awful man is arrested, you can—"

"I'm not quitting."

Daddy clucked like a mother hen. Momma kept throwing her hands around and arguing with me. Bodie stayed in the background and kept his mouth shut. I was acutely aware of his presence.

"I'm not quitting," I finally told them. "And I don't want to hear any more about it."

After a few more remonstrances and pleas, my parents calmed down. Bodie sat down on the ratty loveseat like he intended to stay a while and told them about the old truck. I forgot my quarrel with him long enough to mention the tag, how the colors weren't normal Georgia tag colors and the numbers and letters weren't normal Georgia sequences.

Daddy listened in silence until I finished. "I know some folks, when they get a new car, they keep all the tags they put on it even after they sell it."

Bodie nodded. "That's true. My great-uncle has a muscle car from the seventies. Bought it new. Doesn't drive it anymore except on special occasions, but he keeps the original tag plate on the front."

Daddy scratched his chin. "So if this truck is really an antique, you reckon its owner might have put one of his old plates on it?"

Bodie turned to me. "You saw it, Corrie. Did it look like an old plate to you?"

His question, delivered in the warm tone he'd used before our breakup, left me shaken. During the past couple of hours, my anger of the past three years had been mislaid, and I was left with a large empty hole I didn't know how to fill. I could never make up with Bodie after what he'd done, but . . .

"I saw the tag for maybe ten seconds. All I know is that it didn't look like any Georgia plate I ever saw. Sheriff thinks it's from out of state. I'd say that's the most likely theory."

Daddy's words stuck in my head though. Around midnight,

after James Cleuny showed up and Bodie left, I went to bed mulling it over. What if the tag plate was a really old Georgia plate on a really old Georgia truck? What if the truck didn't come from out of state like the sheriff thought?

At work the next day, when the eight o'clock opening flurry died, I tried checking the state computer for tags beginning with F. As I expected, nothing came up except forestry plates.

Then I got on the internet to search for antique plates.

At first the oldest ones I could find were from the seventies and eighties. Then I finally discovered a site that had older tags for sale. A '56 Georgia plate showed white numbers on a navy background. I stared at it for a long moment, stomach all hollow. It started with an F.

Maybe the sheriff was wrong. Maybe Daddy was right.

I went back to the office and sat down to figure out how I could find out who the tag, if it was really an old Georgia plate, had been issued to. The computer only went back so many years, but the state used to require counties to keep tag records for seven years. At least I thought it was seven years. In any event, I doubted very seriously whether there would be any way to trace tag records from the fifties. Unless—

"Corrie!" Miss Ruby's nasal bellow penetrated my fog. "Come out here. This man wants to know if he needs a tag for his grill."

My daddy's barbecue grill immediately came to mind. The grill we'd bought him for Christmas two years ago was fancy, with a lot of bells and whistles, but I still couldn't see it trundling down the street with a tag on its rear. I shook my head to clear it of the preposterous image and went out front.

The customer had to be talking about the car grill. Bodie's words about his uncle putting his old plate on the front of his muscle car were fresh in my mind. The customer must have moved here from a state that issued two tags, one for the back and another for the front grill.

I smiled over the counter at the young man standing there. "Hello."

He grinned back from under his Atlanta baseball cap. "Morning."

"Georgia only issues one tag for vehicles. You don't need one for the front grill."

"Yeah." He looked confused. "I know that. I've lived in Georgia all my life. But what about this here grill? Do I need a tag for it or not?"

"Ahem." Aware I didn't know the answer, I repeated, mainly to buy some time to think. "Your grill. Uh-hum. A tag for a grill. That's not like a barbecue grill, is it?"

He nodded. "Yeah, you got it."

"I'm a little confused. Why would you need a tag for your barbecue grill?"

He donned the expression Delores uses when she thinks I'm being stupid. "Well, so it can go on the road."

"Your barbecue grill travels?" I couldn't quite see Daddy's grill, swanky as it was, wending merrily down a country lane.

Miss Ruby had been watching with her mouth open. "My gawd. You're putting a barbecue grill on the road?"

"Well, yes'm." He looked from me to her. "Oh, I see what you're thinking." He laughed. "This is a big grill. Got its own wheels and everything. I pull it behind my truck."

Light dawned. "Like a trailer? Like the ones they take to the apple festivals and the county fairs?"

"You got it, ma'am. Now I just picked it up this morning. I got a bill of sale right here. So do I need a tag or not?"

As he held out the bill of sale, something outside the office made a noise.

"What in the name of gawd was that?" asked the ever-curious

Miss Ruby. She craned her neck to see past the man with the grill and into the hallway.

Lucy, busy with renewals, looked up, too, as did the deputy du jour, Tim the Skinhead.

"Sounded like something fell," Delores said, mouth full of Devil Dunky. She laid the chocolate cupcake remainder down by her magazine. "Someone's saying something, too."

I was intent on inspecting the bill of sale for the grill. "If this grill's going on the road, you'll probably need a tag."

"Well, that's what I figured, too. That's why I come in."

Loud voices came from outside the office. Several people in the hall scurried by our glass entrance door toward the reception area.

"Sounds like a mob out there," Lucy said.

Tim went to the hallway and looked out. "Sure is a crowd of people gathering up." He didn't seem inclined to leave his post to investigate.

Delores patted her mouth with a napkin and hopped up. "I better go see what's happening. I'll come back and tell you." She was as bad as Miss Ruby about wanting to know everything going on.

I was curious, too, but the problem I saw on the bill of sale for the barbecue grill kept me from trotting after her. "There isn't an identification number on here," I told the customer as Delores took off.

He didn't hear me because his attention was focused on the commotion in the hallway, too. I had to repeat myself before he shifted it back to me. "What? Uh, no'm. This old boy fabricated the grill for me to my specifications." The voices grew strident. He looked toward the hallway again, losing interest in his grill. "What you reckon is happening out there?"

"Delores will find out." I handed the bill of sale to Miss Ruby. She obviously wanted to hoist her plump little behind off her stool and follow Delores to where the crowd gathered, but I barred her way. "Miss Ruby, treat this like a homemade trailer. Issue him an ID plate. Use the sale price for value. When he gets it fastened on the, um, the grill, and brings in his inspection paperwork, he can get a regular trailer tag." Maybe I wasn't doing anything illegal.

She reluctantly took the bill of sale. "All right, but you better go see what's going on out there, Corrie. Sounds like something bad's happened."

Delores sauntered back in.

Tim looked askance.

"Well?" said Lucy, renewals forgotten.

Miss Ruby eyed Delores, too. "What is it happening out there, Delores?" She sat forward expectantly, paperwork frozen in one hand, customer forgotten.

Her customer didn't care. Like everyone else, he waited to hear Delores's report.

"There was an accident." Delores took her time, brushing past Tim and coming back behind the counter before continuing. "Looks like Billy Lee Woodhallen pushed somebody on the stairs and the railing gave way. They called the EMTs, but that guy in planning who used to be an army medic is out there with him now."

"Broke, eh? Sheriff always said that whole staircase was rotten." That was the longest sentence I'd ever heard Tim put together.

Lucy shook her head. "Billy Lee again."

"Who was it got pushed?" Miss Ruby asked.

Delores aimed her words at me. "That guy who was in here the other day. The one from the college you and Rayla went to lunch with? Oh, I forgot. You'd already eaten."

I ignored her dig because I was too busy gasping. "Professor Random?"

"Guess so, if that was his name. That's the one. I think it's him."

I rushed out past her and pushed Tim aside. Tim, slow on the uptake, caught up to me as I ran up the hall and surveyed the courthouse lobby. "Hey, you hadn't ought to run out like that! Makes you an easy target."

There by the reception desk, in front of a bunch of copy paper boxes newly delivered from our supply company, a crowd huddled around a prone figure. A once-opulent marble stairway led up to the second-floor landing. The railing on the stairwell was broken, part still dangling at a precarious angle above the crowd.

At the bottom of the stairs, Billy Lee flailed some rolled up papers in the air.

"I didn't push him!" he bellowed to no one in particular. "All I did was start past him and he backed up and the railing gave way. He oughta sue the county. Rotten as them stairs are, it's a wonder nobody's been killed on 'em before now."

Sherry appeared next to me, holding a post office bucket and looking scared to death. "Billy Lee's telling the truth. He really didn't push that man," she said in a hushed voice. "I was picking up the landfill's mail and saw the whole thing."

"What happened?"

"The guy on the floor was going up when Billy Lee was coming down. He said something to Billy Lee and Billy Lee told him to go to hell. Billy Lee started on down and the other man got against the rail to let him go by, and it broke."

"Is he dead?" I asked.

She shook her head. "No, but looks like he's hurt bad. Do you know him?"

"I think it's my professor from school." I shoved my way to the front of the onlookers.

Tim caught my elbow. "Bad idea," he muttered. "Too many

people around for me to protect you if anybody tries anything."

I jerked my arm away.

Delores was right. Professor Random lay on the marble entrance tiles, while the man from planning kneeled beside him and talked to a hovering Fred Bauers. "We shouldn't move him. His back may be hurt. Keep everyone away till the EMTs get here. Give him air, people!"

"Come back to the office." Tim pulled at my arm again.

Again, I shook him off. "Leave me alone."

Professor Random's dazed face was white. Someone had thrown a windbreaker over him. Sheila, the commissioners' secretary, bustled up with another jacket. "Here, put this under his head, Owen."

The guy from planning took it. "Don't want to move him, but I'll cover him up with it. He's in shock and we need to keep him warm."

Nausea started in my stomach and rose to my throat.

The old elevator creaked to a stop and Judge Hartley, in full courtroom regalia including his gavel, burst out. "They said someone fell through the stairs! Was it an attorney?" He saw the professor and waved the gavel toward him. "Is he an attorney? Who is the hurt man? Is he an attorney?"

Several people shrugged. One of them said, "We don't know. Just some man going up the stairs."

"He's from the college." My mouth was so dry I could hardly say the words. "His name is Professor Random."

Judge Hartley swiveled toward me. "A professor? Of law?"

I shook my head. "Business statistics."

Judge Hartley visibly relaxed. The gavel fell to his side. "Not an attorney. Thank the Lord." He straightened his robes. "I've told them and told them this place isn't fit for human habitation. I've warned them that if any of my attorneys are hurt, there'll be hel—" He coughed. "There'll be repercussions. Serious repercussions."

About that time, the EMTs arrived with Sam Blanken hot on their heels. The EMTs started toward me. I pointed to Professor Random on the floor.

As they began working over him, others in the crowd gave garbled accounts to Sam.

The judge, imposing in his robes despite his height, or lack of, puffed up so much he reminded me of Miss Ruby. He took two strides and, breaking into a bystander's eyewitness account of the accident, pulled Sam Blanken roughly aside. "This could have happened to an *attorney!*" he thundered.

Trembling with indignation and clutching his gavel, he still managed to grab the startled Sam by both jacket lapels. "Do you understand me? It could have been an attorney lying here!" He emphasized every other word by shaking Sam's lapels. "You have got to get your fat ass off of your soft commissioner's seat and build me a justice building!" His voice rose with each lapel shake till he was screaming.

The flabbergasted Sam tried to pull loose. "We want to, Sutherhold. You know damned well how many times we've had a referendum on the ballot. The voters won't—"

Judge Hartley released him with a contemptuous noise. "I'm not going to stand for this. My attorneys have the right to work in a safe environment. By God, I'll have this place condemned, that's what I'll do."

Alarmed, Sam pulled at the judge's arm. "Now Sutherhold, we're putting it up for a vote again, and maybe this time—"

"Not good enough. I'll be writing up an order as soon as possible, mandating renovations or a new building. We're going to get something done here before an attorn—before anybody gets killed."

He stalked off.

"Can he do that?" Sam asked the county manager who had

made his appearance in time to hear the judge's threat. "Can he make us renovate when we can't get a referendum passed?"

"I'm not sure. We need to get the county attorney's opinion." The manager's Adam's apple bobbed. "He needs to know about a possible lawsuit anyway. Let's go upstairs and see if he's—"

So. Our county leaders obviously felt future court orders and lawsuits were a lot more important than the man currently lying injured due to the dilapidated condition of the courthouse.

When the EMTs started strapping his blanketed and back-boarded form onto the gurney, the professor stirred. Out of all the people surrounding him, his mystified gaze singled me out.

I wanted to cry at his total incomprehension of why this had happened to him. Instead, I pushed past the planning guy to reach the gurney. "Professor, is there someone I can notify for you?"

His eyelids flickered.

I pressed on. "A friend? Your family?"

"No," he whispered. "There's no one. Just me. Thank you, Corrie."

My poor professor.

After they loaded him and carried him away with sirens screaming, I ran back to the office and told Delores I was leaving. "You'll have to take care of things here."

She curled a lip. "I think I can remember how."

Her sarcasm flowed off me. There were too many other things to worry about. Grabbing my purse, I headed for the hospital with my startled bodyguard right behind me.

"Where're we going?" Tim asked. "Don't you need to tend to customers or something?"

No one, he'd said.

Poor, poor Professor Random.

At the emergency room, I had to pull strings to accompany the professor. That meant calling in my mother. After her first startled response of making sure I was all right, she used her influence on my behalf. Thanks to her intervention, they got the professor to waive his privacy rights or something so the receptionist could let me—and a disgruntled Tim—back where Professor Random waited for the ER doctor.

Still strapped to the backboard the EMTs had put him on, he lay with eyes closed in the tiny cubicle. Tim and I tiptoed in to sit quietly in plastic chairs beside his bed. After a few minutes, he turned his head and saw me. "Corrie."

I put on a smile. "Hey there, professor. I'm going to stay with you till the doctor comes. Are you sure there's no one I can call to be with you?"

"No." His eyelids closed. "Thank you for worrying, but I'll be fine."

"After a fall like that? It may take a while for you to feel fine again."

He didn't answer.

I hesitated. "Did Billy Lee Woodhallen push you?"

His face grimaced. He might have tried to smile. "No."

"Someone thought he might have."

"No. I wasn't pushed." He opened his eyes again. "I asked him if he . . . He got angry and yelled at me but no, he didn't touch me. I stepped back and fell. All on my own. Clumsy." He meant himself.

"The railing was rotten. Everyone who works there has complained about those stairs for years." After a moment, I ventured, "Why was Billy Lee angry?"

Some air gusted out as if he'd been holding his breath. He was obviously hurting. I didn't think he would answer or even remember the question, but finally he spoke. Maybe the pain made him forget his usual reserve. "I think Billy Lee's my father. I guess I'll have to get his permission to do a DNA test and make sure. Or maybe a court order."

"Billy Lee?" I repeated stupidly. "Your father?"

Tim in the corner stiffened.

The professor made as if to shift his position, but the effort made him bite his lip. If possible, he turned whiter. When the twinge passed, he told me more. "I'm adopted. I found my grandmother but her daughter, my natural mother, died a few years ago. My grandmother told me what little she knew about my father, and that led me to Billy Lee."

"Your father." This was too much to take in. "Billy Lee. But you don't know for certain?"

"No." His eyes closed. "My grandmother says my mother stayed with her cousins the summer before I was born. One of the neighboring boys got her pregnant. I traced everything here, to Goat Ridge. The cousins are gone, but when they lived there, the only neighbors were the Woodhallens, the Jemsons, the Parsneys, and the Bromfields. The Parsneys were an older couple without any children. They're dead now. The Jemsons had four daughters."

I nodded. Delores was one of that family.

"The Bromfields had a son."

"That would be Miss Ruby and her husband. I think their son's about forty-five or fifty now."

The professor kept his eyes shut. "When I started researching, I found he joined the army before my mother arrived and was in boot camp all summer. That pretty much left Billy Lee. He was the only candidate who lived close enough to be called a neighbor."

"Have you talked to him? Asked him about it?"

Professor Random opened his eyes. He let out something that could have been a laugh except the pain from the movement made him gasp. When he could answer, he said, "On the stairs. Problem with Billy Lee is, as best I can figure, he was only twelve or thirteen that summer. I was coming today to probate court. I wanted to see his birth certificate to make sure."

"Aren't birth certificates confidential?"

He tried to smile. "I don't know. I hoped to see a record but I never made it that far. It doesn't matter, anyway, not really. I don't even know why I was bothering to look for it. Twelve- and fourteen-year-old boys father children all the time nowadays. I don't guess it was any different thirty-two years ago. Anyway, I met Billy Lee coming down the stairs and . . . I lost my head. I thought to hell with it, I want to know. So I told him who I was and asked him if he was my father."

"Oh, wow. That must have floored him."

"Yeah. He denied it of course, had a few choice words to say about it. I guess I'm going to have to figure out how to get him to agree to a DNA test."

"Do you want to know that badly?"

He lay quietly without answering right away. Then: "I want to belong somewhere. My adoptive parents are dead, and I don't have anybody else. Even my natural grandmother wasn't pleased to see me. Seems she pretty much washed her hands of my mother when she got pregnant. Never saw her again. Didn't even go to her funeral."

He closed his eyes again, exhausted.

I took his hand and held it until the nurse came in. I recognized her as one who'd worked with my mother a couple of years back. She knew me, too, which made her a little more communicative.

"Doctor's on his way. Looks like a couple of broken bones, but the back's the main worry. We'll know something for sure once he gets examined. Won't be long now. I'm sorry, Corrie, but you and"—she glanced at Tim with a hint of a smile—"your guard will need to leave."

Did everyone in town know I was under twenty-four-hour protection? How embarrassing.

While waiting, I had programmed my cell number into the professor's phone. I told him so as I got up. "Call me if you need me for anything, Professor Random. I'll be around town, so don't you think twice if you want me to go get some pajamas or your toothbrush or anything else you need. I'll come back to check on you later, okay?"

He gave me a weak thumbs-up.

I managed to walk out without wobbling too much, although my eyes were misty.

"You think Billy Lee's really his father?" Tim asked.

I shrugged, but his words overshadowed pity.

If Professor Random was indeed Billy Lee's illegitimate son, did that mean the professor would be heir to some of the Woodhallen holdings? Could the professor claim them if he was illegitimate?

That conjecture led to other unwelcome thoughts. If Professor Random thought Billy Lee was about to lose those very valuable holdings he might one day be heir to, would he do something to insure they didn't get sold for taxes?

That's crazy, I argued. Professor Random had no way of knowing the route I took home from school. He had no way of knowing Rayla and I were stopping at Scallops Tuesday night. He might possibly, barely possibly, have a motive, but he'd had no opportunity to make any of the attempts on my life.

Had he?

There weren't that many roads from the college to Medder Rose. The professor probably took at least part of the same route I did. He might have noticed me going that way before. And Rayla had invited him to eat at Scallops with us last night. He owned an old truck he was restoring. Could I trust his claim it was from the seventies or eighties and undrivable?

I gnawed my lip.

In a different vein, I had big problems imagining Billy Lee as a ladies' man. Common sense said it only took one gullible girl who didn't think he was totally repulsive. And maybe when he was younger, he wasn't as repulsive as he was now.

Tim the Skinhead strode along beside me.

"You going to tell the sheriff what the professor said?" I asked.

He looked impassive.

"Even if what the professor thinks is true, that doesn't mean Billy Lee's off the hook for killing Mr. Jethro and trying to kill me."

Tim didn't even blink. He wasn't nearly as forthcoming as Ethan.

That night I sounded out my daddy as he reared back in his recliner to read the newspaper. "Do you think Billy Lee might have fathered an illegitimate child when he was young?"

The newspaper fell. "Billy Lee Woodhallen?" Daddy looked at me over his reading glasses as if I were hallucinating. "You think Billy Lee Woodhallen might have got some girl pregnant?" He guffawed so hard he choked.

James Cleuny, my nighttime guard who was in the kitchen fixing himself a snack, heard and stuck his head in. "You all right, Keith?"

"He's fine. Go back to your popcorn." I'd witnessed Daddy's giggling fits before, but this was no time for one. "Come on, Daddy. Calm down. Stranger things have happened."

He collected himself. "Maybe so. But everybody was shocked to high heaven when he come home married to that gal from Atlanta. He never even looked at a woman before then. In fact, nobody ever thought he'd marry, period. Billy Lee ain't known for his sweet-talking abilities, 'specially with women. I always half suspected he was scared of 'em."

"So you don't think oh, thirty years ago or so, he might have got a girl in trouble?"

"Billy Lee?" That set Daddy off again.

James came back in. "Is he choking or something? I can do the Heimlich."

"I told you, he's fine. Daddy, stop it!" I sniffed. "Is that your popcorn burning, James?"

James rushed back into the kitchen.

When Daddy finished laughing, he shook his head and wiped his eyes. "No way, chickadee. Now if you were talking about his brother, it'd be a different story. Vince Woodhallen had girls hanging all over him. I never heard of him getting one of 'em pregnant, but he for sure had plenty of opportunities."

My turn to be surprised. "Billy Lee has a brother?"

The newspaper crackled and went up. "Had. Vince died in a wreck when he was a senior in high school."

"I remember that," James put in. He held a bag of micro-waved popcorn by the corner. It smelled scorched. "Strung out on something, wasn't he? Crack? Coke maybe? Then the dealer supposedly sold it to him went down a few weeks later, rifle shot through the heart. We all thought Billy Lee's father did it, but he had an alibi."

"Alibis can be fabricated," I said tartly.

James looked at me like he didn't have the faintest idea what I was talking about.

I ground my teeth. "When was this, Daddy? Was this brother older or younger than Billy Lee?"

The newspaper lowered enough to let Daddy peer at me. "Older. Four or five years older. Tore his folks up, but what did they expect? You give a boy a new car and plenty of money and let him think he's got the right to—" He broke off. "Enough sermonizing. Why do you want to know?"

"Just asking." I'd have to tell Professor Random about Billy Lee's brother being a more likely candidate to be his father. If he had any sense, he'd be thrilled to mark Billy Lee off his list.

More to the point, being Billy Lee's nephew instead of his son still didn't discount the professor from a share in Billy Lee's inheritance.

CHAPTER 14

On Thursday, Momma dropped me off at work since she was going in late for a sixteen-hour shift. Rayla showed up at nine to relieve James Cleuny, despite her foot being in a splint thingie.

She was blunt. "Ethan says your bad luck's rubbing off on me."

"*What!*" That did it. No matter what our mommas hoped, there was no way Ethan and I would ever get together. We might not even continue to make it as friends. He was too darned critical.

When Momma got to the hospital, she called to let me know Professor Random was in better shape than expected. It seemed the boxes of copy paper stacked by the reception desk in the lobby had padded his fall. He escaped with a broken arm, a fractured ankle, and a concussion.

I was glad. Further reflection the past night had convinced me the gentle professor couldn't possibly be a murderer. "So they're letting him go?"

"They've already discharged him. He's headed toward the orthopedic surgeon's office now so they can put casts on his arm and ankle. He can probably go back to work in a day or two, unless he's hurting too bad from the fall."

Who was taking him to the orthopedist?

My office window overlooked the front lot. Yep, his Mustang still stood where he'd left it before the fall, and he said he didn't have anybody to help him. "His car's here. How's he getting around?"

"His boss and her secretary came over. They're going to take him to the orthopedist's office, and they're also going to shuffle cars so they can take his back to his house."

"Oh." I was put out. After he'd confided so much in me yesterday, I thought he considered me his friend. His only friend. "I offered to help him out. He doesn't have any friends or relatives close by."

"That was nice of you," my mother approved, "but I guess he's got at least a couple of people to look after him, so you're off the hook."

Yeah, and out of an opportunity to pump him about Billy Lee and any tenuous ties to the Woodhallen estate.

The big question so far as I was concerned, of course, was whether my meek college professor would do away with the tax commissioner in order to keep a questionable inheritance intact. I didn't think he would, but as I kept learning from my job, you never could tell about people. "I'm glad he's well enough to be released, Momma. Thanks for letting me know."

While my intuition said the professor wasn't out to get me, other doubts needed resolving. Was the professor really related to Billy Lee? If so, how could he prove it without getting a DNA sample that Billy Lee would never willingly give?

For a Thursday, we were abnormally busy. Between helping Miss Ruby with customers, worrying about Professor Random's motives for proving he was related to Billy Lee, and thinking about the tag on the pickup that had run over Rayla's foot, the morning flew by.

I forgot about the appointment I'd made with the owner of a delinquent tax service business. He showed up at eleven, looking professional in a navy suit and maroon tie, middle-aged but fit, ready to sign me up.

He talked about the procedures leading up to tax sales, emphasizing all legal and advertising costs were borne by the delinquent property owners and not law-abiding taxpayers.

After we talked about what they would do regarding the sales, he moved on to a friendly conversation, mentioning the houseboat his company owned. "We give classes on it three, four times a year. A lot of tax commissioners we service come. Then we throw a big party in Athens for our customers, too. And at the Savannah convention. You like to dance?"

"Um, yes." Not with other tax commissioners, though.

He leered. "You'll like our parties, then. We throw one in Atlanta, Savannah, Athens, and any other place the state gives classes. We got other perks, too. You like football?"

"Um, not especially."

"How about baseball?"

"Not really."

"Hum."

I watched him size up my frumpy pants and modest shirt and head with hair barely covering the spot where the bird hit me.

"How about shows down at the Fox Theater in Atlanta? Ever been to any of them?"

"Actually, I have." *The Nutcracker,* when I was fifteen.

He brightened up. "We got an in there, too. Get you tickets to nearly any show they put on."

I'm naïve. It took me that long to finally understand what he was offering. I stood up and fell back on my, by now well-practiced, reply in all daunting situations. "I'll consider your collections company. I have two other people I'm interviewing." I held out my hand. "Thanks for coming up. I know Medder Rose is a lot out of the way for you to travel." I used my hand-hold to gently maneuver him out of my office. "I really appreciate your taking the trip all the way up here."

"I'll be glad to leave you a copy of the contract." He started to open his briefcase.

"Miss Ruby?" I called. "Can you see Mr. Porrenge out?"

Miss Ruby hopped off her stool and grabbed him while he was still looking for his paperwork. "Come on with me." When she shoved him toward the exit, I could tell he didn't like not getting my signature on his contract.

Too bad. He'd have to lump it.

At lunch, Delores had a dentist's appointment, so the hobbling Rayla and I went to MoJo's Magic Eatery while Lucy and Miss Ruby watched the tax office. Ethan, the dweeb, showed up and sat with us. Rayla flirted with him outrageously even though he was several years her junior. He lapped up the attention so much, he didn't notice how little I had to say.

When we got back to the courthouse, Lucy went to lunch, but Miss Ruby pulled me aside. "I put Sukey Woodhallen in your office," she whispered.

It took me a minute to figure out who she was talking about. Then I hyperventilated.

"Billy Lee Woodhallen's wife?" I whispered back.

"Uh-huh," she said.

I tried to stop breathing so hard. I was getting dizzy. "What does she want?"

"How the devil should I know?" Stealth forgotten, Miss Ruby puffed up like a little hen and asked hopefully, "Do you want me to go find out? I can if you want me to."

Breathe slowly, breathe slowly. "No, no. Not now. Go on and eat your lunch." I hoped Billy Lee's wife wouldn't yell at me. The only thing I knew about her was that she had moved up here from Decatur when she married him six years ago. Like Billy Lee, she kept pretty much to herself. She might be from a big Atlanta suburb, but odds said she was white trash like him.

When I went into the office, my mouth fought to stay closed.

Sukey Woodhallen was maybe five years younger than Billy Lee, in her late thirties or early forties. She was definitely not big and fat and loud as I had imagined.

No, indeed. While she wasn't pretty by any standards, the clothes on her petite form looked like they came from Saks or Neiman Marcus. Small gold hoops in her ears and a gold wedding band abutting a modest diamond solitaire were her only jewelry. And her dark hair was styled in an expensive bob that I doubted any beautician in town knew how to cut.

My sister, who'd married into money, wore her hair exactly like that, and I knew what she paid to get it cut.

Looking up at my entrance, the woman in the visitor's chair gave me a friendly smile and got to her feet. Tanned and fit, she had tiny laugh lines that she made no effort to conceal with makeup. "Hello, I'm Sukey Woodhallen. I need to talk to you about William's taxes."

William? Who the heck was William?

Good grief, she meant Billy Lee.

Noticing the hand she was holding out, I shook it gingerly. "Um, sit down then and we'll, um, talk, Mrs. Woodhallen." I pulled my chair up to the desk and held on with my fingertips.

She hitched her visitor's chair forward so she could look directly at me across the desk. Kind of like Billy Lee had done the other day when he wanted to make payments. Her angular face was a lot pleasanter than his though, with the kind of homely features that belonged on a favorite aunt.

A sensible aunt who'd never marry a loser like Billy Lee.

Without hemming and hawing, she got right to the point. "I found out this weekend about our unpaid taxes. I wondered why I kept getting sly looks whenever I went to the grocery store or took my daughters to school. Now that I know what's going on, I see those taxes need to be paid. William's on his high horse, so I guess it's up to me. Can you please tell me how much we owe?"

I had to go out front to use a terminal since Mr. Jethro, suspicious of all technology, would never let IT put one in his office. Though I had entered a work order for one, who knew when Dyson, the pothead, would get around to installing it?

Nevertheless, in a few minutes, printouts on Billy Lee's parcels started spewing out of the front printer.

When I handed them to Mrs. Woodhallen, she looked at each one carefully, counting to make sure I had all the property Billy Lee owned. "These bills are on the four pieces of property William has right now, this one is on his mother's house—William really ought to put that back in her name and let her claim homestead again since he never could get her qualified for any kind of government aid."

Yeah, aid like free groceries from the charity he set on fire. Did his wife have a clue about Billy Lee's proclivities? Probably not.

"And this one is for the trust, this one is for the farm, so what's this one? Oh, it's in my name. For the boat. Okay. And what's this other one in my name?"

I looked at it. "That's all the farm equipment, like tractors and combines. It also includes cattle and horses."

She inspected it with an eagle eye. "The assessment looks high. Then again, we bought that new bull last year." She leaned back in her chair. "That's probably about right. What's the tax total?"

I used Mr. Jethro's old desk calculator and gave her the bad news.

She took the calculator tape without batting an eye. "Does that include interest?"

"And penalties and fi-fa fees." I wanted to make sure she knew she wasn't getting out of paying anything.

She laughed. "Like fee fie fo fum? No," she quickly added,

seeing my face. "I understand. But I've always wondered. What exactly is a fi-fa fee?"

"It's from Latin. *Fieri facias.* It means 'to cause to be done.' " I butchered the pronunciation but I wasn't about to haul in Delores to explain. "It's a court cost we have to charge when we place liens on property for unpaid taxes."

"Like ours."

"Yes, ma'am."

"That makes sense." She drew a pretty silver pen from her purse that looked a lot like my sister's Chloe bag her husband had given her for her thirtieth birthday. Carley's husband is a big wheel with a large international company and could easily afford it. I wondered if Mrs. Woodhallen's purse was a knockoff or real. If it was real, I wondered whether this nice woman had any idea hers might have been bought by drug money.

You don't know that! I slapped myself mentally.

Mrs. Woodhallen used the expensive pen to circle the total on the tape. "So this amount is what I need to pay to keep the liens from being sold."

"Yes, ma'am, that amount is what's owed."

She brought out a checkbook and looked at it with a slight frown. "I can't pay all of this today. I have a certain balance I have to leave in my household account."

Uh huh. Here we go again.

Other taxpayers had pulled this same routine in the past. They came in, pretended they wanted to pay, and then went back to the same old waffling. I held my chair up to the desk with my fingertips, steeling myself. In the past, Mr. Jethro had been the one to withstand the pleas or threats that usually came. Today I'd be on my own.

Sukey Woodhallen looked at me over her open checkbook. "If I pay eighty thousand today, will the interest change before tomorrow?"

Surprise, surprise! Eighty thousand? Wheeee!

I hid my excitement. "Tomorrow? No, ma'am. It's already past the fifteenth, so you have nearly a month before interest goes up again."

She started making out the check. "It won't take that long. My cows go to auction tonight, so I'll come in tomorrow sometime with the remainder." She stopped writing and looked up. "You won't do anything with the tax liens before then, will you? Sell them, I mean?"

"Me? Oh, no! Not if you're paying that much today."

"Good." She laughed ruefully and went back to writing. "I didn't intend to take all my cows to auction this month, but I think getting taxes paid is more important."

I wanted to do a jig. "Oh, yes, ma'am. I agree. Absolutely."

She tore the check out and handed it to me. "How will you apply it?"

"I'll start by paying the smaller bills and go up. That way both the personal ones and the property ones will get paid except for the largest one. The seven thousand or so still due will owe on it."

"That sounds good. May I have a receipt?" she asked as I got up.

"You most certainly may!" *Eighty thousand in one swoop!*

I danced out front with the check and processed payment myself.

Back in the office, Sukey Woodhallen looked at the receipt, noted where I'd highlighted the remainder due on the unpaid parcel and stood up. "Men are such fools, aren't they?" she said with a confiding chuckle. "William could have cashed out one of his treasury notes early and paid those any time this past year, but he was so annoyed with Mr. Jethro for nagging him—poor man, that was such a terrible thing that happened. Have they ever found out who did it?"

"Um, not that I've heard." If she didn't know her husband was the prime suspect, I wasn't about to tell her.

"That's a shame. I only met Mr. Jethro a couple of times, but he was always charming. I know William thought a lot of him. When Mr. Jethro threatened to sell those liens, William couldn't believe he really would. Then he got his back up and . . ." She shook her head ruefully. "I hate it when William digs in his heels. He's really a fine person except for that little stubborn streak. Thank you so much for your help."

She held out her hand. I shook it in a daze.

Little stubborn streak. Was she talking about the same man I knew?

"I'll see you tomorrow," she chirped and waved goodbye.

Along with Delores, back from her dentist appointment, and nosy Miss Ruby, poking her head out of the vault where she was eating her sandwich, I watched Billy Lee's wife leave. I said, "She seems real nice."

"Yep, I heard that about her, but I don't know her personally," Miss Ruby said in her nasally tone. She started back toward her lunch in the vault. "She don't do much of her shopping and stuff in town. She's Catholic, too, so she has to go over to the next county for church."

"Bet Billy Lee's gonna be fit to be tied." Delores might have just come from the dentist, but she was already unwrapping a Devil Dunky cupcake. "When he finds out she went behind his back and paid up his taxes, he'll have a fit." She shook her head solemnly but couldn't hide her satisfaction.

Hearing Billy Lee's name brought Rayla out from behind her magazine. She was inside with us today, sitting on a ratty side chair with her splinted foot resting on a filing stool. "That was Billy Lee Woodhallen's wife?"

I nodded. "Hard to believe, isn't it?"

"Nigh impossible," Rayla said.

"She came to pay his taxes," I said.

Rayla's mouth formed an O. "And she paid 'em?"

"Except for about seven thousand dollars. She says she'll be back in tomorrow to take care of the rest. After she sells her cows tonight at the auction."

"Wow." Rayla ran a hand through her recently colored honey-blond curls. "Maybe I better take up raising cows. I didn't know there was that kind of money in that kind of stuff. She sure doesn't look like a cattle person, did she?"

"Nope. She sure doesn't." Sukey Woodhallen looked like she belonged to the country club and the junior league. Which, for all anybody knew, she might very well have done before she married Billy Lee.

"You gonna let Duke know the taxes got paid?" Rayla asked.

"I hadn't thought about it. I guess I better." That made me brighten up. "Now Billy Lee doesn't have a reason to murder me, does he? I can quit being shadowed all the time!"

Calling the sheriff to tell him about Sukey Woodhallen's visit, I was surprised he didn't agree I no longer needed protection. "Maybe, maybe not," he said. "Assuming that Billy Lee's the murderer—"

"Who else could it be?" I put aside Professor Random's confession.

"He's got alibis," Sheriff Duval said patiently.

"Yeah. His wife." I thought back to the woman in the office. She didn't look like she'd lie, but in this business you learned fast that you can't always tell what people will do.

"Regardless, I think we'll keep someone with you a little longer," Sheriff Duval said.

To tell the truth, I was kind of glad.

CHAPTER 15

About four thirty, my little Hyundai showed up at the office, all fixed up and shining like new. I was so tickled, I did a happy dance around it.

I wasn't so tickled about the bill the mechanic presented, but I'd have to pay it because my insurance agent had put in to have the reimbursement check come to me. I hoped that, when it came, it would cover most of what I had to shell out.

After work, since I had wheels again, I went up, followed by Rayla, toward Goat Ridge to look for Professor Random's house. If he was feeling up to it, I wanted to tell him about Billy Lee's brother.

On the way, I went past Delores's brick ranch with its clean red shutters and perfect landscaping. She and her three sisters had built houses next to each other on land their parents had given them. From tidbits Delores let drop, I knew their widowed mother lived directly behind them. You couldn't see her house from the road because of a high yew hedge that ran behind the sisters' properties, but you could catch a glimpse of a couple of derelict chicken houses.

A commune of women like Demon Delores.

I shuddered. Oh, the horror.

A mile down the road, Miss Ruby's house came into view. She lived in a shabby white frame with empty chicken houses in the back. Poultry farming had once been a big industry in the county, and a lot of people still did it, but Miss Ruby had given up raising chickens years before. Like Mr. Jethro and Delores's parents, the Bromfields had parceled out their acreage to their children, and their son and daughter lived beside them.

Ten minutes past Miss Ruby's, I came to Billy Lee's driveway. I'd heard about the eight bedroom mansion he and his wife had built on top of the ridge, but the only thing visible from the road was the roof. It looked huge. According to recent tax records, the mansion stood among five hundred acres that had been in his family since the Cherokee got pushed out.

Of course, Billy Lee had conservation exemptions on most of his farmland so he didn't have to pay so much in taxes. I couldn't fault him for that, since every landowner with good sense filed for the same exemptions. Seemed kind of unfair on the rest of us because we had to make up for what they got out of paying, but that was the law.

And the conservation law really helped Billy Lee, too. The fair market assessment on his house and acreage and businesses was over two million dollars even with our assessors' usually lowball figures. Still, his house and lands might be worth less in this economy.

Or maybe not.

A farmer in the south of the county had recently sold eight acres partly on the river for over twelve thousand an acre despite housing's downward spiral. I tried to figure out how much Billy Lee's property would be worth. Five hundred times ten thousand dollars an acre, a conservative estimate since a lot of it was waterfront, would be . . .

Five hundred thousand dollars?

No. Five million dollars. I almost drove into a ditch in shock, but corrected without jerking the wheel too much.

Five million dollars. And that wasn't counting the house and the separate farm parcels and the commercial stuff owned by the Woodhallen estate.

Good grief.

If you looked only at his land values, Billy Lee Woodhallen, despite his crude appearance, was still a multimillionaire.

And the professor might be eligible to claim part of that wealth?

When I finally pulled up at Professor Random's, his home was a far cry from Billy Lee's mansion. This house looked like any other wooden farmhouse built in the early part of the twentieth century. Some scaffolding on one side revealed the professor was in the process of remodeling, but no one was at work today.

A canvas-covered vehicle sat in the side yard. The old pickup the professor was restoring. Maybe I should go look under the canvas. Just in case.

I didn't really think this was the same pickup that had stalked me. The professor had said it wasn't drivable. But if he had lied . . .

"What're you standing there for?" Rayla, out of her patrol car, interrupted my reverie.

With her limping along beside me, I went to the door and rapped lightly. Taking an indistinguishable response for a welcome, I turned the unlocked knob and we went inside.

Professor Random reclined on a low leather sofa, one arm and one leg from ankle to hip encased in plastic. "Hello, Corrie. And, um, Rayla." He didn't seem pleased to see us, but he didn't seem displeased either. He did look tired. "Come in and sit down. Sorry I didn't get the door. I'm still a little woozy from the painkillers."

"Not to worry." I sat down and nearly fell to the floor. The chair was one of those squishy ones that sink under your weight like it's about to swallow you.

While I got myself arranged, Rayla looked around. "Hey, can I borrow your powder room, Jeff? Corrie rushed me out before

I could use the facilities at the courthouse."

Like it was my fault she hadn't gone before we left.

He gestured down a hallway. "On the right."

Pep him up. Be cheerful. "Even woozy, Professor Random, you look like you're feeling better."

He didn't, but what do you say to somebody who's broken an arm and ankle, and has nobody who cares?

He tried to smile. "I'm fine. I'm sure tomorrow I'll feel more like myself."

"The school isn't pushing you to come back to work, are they?"

He shook his head. "Oh, no. My dean's been great, insisting on coming and picking me up and bringing my car home. She's going to teach my classes herself tomorrow and next week if I don't feel like coming in. She said I shouldn't worry about a thing except getting better. She's even bringing me lunch every day."

I had met the dean. She was a good-looking woman for her age. Forty maybe. I wondered if she was married and if she had her cap set on . . .

This was no time to dwell on such matters. "Well, that's good." Taking advantage of Rayla's absence, I said, "I, er, learned something about the Woodhallens you might be interested in."

He didn't perk up as I hoped. "I don't know that I care now. After what happened in the courthouse, whether or not . . . If Billy Lee's my father, he'll never admit it. I've been thinking about it and I'm not sure I want to know anymore."

"Well, that's the thing. He may not be your father."

His head snapped up so abruptly as to make him wince. "What do you mean?"

"Billy Lee had an older brother who died when he was seventeen. And evidently the girls liked him. A lot. He was several years older than Billy Lee, so I'm wondering if he died about the same time you were born which would mean—"

"The brother could have been my father." Professor Random nearly came off the sofa. Relief, joy, hope flooded his face. "So I may not be Billy Lee's son after all!"

For the first time since I came into the room, he looked alive.

This man couldn't possibly be responsible for Mr. Jethro's murder. After meeting Billy Lee, he didn't *want* to be Billy Lee's son.

Nevertheless, on the way out, I detoured by the covered vehicle and gave the canvas a tweak.

Gray primer covered the exposed hood. I looked at it a moment, then checked the back. To my relief, the wheel was under the truck bed. No exposed fender like the old truck that ran me down.

Rayla caught me. "What're you doing?"

"Nothing."

"This isn't the truck Duke's looking for. They went over this area with a fine tooth comb."

"Of course it isn't. Never thought it was."

CHAPTER 16

On Friday, I woke up more cheerful than I'd been since I took on this miserable job. Not only would Billy Lee's taxes be completely paid today, meaning he should have no reason to murder anybody else, but it had occurred to me that there might be a way to find out if the tag I'd glimpsed was an old Georgia tag as Daddy suggested.

If Billy Lee's father had bought the truck new—which was probable since he was a Woodhallen and they'd always had money from illegal moonshine or, in today's society, most likely drug running—and if Billy Lee still had the original tag—which was entirely possible—he could put the plate on the truck anytime he wanted to. If anyone saw the numbers, as I'd done, they would assume the truck was from out of state. Since the tag wasn't currently registered, it would be untraceable.

Unless . . .

Last night I'd woken in the middle of the night, a little voice in my head saying, *You need to check the attic.*

The courthouse attic held all the county's old records, going back almost to when the courthouse was built. I knew there were old tag receipts up there, too, because I had run across them last year.

For income tax purposes, a woman selling inherited land needed the value when her grandfather originally bought the property in the 1960s. As always, Mr. Jethro believed in being helpful even if research wasn't strictly his job. He had sent me

193

upstairs to the attic to dig out the information she sought from one of the old tax digests.

I didn't want to go into the attic, because people said there were mice and scorpions lurking among the boxes. Luckily, I hadn't seen so much as a spider on that previous trip, so I should be okay if I went up there today.

Should be.

Anyway, if a couple of hours poking around turned up a receipt on the F411-something tag, it would be worth confronting a varmint or two.

As I was leaving home, Daddy caught me. "I'm going to get your tires rotated and balanced," he said. "The repair shop didn't do it, and you don't want to wear 'em out. Momma's off and she says take her new car."

That stopped me cold. "She trusts me? After I wrecked her old car?"

"No, but she figures you aren't due for another accident anytime soon so it should be safe."

A little put out at Momma's reasoning, but not enough to keep me from snatching up the BMW keys, I rushed out before she changed her mind. The sporty little convertible was fun to ride in. The weather wasn't quite warm enough to put down the top, but next month it would be. Would Momma let me borrow it on a pretty day if I promised to drive no more than fifty miles an hour?

I arrived at work in a pretty good mood till I tried the tax office door and couldn't get in. Delores got to work at seven fifty-five on the dot every morning, and it was only seven forty.

I had fifteen minutes to cool my heels because the inept commissioners still hadn't come up with a set of keys for me, darn them! I called their secretary on my cell.

"Are my keys ready yet?"

"Hi. Corrie." Sheila recognized my voice. "What keys are you talking about, hon?"

"The ones to the office you were supposed to order a couple of weeks ago for me."

"Nobody told me to order any keys for you."

"Sam Blanken promised me I'd have keys by now. When the sheriff wouldn't release Mr. Jethro's set right away, Sam said you'd order me some."

"Well, he forgot to tell me. Most likely he told the county manager, and he's the one forgot. Sounds like something he'd do. He is the most incompetent . . ." She remembered he was her boss. "Never mind. The locksmith's coming out next week to rekey the upstairs attorney-client conference room. I'll get him to make a set for your office and also for the building while he's here."

I shoved the cell back in my purse, still annoyed. If I were a man, I would have had those keys in hand by now. I could see that one of these days, a confrontation with the commissioners would be inevitable. Another peril of being tax commissioner.

Not until I'd waited on my first customer did it occur to me that I'd forgotten to ask Sheila about borrowing a key to the attic so I could prowl around the tag records. Mr. Jethro had one, but it was on his keychain with his other office keys at the sheriff's office.

Great. I'd have to see if Demon Delores had a key for upstairs. Since it was Friday, we were swamped, but I approached her at the first lull.

She looked up from her bill paying (Delores always wrote checks for her personal bills out at her desk and used the office stamp machine to put postage on them) and gave me her usual *you've got to be kidding* look. "What do you want up in the attic? Whatever it is, you need to get one of the trusties to bring it down for you. Those boxes are too heavy for you to be shifting."

She should have told Mr. Jethro that last year when I was

researching tax bills for him. "I, um, just, um, need to look for some old paperwork."

She waited for me to tell her more.

I didn't.

After the silence lengthened, she finally said, grudgingly, "I don't have a key for the attic, but I'll get Carl's for you if you want. He comes in at two. I can catch him at the buildings office before he starts work."

The buildings and maintenance department nestled between other county offices housed in the next block, but chief custodian Carl Brockaway oversaw cleaning crews in the courthouse, sheriff's offices, and parks offices. He also acted as occasional trash collector, drink machine filler-upper, bathroom inspector and whatever else necessary to keep the buildings clean and running.

We women employees loved Carl. He kept the ladies' room neat and, more importantly, stocked with abundant toilet paper and paper towels. When he went on vacation, we had to shift for ourselves and we really missed him. Running out of toilet paper is the pits.

Suspicious of Delores's offer, I demurred. "You don't need to chase down Carl. I can walk over and see him myself."

Rayla, in her splint, groaned. "That means I'll have to walk over with you."

Delores shrugged. "No skin off my nose. I'm going over to fuss at him about the cleaning crew anyway. This is the third time in two weeks they haven't picked up our trash." Her nostrils quivered with suppressed anger. "The county let the last crew go because they got a lower bid but, I swear, these new people are the laziest group I've ever seen in my life."

Sloppy cleaning ticked Delores off. Among other things.

"Let Delores pick up the key for you," Rayla pleaded.

I couldn't make Rayla limp that far. "Okay, Delores, if you're sure you don't mind, then I would appreciate your asking Carl for his key. Tell him I want to go upstairs right after we close at five. There's no way I can do it now with all these people still coming in from the days we were closed."

Rayla breathed a sigh of relief.

Poor Rayla. "And you can wait for me down here when I go up. The courthouse will be locked. No sense in your climbing those stairs to the attic. They're more rickety than that second-floor railing. With your bad foot, you sure don't need to be on them."

A group of people came in, chattering and laughing. It is a proven fact that tax customers congregate in the parking lot until they have five or ten people gathered; only then do they wander inside to continue their conversations and enjoy the camaraderie.

When they lined up, I took the opportunity to get back to my workspace before Delores could pry any more about what I wanted from the attic. I didn't want to look foolish if nothing was there.

Billy Lee's wife, true to her word, showed up that afternoon to make the final payment on their taxes. When she handed over a fistful of hundred-dollar bills, Rayla's eyes got big. "Mercy, I'm definitely going to get me some cows," she said after Sukey Woodhallen left with her receipt. "I never thought there'd be that much money in raising cattle."

"There ain't, once you figure the fencing and the feed and losing 'em to coyotes and such," Miss Ruby opined. "She's got all her capital outlay done so all the costs she's got now is the normal overhead. But you'd have to buy some pasture and put up a fence, Rayla. Then you'd need to buy 'em hay in the winter when there ain't no pasture. And somebody'd have to stay close by and check in every so often to see that none of 'em get out of the fence. And fences are always needing—"

Rayla's eyes glazed. "Maybe I won't raise cows."

"Not that they ain't better than raising chickens," Miss Ruby said. "With layers, you got to pick up eggs every blooming day. Fryers are a little better, but you're still tied down for the six weeks they're growing. Then when you finally get shut of 'em, you got to muck out all the litter, and if you think cow manure is bad, just start messing in chicken shit and you'll think—"

"I'll just keep on doing what I'm doing," Rayla said hastily.

About four, when Rayla was yawning over her magazine, a group of young Hispanics came in. Hispanics don't meet and gather in the parking lot; they arrive together and leave together. I've decided the reason is that a few of them know some English words and a few of them know other English words, so it takes a group to figure out what we're saying and what to answer. Occasionally, a family comes in relying on a small child to interpret.

For the most part, the Hispanics in our county mind their own business, work hard for minimum wage, and line up at the post office every Saturday morning to send money to their relatives back home. My only quarrel with them is that they don't speak English. I always worry that they don't understand everything we tell them, especially when a five-year-old child is translating between the parents and me.

This group today had their stuff together. The car was going to Mexico so they needed a title even though the Chevrolet was fifteen years old. In Georgia, anything that old doesn't have to be titled, but if you have a Georgia title properly signed over, you can still get one if you choose.

The title looked good. The information was filled out correctly. The only problem was the insurance, but after some consternation when they talked among themselves for about ten minutes, one pulled out a card with their agent's name and number.

I tried to explain a card wouldn't do, that the information

had to be in the computer. In the end, a phone call to the agency elicited the assurances that yes, the vehicle had insurance and yes, they would fax us the forms we needed.

Naturally, that didn't happen for another forty minutes, but the fax finally spat out and it contained the correct forms. The patient Hispanics were there for over an hour by the time I handed them their title application and registration receipts. "Okay. You should get your new title in the next week or so. Good luck." I waved the pleased group out the door.

Taking advantage of no customers in line, I dragged myself off my stool to get a root beer.

Delores caught me at the small fridge. "Carl wouldn't give me his attic key, but he'll leave the door unlocked for you when they start cleaning at five. Then he'll go back upstairs and lock up about eight or nine. That'll give you enough time to do whatever it is you need to do." She gave me a speculative look. "Won't it?"

"More than enough." She was being nice but I knew why: she was dying to know what I was searching for. Well, she could just keep wondering. I popped the top on my root beer. "Thanks, Delores."

"You're welcome," she said, seeing I was through talking. "Guess what Judge Hartley's gonna do?"

"No idea."

"Call in the fire marshal to condemn the courthouse."

"Condemn the courthouse?" I remembered the judge's threat. "Does that mean we can't work in it?"

She shrugged. "All Carl heard was that the judge is mad as fire over that railing breaking, and he's threatening all kinds of things."

As if I didn't have enough on my mind right now. Yes, the courthouse was old, but to condemn it out of hand without giving the commissioners a chance to renovate or get the bond passed? Where would the offices go if we had to move out? How would we get moved? The heavy safe alone would require a fork lift.

Oh, well, I couldn't worry about that now. Another cluster of tag buyers had congregated outside and now poured inside *en masse,* laughing and chatting among themselves like old home week. I put on a smile and went to help Miss Ruby.

When we closed at five, Rayla said, "Let's order some pizza or something before you go upstairs. I'm starving."

"Can't you wait till your relief comes?"

She made a face. "I'm on duty till eleven tonight. Duke has Ethan doing something else before he takes over for the weekend."

That was all right with me. Ethan was still on my list.

Delores came out of the vault. "I've closed and locked the safe. Don't forget to lock the office door when you get through in the attic."

"I'll do it," I promised.

She got her purse and went out. When she got to the door leading into the hall, she stopped and turned. "Don't forget, Corrie. Lock the door before you leave. No telling what kinds of groups might be in and out this weekend. We had kids from DUI school who met here for classes one year. They got in and it took Dyson two days to get the computers back to normal."

"I will definitely lock the door. Rayla here will remind me."

Rayla nodded as she picked up some magazines.

Delores closed her eyes as if in prayer. I could tell she wasn't happy about depending on me to take care of what was usually her job, but that was Delores. She wanted things done her way.

After she finally left, Rayla ordered us sandwiches from Mo-Jo's Magic Eatery. About five thirty the cleaners breezed through, doing their thing with trash cans. By the time the sandwiches came and we ate, it was after six o'clock.

Carl should have opened the attic door for me by now. I dreaded going up there in the eerie gloom with the stale air, but I could stand it for a little while.

"I shouldn't be gone but about an hour or so," I told Rayla as I headed for the attic. "I'll hurry fast as I can."

She yawned. "Don't worry about it. I'm not. The courthouse is secure after five. Nobody can get in but county employees or the cleaning crew, and I don't think any of them are after you."

"I don't even believe Billy Lee's after me any more, not now his taxes are paid."

"You're probably right, but Duke hasn't relieved us yet." She settled herself on the sagging loveseat in Mr. Jethro's—my!—office and put her splinted foot up on the visitor's chair. "I may close my eyes for a few minutes while you're up there."

"Feel free. No reporters are around to whine about county employees sleeping on county time."

She grinned. "And won't be, 'cause they can't get in. By the way, don't let the rats get you."

"That's just an old wives' tale."

"Little you know. There was one in Judge Hartley's secretary's office a few weeks back. Tore into salsa and ketchup packages, and got every last one of her candy bars. Big fellow, Carl said. Big as a cat."

Great. Stale air, dust, and huge rats who thrived on candy.

The elevator only went up to the third floor, meaning that the attic had to be accessed by stairs. A shaky stairwell led up to an area as large as the entire courthouse beneath it, except for one part in the middle leading up to the clock tower. The county used the space for storage of seasonal decorations and mainte-nance supplies, as well as old records and unusable furniture.

The lighting left a lot to be desired. There were two dormer-type windows, one in front and another in back, though precious little daylight crept through this time of day. Random bare bulbs dangled, but they couldn't have been over forty watts apiece.

I looked around for scurrying figures but didn't see any.

From my trip up here the previous year to find digests, I remembered where the tax commissioner's records were stored. After I picked my way through boxes of cleaning supplies, record file boxes, and mutilated office furniture, I reached the northeast corner where the tax office's Christmas tree, still decorated from the holidays, marked the beginning of our portion.

One ear listened for little feet as I shifted accounting boxes. In fifteen minutes, the ones housing tax records came into view. Stacked neatly against the wall, the cartons contained well over seventy years' worth of copies of tax bills, tag receipts, and mobile home decal receipts.

I was only interested in the ones labeled "1950s." Everyone agreed that was the era the mystery truck came from. So I broke into a taped box containing receipts for 1950–1959.

What the heck. Copies of tax bills, tag receipts, and mobile home receipts were filed together.

And they were not in order.

"Arghh!" The dismal attic echoed. "I'll never find one stupid tag receipt. Even if it's here."

But no giving up now. I spied a clerk's chair missing its back in what must be the sheriff's section, and rolled it over to the tax boxes. The seat stuffing was coming out. Something had gnawed at it.

Rats! I knew it!

After a brief coughing spell provoked by the musty air, I peered around. Everything seemed kind of spooky but quiet. No rodents playing hide and seek anywhere.

There didn't seem to be any roaches or anything crawling on what was left of the chair, so I perched on it and started thumbing through the tissue-thin sheets. First, I sorted out the tag receipts from the property tax and mobile home papers. Each section took about twenty minutes to go through before every tag number on every tag receipt had been checked.

This wasn't as easy as it sounds. Back in the fifties, the state got the original, the customer the first carbon copy, and our office the third. That meant our files contained barely legible handwritten figures. I had to pull each receipt out and pore over it under dim light to decipher the squiggles.

This Friday night was shot. What was I doing shutting myself up in this horrible space where only rats visited? Why was I engaged on such a hopeless task? Duke Duval had decided, and part of me agreed, that the truck's tag was from out of state. Why did I think I knew more than the sheriff?

He might be wrong, though. The tag I'd seen might be an old Georgia plate. It was possible. Like Daddy said, some people put them on their old cars. Antique cars with matching tag plates were pretty hot commodities to auto collectors.

Brushing aside doubts and keeping an anxious eye out for unwanted pests, I plowed on.

In the third section, labeled "1955–56," I hit pay dirt and shrieked, "Ya-hooo!"

In 1955 our office had issued a series of tag plates starting with F. F4100 through F4159 were among them. Only three plates had gone to truck models from the fifties: a 1951 GMC truck owned by Barrow Mangrove Smith, a 1956 Chevrolet owned by W. John Fieldwick—hmm, must have bought it brand spanking new—and a 1955 Ford truck in the name of Clark F. Williston. The last had been bought new, too.

I knew some Smiths, but not the Barrow Mangrove listed on the tag receipt copy. He was either dead or gone from the county. I didn't know of any Fieldwicks from around here, nor could I remember any Willistons, although that name sounded vaguely familiar.

Still, I took the three thin papers from the box to give to

Sheriff Duval.

Too bad the old receipts didn't list vehicle colors. No matter. The paint could have been changed several times over the decades if, by chance, one of these trucks still traveled the roads.

And the blue or silver truck that had squashed Rayla's foot was certainly running and in use. Legally it should be tagged, but if its owner hadn't registered it, someone could have put one of these old tags on it. If the fifty-five tag was issued to one of these trucks, we'd have a VIN number to work with. It might even be listed on the state computer. If not, Sheriff Duval still might be able to trace a person with access to the old tag.

You're assuming a lot. I laughed at myself. Didn't matter. This was a feasible theory. I'd already done the legwork. Now I needed to follow through.

My watch said eight forty.

Eight forty! I'd been here two and a half hours. Carl would be along any minute to lock up, and Rayla would be worried.

Hah. More than likely, she was sound asleep.

I stretched, then yipped as a muscle caught in my back.

Before I left the courthouse, I'd go down and check the computer for the VIN numbers on these trucks to see if any of them had current registrations. Wouldn't it tick Ethan off if I solved the truck mystery? Feeling pretty smug, I bounced through the clutter to the heavy door leading from the attic.

The door didn't open.

Stuck. Everything in this ratty courthouse was out of alignment. Maybe Judge Hartley was right. Maybe the old building did need to be condemned.

I pulled harder.

The door didn't budge.

"Come on, you stupid door!"

I yanked at the handle several times before the realization hit me.

"This blooming door's locked!"
Carl had locked me in.

CHAPTER 17

As my panicky voice echoed round the deserted attic, I hyper-ventilated.

All right, the door is definitely locked. Breathe. In. Out. Calm down. Why didn't Carl call out before he locked up?

I checked my watch again. Eight forty-five.

Common sense kicked in. Would Carl lock the door without checking to see that I was gone? It would be very unlike Carl. He was conscientious to a fault. No, Carl hadn't locked the door.

Maybe another person had noticed it was unlocked and locked it, not knowing I was inside.

No, surely anyone would have seen the lights and yelled to see if somebody was working up here.

Unless someone had locked the door deliberately.

I pooh-poohed the idea. Too implausible. Most likely somebody came along, didn't realize I was here, and . . .

Who had a key?

Never mind. Carl would never lock the attic door without making sure I was out. He should be along any minute. I'd wait for him at the door.

And if by some chance, Carl forgot me, Rayla would come looking when I didn't show up.

Relieved at this rational scenario, I stationed myself beside the door. In fact, I'd just call Rayla now and save . . .

Except my cell phone was in my purse and my purse was

downstairs in my desk.

Crud. I'd have to wait for Carl.

After standing quietly for several minutes, I heard rustling.

Rats!

I looked around. Was that a shadowy figure near the clerk's area? I stared into the gloom, trying to see.

Yes, there was something there. Oh Lord it must be rats. Didn't they come out at night? Surely Carl would be here soon.

Nothing moving now. Maybe I was imagining things.

Nine o'clock came and went without Carl or Rayla appearing. What did happen were soft scuffling noises occasionally coming out of the dark corners, too many to be imaginary.

I yelled whenever I heard them in hopes of discouraging any close-up appearances.

Thud! A box fell followed by loud scrambling.

I screamed. At the same time, my heart sank to my toes.

By this time, someone should have been searching for me.

Carl and Rayla had forgotten me.

Or else something had happened to them.

Like what? Billy Lee's taxes were paid. Why would he care about me now? What had Delores said? He might decide to demand his wife's checks back? What if he had done something to Rayla and Carl?

No, I was getting hysterical.

Why not? Someone should have missed me by now and come looking for me.

One thing was certain. If I didn't want to stay here and be attacked by rats, I was on my own. "I've got to get out of here." I eyed the dim attic that had become a prison.

What am I going to do?

You could have called for help, you idiot, if you'd brought your cell with you.

Why in heaven's name hadn't I?

Too late for regrets. Surely Rayla would eventually wonder where I was and come to see about me.

If she was able. If Billy Lee hadn't . . .

No. More than likely, she was asleep on the loveseat. She might sleep for hours.

"I can't stay here all night!" I didn't hear the creatures stirring anymore, but they were there. I was positive they were there. Big fat rats with sharp white teeth.

Moving warily and singing "Old MacDonald" to scare any nearby rodent (my singing should traumatize the bravest rat) I went over to the closest window. Though dirty panes, I could make out dim streetlights illuminating the front walkway and lawn of the deserted courthouse.

No passersby or people leaving work on the sidewalks, only cars rushing past trying to get home. Not much hope of flagging down one of them.

"—and on that farm he had a pig." Singing at the top of my voice, I trotted to the only other window. It overlooked the brightly lit dumpster at the back of the courthouse where cleaning people brought trash from the different offices.

The dumpster was the best bet to see someone I could yell at.

"Ee i ee i o-o-oh!" Okay, first thing was to open the window.

Easier said than done. Multiple coats of paint over the years had glued it shut. I looked around for something to use to pry it open. Nothing.

Wait, what was that sticking out from the pile of discarded furniture?

I sang, "—a baa baa here, a baa baa there," as I cautiously approached the pile and saw a pedestal off a broken table. I picked it up. It was heavy enough to break the glass. Or fend off a large rodent.

Protection or help. Summon help or hit a rapacious, sharp-toothed attacker.

How much would it cost to replace the window? Was the glass original or a cheap replacement? How much money were we talking—?

What difference does it make? I've got to get out of here!

The glass broke but some chips stung me.

"Owww!" I let the heavy wood fly out of my hand and out the window.

It sure wasn't safety glass.

I watched the pedestal leg fall to the parking lot below. It landed on the pavement with a clunk.

My weapon was gone. I whirled frantically, but heard and saw nothing. Maybe the rats were as afraid of me as I was of them.

Maybe my singing had frightened them away.

I looked back down. Too bad the parking lot was empty. A falling chunk of wood would have attracted some notice.

Oh, well. Maybe someone would see the broken pedestal and look up.

"Help!"

My experimental yell sounded loud in the quiet. Someone should hear that. Someone had to hear that.

My hand was bleeding from the glass splinters, so I rummaged around and found a box of paper towels for the bathrooms. Pulling some out, I wrapped a couple around my hand and went back to the window.

Would my bleeding attract the rats like blood attracted sharks? I could be gnawed to death.

"Old MacDonald had a farm," I started again.

After a bit, two workers approached with their cleaning barrels full of trash.

I yelled.

Deep in conversation, they didn't hear me. An eighteen-wheeler approached the front side of the courthouse.

I screamed.

Against the sound of traffic and the semi crawling by the courthouse at twenty miles an hour, the legal city limit, I could see the cleaners chatting and laughing. They never once looked up.

I could be up here getting murdered, and they wouldn't hear a thing.

Frantic, I looked around for something to throw at them. There was nothing. Remembering where I'd found the towels, I rushed over to Carl's supply section. A box of towels wouldn't be heavy enough.

I tore into a large carton.

Toilet paper. Industrial-sized rolls of toilet paper. Nice and heavy.

I grabbed one—it took both hands to lift it—and ran back. Preparing to heave it out the window, I looked down and saw retreating backs of the workers rolling their barrels away.

Shoot.

Never mind. They'd be back. I would stockpile some more rolls of toilet paper to throw down at them.

A few minutes later, prepared and armed, I waited beside my stack as the minutes dragged. The scurrying started again.

Oooh, closer than last time.

I started my medley again. Loudly.

Nine fifteen, nine twenty, nine twenty-five came and went. I made up animals for the farm. Giraffes, emus, walruses. My throat started aching, and my voice got hoarse. Finally . . .

Headlights. Glory be, someone was turning into the back lot. I peered down to see a pickup park across from the dumpster. Not an old one, thank goodness. The lights illuminated a big black extended-cab truck.

"Arghhh!"

Billy Lee Woodhallen heaved himself out of the driver's seat, pulled his jeans out of his back crotch, adjusted his front crotch, and ambled toward the back door of the courthouse.

I shrank back.

Common sense prevailed.

His taxes are paid, I told myself. He's got no reason to murder me. He couldn't have locked me in because he only just got here. He couldn't have done anything to Rayla or Carl, because he just got here.

Billy Lee or rats.

Rats or Billy Lee.

A fleeting shadow on top of some banker boxes to the side made the decision.

Gritting my teeth, I flung a heavy roll of toilet tissue out the broken window.

It landed to the side, causing Billy Lee to stop and look around in bewilderment.

I yelled. "Billy Lee! Billy Lee!"

He scratched his head, still mystified as he gawked round the parking lot. Like the cleaning people, he didn't hear me against the Friday traffic busy heading home or out to eat or to the movies or . . .

Who cares where they're going?

I screamed again. "Up here! Help me!"

Billy Lee finished surveying his surroundings and started his hemmorhoidal amble toward the courthouse. He never once looked up, the idiot.

I chucked another roll down in front of him.

Well, I meant it to land in front of him. It actually hit him on the head.

He staggered, grabbed his hat that the tissue roll knocked onto the pavement, and leaned over to peer at the tissue roll. Finally, at long last, he looked up.

I wedged as much of me out the broken window as I could, which was like my head and a hand and part of an arm, and waved frantically. "I need help!"

Billy Lee was hopping mad, literally. He jumped up and down and shook his finger at me. "I don't know who the hell you are, but you're lucky I don't come up there and beat the crap out of you!"

I could hear him plainly. I don't know why everyone down below had such trouble hearing me.

I gave it another try. "Billy Lee! It's me! Corrie Caters! I'm locked up in the attic!"

He stopped and cupped his hand to his ear. "Who the hell—?" He peered up at me. "Corrie Caters? Is that you? What you wanna hit me for?"

"I need help! I'm locked in! Help! Get Carl Brockaway with his key!"

"Why'd you hit me?" His finger wagged at me. "You oughta be ashamed of yourself! I'm gonna come give you what for!" His whole posture signaled outrage before he jogged into the courthouse.

Oh, drat the man. He probably didn't know who Carl was. If he'd even heard that part. Maybe he'd have enough sense to find his way to the attic. If he decided to try.

Maybe he wouldn't beat me up.

After a few suspenseful minutes of playing would he, wouldn't he, I heard him at the door. I flew over, yelling, "Billy Lee! Thank heavens. You're going to have to find Carl, our janitor, so he can unlock the door and let—"

The door opened.

Billy Lee's round face stared at me in amazement. "How'd you get in there with the door locked?"

He wasn't the only one amazed. "How'd you unlock that door?"

"Key was in it."

"The key was in it? The *key* was in the door?"

"Uh-huh." He scratched his head under his ball cap with its big orange letters saying FAT MAN CLUB. He looked from the door knob to me and back again. "How'd you manage to lock the door out here while you was in there?"

"I didn't. Someone locked me in."

We looked at each other. For once, I could see wheels turning in the man's head. Billy Lee might not be as stupid as we all thought.

He wet his lips. His beady eyes bored into mine. "Did you call me to come over here tonight?"

"Me? No."

"You didn't tell me to be sure and park back of the courthouse? Say you'd leave the back door there unlocked so I could get in?"

"No, I didn't call you and tell you anything. I've been up here all evening. Why should I call you?"

"Someone did. A woman. Said she was you. Said something about a tax bill left out when my wife paid up today. Said if I'd meet her here at nine thirty, we'd take care of it before liens got transferred tomorrow."

Cold made me shiver. "It wasn't me. Your wife finished paying all your taxes this afternoon. She made sure of that."

"Yeah, thought so. Sukey don't mess around when she gets her mind set on something. And she was pretty dam—uh, darned mad with me." He paused, pursing his mouth in disapproval, eying something behind me. "Look at the gall of that squirrel."

I whirled to look. "Squirrel?"

The little booger jumped from one banker box to another before standing up on its hind legs with a curled bushy tail and bright curious eyes. It stared straight at me.

Billy Lee coughed. "You know what I think?"

I was distracted. "That's not a rat?"

"Never mind what it is," Billy Lee said impatiently. "Courthouse is probably eat up with rats and squirrels both. The important thing is somebody's out to frame me. Looks like they been trying all along."

An unnamed fear rendered the squirrel forgotten and turned me frantic. "Let's go. Right now."

He wasn't waiting for me to tell him. As I followed his bulky shape tramping down the rickety stairs, I remembered Professor Random who'd broken his ankle and arm after falling through the railing. "Don't lean on the banister, for heaven's sake."

Billy Lee kept on trucking. "I ain't no fool," floated back.

A stray bit of rationality said I should have gone first in case he broke the stairs and I couldn't get down. Too late now. He wasn't stopping.

I was on tenterhooks the whole time we fled, praying the steps would hold under his weight.

Finally, we made it safely to the third floor. From there we took the elevator down to the first. Emerging in the lobby with its cordoned-off staircase, the dim lighting turned familiar hallways into shadowy corridors where unknown threats lurked.

"I've got to get my purse from the office." I didn't move. I hoped Billy Lee would volunteer to go with me or at least wait for me.

"Leave it." His head twisted as he inspected the deserted building.

"I can't. My house keys are in it. And my car key. And Rayla's waiting for me in there, too." I wouldn't give voice to the alternative.

"Leave 'em. Call Duke afterward. We got to get out. Now."

"I don't think so," a third voice put in.

We wheeled.

Delores stood holding the revolver Daddy had insisted I bring to work. It pointed directly at me.

"My desk drawer was locked," I said inanely.

She snorted. "You think after thirty-four years I don't have keys to everything in this here courthouse, including old Jethro's desk?"

"You the one called me?" Billy Lee asked.

Williston. My daddy's words about Delores's ill temper came back: . . . *bipolar or schizoid like her grandmother Williston.* Williston, the name on the tag receipt. "It was you, Delores? You killed Mr. Jethro?"

She didn't deny it. "Both of you get in the tax office." She waved the gun. "Now."

"Nope." Billy Lee crossed his arms. "You'll kill us if we go so we're better off—"

The gun spat flame. The boom hurt my ears.

I screamed.

Billy Lee yelped. He looked down and touched the blood seeping out of his thigh. "You shot me!"

My eardrums reverberated. I had to strain to hear.

"Yeah and next time I'll kill you if you don't get in that tax office. Now! Maybe I'll kill you right here anyway." In the muted light, she looked alien, like a woman out of her mind. "It won't matter in the end anyway."

Rayla. "What have you done to Rayla?"

"She's inside. Go on. Move."

"Have you hurt her? Is she all right?"

"For now. Get going!"

This woman would kill us whether we obeyed or not. I knew this. Billy Lee knew it, too, but he submissively dragged his leg toward the tax office door. I followed. Anything to put off the inevitable.

Picturing Delores as a murderer—murderess?—took a radical

mental adjustment. She was mean-tempered and hard to get along with, but still . . .

I'd worked with her, grumbled about her moods, seethed about her sarcasm.

But a murderess? Delores was the one who'd killed Mr. Jethro and Briant? The one who'd nearly killed me? "Where did you get that truck? Was it yours?"

"It was my grandpa's. It's my son's now. Benjy restored it. He keeps it up and running so when he comes into town on leave, he'll have a ride."

"He didn't tag it."

"He's not here but a couple of times a year. No need to pay to tag it when it's hardly ever driven."

"It's illegal to d-drive without a tag. You s-still owe taxes—"

"Duh. Like I'm gonna pay taxes on something driven twice a year."

Delores was a lawbreaker. "But he'd get caught driving without a tag."

"So sue me. Sheesh, ain't you got any sense? I always put a temporary on it while he's here. Except for lately when I used it. Then I put one of Grandpa's old tags on it so nobody'd know. Did you find the old tag receipt?"

I nodded.

"I thought that's what you were doing up in the attic," Delores said with satisfaction. "I always figured even if somebody saw the tag, they wouldn't realize what it was. And then you did."

"But they looked for the truck." I kept trying to make sense of everything. "After you threw the block from the bridge, the sheriff searched all the houses in the surrounding area. Including over by where you live."

"Hah. Those dumbasses couldn't find their fingers in their assholes. It was in Ma's old chicken house the whole time, behind some stacked up bales of hay. Those deputies were too lazy to move 'em."

We had reached the office door. "I don't understand, Delores." I was still reeling. "Why?"

"Honest to gawd. You got no clue, do you?" She gave an exasperated sigh. "I'm gonna be tax commissioner now. Once you're out of the way, they'll have to appoint me. There won't be anybody else left that can do the job."

My jaw fell. "You actually *want* to be tax commissioner?"

"Wanted it five years ago. I could of retired by now. I got my thirty years in. But old Jethro wouldn't give it up. He just kept on a-going. That day Billy Lee here came in and made such a ruckus, I saw old Jethro meant what he always said about dying in office."

"Mr. Jethro was good to you. He never hurt you."

"Never had no problems with Mr. Jethro except him not leaving when it was his time to go." She laid her reasoning out calmly. "He wouldn't step down and I'm at retirement age. Only I can't afford to quit work on what I'll be drawing. If I'm tax commissioner for a couple of years, though, I end up getting nearly double in my state pension, and it'll help my social security, too. And my four-oh-one-kay. All I needed was a couple of years drawing Mr. Jethro's salary."

"You killed Mr. Jethro and Lucy's husband so you could retire?" There had to be more to her story.

"Duh. Ain't you been listening? Besides, I deserve to be tax commissioner. I put in my time. Excepting after I went to all the trouble of making up a story about losing my keys and getting Mr. Jethro to come unlock the office that night, them three stooges upstairs go and appoint you instead of me. I couldn't believe it. I knew they was dumb, but that took the cake."

Inside the office, Billy Lee quietly sidled away from me.

Delores noticed and flourished the gun. "You get back there

next to her, Billy Lee. Stay together."

Billy Lee shuffled back toward me.

"Where's Rayla?" I asked.

"Back in the vault. She can't help you."

My chest tightened. "Did you kill her, too?"

"Not yet. Figure it'll be better for you all to go together. Make more sense that way. Billy Lee come in here, you pulled your gun while she tried to stop him, but there was a fight and in the commotion you all ended up dead."

My skin crawled.

Rayla was still alive. If I could keep Delores talking, maybe we could figure out how to get away. I wet my lips.

"Briant," I croaked. "You tried to kill me and killed him instead. He never did anything to you, but you killed him anyway."

"That was your fault. It was your cookie bar. You should've kept it instead of giving it away."

"What'd you put in it?"

She smiled, a cold superior smile. "Simplest thing in the world. Yew seeds. We've had yew hedges between me and Ma's house for years. I ground up some seeds when I heard Miss Lavinia say she was baking for us the next day. I knew I'd have a chance to put them in your bar. It was your own fault Lucy's husband died. You shouldn't have given your cookie bar to her."

She was right. I was responsible for Briant's death. But I hadn't known.

Deal with the guilt later. Pull yourself together.

"You can't get away with this, Delores. Billy Lee's taxes are paid. Nobody's going to believe he—"

"Huh. Think I'm dumb, don't you?" She smirked. "The checks aren't deposited, Miss Smarty Pants. Billy Lee came in to burn down the place along with his wife's checks before they could get to the bank. Everyone knows he was set against paying those taxes. He was probably real riled with his wife for coming in here and paying them. So while you and Rayla struggled with him, the fire took hold."

"Fire? What fire?"

"The one Billy Lee is gonna set."

I hadn't noticed the smell in the tax office until then. Lucy's burning vanilla candle on the counter couldn't hide the acrid odor of . . .

"You've poured gasoline in here." The upholstered chairs were dark while the wooden floor gleamed with spilled liquid.

Delores rolled her eyes. "Oh, gawd, you're so dumb. Kerosene. Safer. Not as explosive. And that's what you used to burn down the Sisters' charity shop, wasn't it, Billy Lee?"

He recoiled as if shot. "Nobody never proved that!"

She giggled. I hadn't seen Delores laugh before, much less giggle. That sound scared me more than her gun waving.

"I've been stockpiling gallon jugs of the stuff for this. I went home after work and got them. When I came back, I told Rayla I'd forgotten a sympathy card I meant to mail this weekend. Silly thing believed me. When she turned her back, I knocked her in the head with the doorstop and dragged her in the vault." She smiled, a hideous gloating smile. "She's a little thing, isn't she? Stupid, too, thinking she's tough enough to be a deputy. After that, I went upstairs and locked you up in the attic."

"You didn't need Carl's keys, did you?"

"No, but I borrowed his attic key for you. Told him you'd leave it on your desk for him to pick up when he did his Saturday rounds." She frowned. "You'd of made it a lot easier for me if you'd stayed locked up." The brief annoyance faded. "Never mind. Now that Billy Lee's here, we can start the show. We have to work with what we got, don't we?" She waved the gun toward the door leading behind the counter. "Get on back there. Both of you."

Billy Lee and I took our time complying, but my mind raced. If I could close the door before she got back there with us, maybe we'd have a chance to escape.

She slipped through while I was working out logistics.

No chance now.

I stopped and looked around the familiar office. No weapons, no staplers, no letter openers, no Scotch tape dispensers. Delores's desktop and the counters were clean except for the candle burning sweetly at Lucy's work place.

"Go on." Delores motioned toward the vault. "In there. Rayla's waiting."

She intended to lock us in the vault and set the place on fire with Lucy's candle.

I hyperventilated. Black dots danced before my eyes. I leaned on the counter for support.

"No way." Billy Lee was pale. His right trouser leg was dark from his wound. "I ain't gonna be roasted like a marshmallow."

"Suit yourself." Delores raised the gun toward him. "Let's see. During the struggle, you got shot but still managed to lock Corrie and Rayla in the vault. You passed out before you could escape though, and the fire got you. That'll work, don't you guess?"

The dots were clearing from in front of my eyes. "That's ridiculous. Forensics nowadays can tell exactly what happened at a crime scene." Not for nothing had I watched *CSI* and *NCIS* and all the copycat shows. "You won't fool anyone."

She snorted. "I'll take my chances. They may not believe it happened that way, but they still got to prove what did happen."

In one single movement, I swept up the vanilla scented candle and threw it in her face.

The gun roared but missed. My ears roared. Plaster fell when the bullet hit the ceiling.

I jumped for the gun, grabbed her arm.

Weak as he was, Billy Lee tackled her legs.

She fell backward against her desk, taking me with her. A flame blazed up where the candle hit the kerosene-soaked floor.

I clawed her face.

The pistol exploded again but it sounded kind of muffled.

Billy Lee yelped in pain and fell back.

I caught the wrist of her gun hand, forcing it back and up.

She kneed me in the stomach. I grunted but held on.

She let off another shot. It whizzed by my head so close I felt the breeze, but it sounded faraway.

I clung to her wrist for dear life. My ears were stuffed up, but I could still hear a high-pitched scream of *aiiigh* like it was somewhere in the distance.

The fire spread around us. The flames flickered, but there wasn't any crackling.

Delores slumped suddenly and fell over without resistance.

The screaming from somewhere continued.

Billy Lee stood there, holding the iron doorstop he'd hit Delores with.

I froze, mouth open. The dachshund dropped from his hand. He staggered and slowly folded. A last-minute twist of his huge body left him lying across Delores's back and legs.

The *aiggghh* went on and on. I needed to reassure someone, but I couldn't take my eyes off Billy Lee. Was he dead?

The blood on his pants had turned black, but a fresh dark stain spread over the colors in his flannel shirt.

How could he yell like that with his mouth shut?

That wasn't Billy Lee yelling. That was me.

I closed my mouth. The long-winded scream stopped. I'd only heard it because it was in my throat. I was deaf from the gunfire.

The fire continued to grow. The burning smell snuffed out

the gunpowder acridity.

Delores lay with Billy Lee on top of her. His barrel legs were spread apart, and his head rested on the soaked carpet. The flames neared them.

I pulled the gun from Delores's still fingers. "Billy Lee." I shook him. "Billy Lee, we've got to get out of here. Get up, Billy Lee."

He didn't respond. I couldn't hear myself. Maybe he couldn't hear me either.

Leaving him, I rushed into the vault. Gray duct tape fastened Rayla's hands and feet. Another strip covered her mouth. Her eyes were alert and terrified.

I fumbled in the supply cabinet, found some scissors and cut her arms loose. My hands shook. "You do the rest." I gave her the scissors. "We've got to get out of here before the fire traps us."

She said something but I couldn't hear what. When she started cutting at her ankles, I ran back to check on Billy Lee. He lay unmoving on top of Delores. Smoke was filling the room.

"Come on, Billy Lee." I got under his shoulders and tried to shove him up.

Groggy, he struggled to open his eyes.

"You're going to burn up if you don't help me!"

With my pushing, he got to a sitting position and braced his big hands on his knees. "Lemme rest a minute," I thought he said.

I looked around. The fire was spreading. Black smoke thickened. "We've got to get out."

He made no move. I rushed out to the hallway and broke the fire extinguisher box. The courthouse fire alarms started wailing.

For once, there was a reason.

Coming back into the smoke, I tried to pull Billy Lee up. He and Delores would burn to death if we didn't get out.

I would burn to death.

Rayla staggered out of the office, limping on her splinted foot with her arm over her nose.

I grabbed the fire extinguisher and tried to remember the instructions the cute firefighter had given us last fall.

KISS? No, that didn't sound right. PASS; that was the key thing to remember.

P for pull. Or maybe it was pin.

My fingers fumbled, pulled out the pin.

A for aim. I aimed.

S for sweep. I gripped the handle and started sweeping the flames directly around us. The foam put the fire out wherever it hit but the smoke continued to roil.

What the heck was the other S for? Swim? Save? Sear?

Rayla got Billy Lee to his feet. He had recovered enough to mumble something that sounded like, "We got to get out. We got to get out."

No kidding.

"About time you realized that." I pointed the extinguisher toward the door and sprayed a pathway with foam. "Rayla, Billy Lee, help me with Delores."

Billy Lee staggered, caught himself on the counter. "Let her burn."

I heard that. "Billy Lee!"

"I'm with him," Rayla said.

I heard that, too. "Help me!"

Rayla took one of Delores's hands, but Billy Lee could barely keep his own bulk upright. He held onto the counter and felt his way toward the door.

I threw down the extinguisher. Delores was bigger than Rayla, but she was skinny. Together, Rayla, despite her bad foot, and I managed to get her into the lobby and then the hallway. All the while we urged Billy Lee onward.

By that time a few curious onlookers had gathered out front. They pressed faces to the locked glass doors. When I pushed the exit bar, they surged in and carried the unconscious Delores outside. Rayla, Billy Lee, and I staggered after them as far as we could, gulping in fresh air.

We collapsed at the edge of the parking lot, Rayla sitting down on one side of me with her splinted foot stuck out and Billy Lee falling to his knees on the other. He teetered a moment, then flopped sideways, and lay still.

James Cleuny and Tim the Skinhead raced toward us from the sheriff's office across the street. Rayla told them as best she could what had happened. She looked like she was about to pass out.

I caught words here and there. My ears still weren't operating right. When I put in my two cents' worth, the words sounded garbled and incoherent, even to myself.

"Dang it, just lock her up." Rayla pointed to Delores. "Don't let her out of your sight."

"I'll take care of her," James told Tim. He eyed Billy Lee with some perhaps not unwarranted suspicion. "You cuff Billy Lee. I always knew he was involved in all this. He the one started the blaze, Corrie?"

Billy Lee heard and lifted his head off the concrete where he lay. "By gawd, I'm gonna beat the crap out of you when I'm able to get up off this here cee-ment. Ain't you ever heard of slander?" He made as if to get up.

"Don't try it, Billy Lee." I pushed him back down, which didn't take much strength, and scowled at James Cleuny. "For your information, Billy Lee saved my life tonight. If it wasn't for him, I'd be toast. Rayla, too."

Billy Lee's head fell back to the pavement. "Yeah," he mumbled. "You tell him, tax lady. Not that the old place don't need burning. Wonder nobody ain't already fell through those floors, sorry a shape as they're in. Shame it hadda go like this though."

In the background I heard sirens loud enough to overshadow the courthouse alarms. My ears were recovering.

The fire station was about half a mile away, but by the time the fire trucks arrived, flames could be seen all over the courthouse. The heat became so intense we had to move down the street. James and Tim dragged and carried Billy Lee along, a herculean task since he'd lost so much blood he couldn't help them bear his weight.

The emergency crew and more deputies followed close behind the fire people. Lights flickered everywhere. Blue lights, red lights, white lights, spot lights, whirling lights, flashlights. Their illumination and the eerie fire glow, along with the uniformed people swarming over the streets and trampling the grass, made the square look like a movie scene.

The EMTs saw me and started to detour.

I waved them away. "I'm all right."

Next, they spotted the handcuffed and still unconscious Delores, and loaded her up. When the ambulance squalled away, Tim the Skinhead rode with them to guard her.

By that time another EMT crew had found Billy Lee and started work on his wounds.

It took six men to get him on the gurney and into the ambulance. He was deathly white but still ranting as they loaded him up. "I don't know why the hell when anything like this happens, everybody tries to blame me. It's that girl's fault the old place is burning down. She's the one throwed the candle. I never did nothing. I was just trying to see about my tax bills like any good citizen, and that crazy woman that works there . . ."

I heard him grumbling till his ambulance followed the other down the crowding streets. After that, the billowing black smoke from the courthouse claimed all my attention.

"Damn," said a man coming up alongside me as he watched the blaze. "They should of known this would happen one day. They used oil cleaners on them pine floors for years and years. Don't reckon they can save it now, not with all that oil soaked into the wood the way it has."

Through the smoke I spotted Rayla's patrol car at the front of the courthouse entrance, in eminent danger from the scorching heat. Parked right next to it was . . .

"Momma's new car!" I had left it in the front by the entrance and it was still there. Adrenaline helped me stand up. "I've got to get my mother's car out!"

I lurched down the street, only to be stopped by a fireman. "Stay back!"

"My mother's car is in there!"

"No help for it now. Too dangerous. Stay back, miss. Have to let it go."

"Let it go?" I screamed. "It's my mother's *new* car! She just got it last weekend! She'll kill me!"

"Get back, miss."

"Come on, Corrie." The peanut-eating deputy who'd been with us on our car-shopping trip dragged me back well outside the perimeter of firefighters and deputies. "Your mother'll understand. You stay here where it's safe," he said with more kindness than I deserved, and then was gone.

So I sat on the curb down the street from the courthouse and watched the clock tower poking proudly up through the flames. Bitter smoke filled my lungs while ashes drifted down. Sparks flew up to swirl in the night sky like fireworks.

But this was April, not July, and these fireworks weren't a joyous celebration of liberty.

I hiccupped, tried not to cry. The heat pushed at my face, but I couldn't move.

The lovely courthouse where, as a little girl, I'd gone with my daddy to pay his taxes. The place where I'd bought the tag for my first car. The place where I'd come to get a copy of my birth certificate when Momma mislaid it before I signed up for soccer. The probate office where Bodie and I had got our marriage license.

Yes, the stairs were dangerous and the roof leaked and the bathrooms sucked. But it was *our* courthouse. Even the uneven floors and bad lighting I'd cursed while I worked there. All of that was part of my past, part of our county's heritage.

Gone. All gone.

Already the firefighters had switched their efforts toward the surrounding buildings. The tacit admission the courthouse couldn't be saved made me bury my head in my arms on my knees.

The crowd around me grew as word spread. Grim eyes turned toward the old building and watched the swelling flames in near total silence. Tears gleamed on nearly every face. Like me, they recognized that some of their history was forever lost.

As the fire continued to burn, Duke found me. "I heard you and Billy Lee were in the thick of it. Want to give me a quick recap of what happened?"

I looked at him blankly and thought about it.

I had flung the candle. I had set off the kerosene, let the fire get a toehold.

This was one time I really was to blame.

"It's my fault." I sniffed, blinking back tears. "All my fault. They should have made Delores tax commissioner like she wanted. I never should have let them talk me into taking the job."

"Now, now." He patted my back. "I'll talk to you when you're more composed," he said and moved away.

Just like a man. Disappearing when you most wanted to howl it all out.

I put my head back down on my knees. The courthouse and all its records were destroyed, and all because of me.

I should never have agreed to be tax commissioner.

Judge Hartley stood nearby talking to the sheriff. "They'll have to get me a new court building now." He didn't attempt to hide his satisfaction. "This can only be seen as due justice after all the years I've begged for one."

I scrambled to my feet, started to go after him like Billy Lee Woodhallen had gone after Mr. Jethro. How dare he talk about justice!

Someone held me back.

"Don't do it, Fluff," Bodie Fairhurst said in my ear. "Think of the headlines. Tax commissioner arrested for attacking state court judge."

I leaned back against his shoulder and began to weep.

CHAPTER 18

Late Saturday afternoon, I sat, soot scrubbed from my hair and skin after one hot shower the past night and a long soak in perfumed bath oil this morning, ensconced on our ratty den loveseat. My friend Sherry and her husband took up the matching sofa, while Daddy sat in his recliner, and Ethan stretched out in Momma's.

Momma herself worked in the connected kitchen on a chicken casserole for supper. When she and Daddy got to the fire the past night, she'd grabbed me from Bodie, hysterical. She'd boo-hooed and refused to let me go for the longest time.

She never mentioned a word about her destroyed car.

Have I mentioned how much I do love my momma?

As we continued to talk over the past night's events, Ethan was still trying to make sense of what had happened. "Delores probably grew up knowing that yew hedge she lived next to was poison. Sheriff reckons the eagle diving into your car windshield gave her the notion of throwing the cinder block at you. And you said she knew you were eating at Scallops when Rayla shot at her truck. We found it, by the way, in that old chicken house behind the hay bales, just like you said. Somebody's gonna get written up for a careless search," he added smugly.

Daddy shook his head. "I always thought ol' Delores was cranky, but I never knew she was nuts."

I pleated my t-shirt hem. I didn't have much to say.

Sherry read my mind. "It isn't like any of this was your fault."

"I know." I felt drained. "But I keep thinking if I hadn't taken the job, if I hadn't thrown that candle . . ."

"You ask me, that courthouse needed burning down," Sherry's husband Caleb said.

We all looked at him.

"It was a firetrap," he insisted.

Caleb was from out of the county—out of the state—so we forgave him, but he was pushing his luck. Guess our expressions warned him because he shut up.

"It could have been renovated," Ethan muttered.

Daddy, ever the peacemaker, said, "It was in bad shape. Shame we didn't ever get to see how much it would of cost to redo it though."

From the kitchen, Momma rattled a pan. "It's a bigger shame your male commissioners let it get in that shape to start with."

"Now, honey," Daddy started.

"If a woman had been on the board, she would have seen something got done." Momma slammed a drawer shut.

"Maybe so," Daddy conceded in the interest of harmony. "I got to say, this gives us a chance to build something for today's times. The old courthouse was pretty, yes, but it wasn't functional anymore."

"That's right," Sherry put in loyally. "That fire'll give us a chance for a fresh start, so to speak. Sure, we'll miss the old courthouse, but how long has everyone been complaining we needed a new one?"

I appreciated my friends trying to cheer me up, but I knew quite well what had been lost because of me.

The doorbell rang. "Sit still," Momma told Daddy as she went to answer it. She returned beaming. "Look who's here." She led Bodie Fairhurst in.

He nodded to the others but came straight to the loveseat where I sat. He wore a t-shirt and his University baseball hat and held a plastic grocery bag. A faint scent of the cedar after-shave I remembered from the past clung to him. "Thought you might need some cheering up."

After crying on his shoulder half the night—I remembered sobbing I should have listened to him, that I didn't know how to be tax commissioner, that I was going to give up the job, and saying a lot of other things in the cold light of day I wished I hadn't said—I couldn't get up the energy to snap at him. I silently took the bag he offered.

He looked rested, while his eyes, bright with laughter, emitted the old charm. "Can I sit down?"

I shrugged. "Do what you like. You always do."

"Hmm. You must be sick." He sat down. "If you don't want to open the bag, you need to put it in the freezer."

I looked inside.

Cold Churn Dash ice cream. Mocha Almond Fudge.

I got up without a word and went into the kitchen, got down a bowl, and scooped out a generous portion.

Momma saw me. "You won't eat any supper."

"Won't need any after eating this."

Momma frowned at me as I got myself a spoon and headed back to the den. "Does anyone want any ice cream before supper?" she called loudly. Making sure I knew she disapproved of my manners. "It's Mocha Almond Chocolate that Bodie brought."

The others allowed as how they might. Even Sherry trooped into the kitchen to get a bowl.

Everyone went except Bodie. One long leg stretched out in front of him while one arm rested on the back of the loveseat.

Not wanting to let him run me out of my place, I plopped down beside him with my bowl.

My cat Bill stuck his head in, slunk toward the kitchen and stopped, paw frozen in midair as he surveyed the crowd. Bill

231

didn't like a lot of people in the house.

"Thought that would make you feel better," Bodie said complacently, nodding at the ice cream.

Why did he have to smile at me like that?

"—women's league talking to Lavinia about running a woman for county commissioner," Momma's voice came from the kitchen.

Bill decided too many people trumped his hope of getting food and stole back toward the stairs. Unsociable animal.

Bodie and I watched him disappear. "It's a good thing you're in Atlanta now," I said. "Bringing me ice cream like this will make me fat."

"I won't be in Atlanta anymore."

Daddy's voice rose. "—too dadgummed old. If you plan to make a decent showing, you need a younger woman than Miss Lavinia. Younger voters can't—"

"Where will you be?" I asked Bodie, spoon raised halfway to my mouth.

"I resigned from the GBI yesterday."

The spoon clattered on the bowl. "But . . ." I remembered the rumors about him being investigated. Had he been forced out?

I took a firm grip on the spoon. This was none of my business. I didn't want to get involved with Bodie and his problems. I had enough of my own. I spooned up a big luscious chunk.

In the kitchen Momma sounded heated. "—know that, Keith, for pity's sake. We have several capable women who—"

"I'm coming home," Bodie said. "You're not still thinking about giving up your job, are you? The hard part's over now Delores is in custody."

I searched his face, remembering what he'd said to me at Scallops. About me not wanting to leave Medder Rose. Was he coming back because I wouldn't leave home?

No, I was reading too much into this.

"I'm leaning toward quitting," I said slowly. "If I hadn't taken the job to start with, none of this would have happened."

Momma listed candidates. "Loretta Swensin or Sally McEverly or Barbie Ruth Dempsey—"

I stuffed my mouth with ice cream.

"That's too bad," Bodie said. "I was hoping you might have an opening for me. Since I'm out of a job now."

"An opening!" I almost spat out my ice cream. "You think I'd hire you?"

He gave an exaggerated sigh. "Guess it was too much to hope for. Doesn't matter, though. I'm still coming home."

"And I care about this because . . . ?" I asked him when I finished chewing.

Ethan's smug voice floated toward us. "Sally McEverly has an arrest record. She can't qualify."

Blue eyes crinkled. "Because I thought you'd want to know I'll be available. Whenever you need an ice cream jump start, I mean."

Momma shrieked. "Sally has an arrest record? For what?"

I never did hear Ethan's answer.

READER QUESTIONS
FOR DISCUSSION

1. Did the setting seem appropriate for the story? Could you visualize the courthouse, the square? Would the same story have worked as well in a small town in a different region of the country?

2. Were all the characters believable? Did any characterizations seem off-key?

3. Corrie is only twenty-three when she's appointed tax commissioner. Did her actions throughout the story reflect her age, experience, and personality? Could you follow her growth process?

4. Did Corrie's problems make you wonder about the qualifications a tax collector, whether elected or appointed, should meet?

5. Did the plot give away too much too soon regarding the murderer and motivations?

6. Were there loose ends you wish could have been tied up better?

7. Did you learn something about the workings of a tax/tag

office? The behind-the-scenes maneuvering of politicians?

8. Was the writing craft sufficient so as not to take you out of the story? Did you understand what the author was trying to say?

9. Was there anything about the book you especially liked? Disliked?

ABOUT THE AUTHOR

Cheryl B. Dale wrote *Treacherous Beauties,* a romantic suspense under the pseudonym Cheryl Emerson. Published by Silhouette, it was made into a television movie. She has three romantic mysteries from MuseItUp in March, July, and November 2012.

In nearly twenty years working for a Georgia tax commissioner's office, she sold tags and collected property taxes. That's now in the past. She's nostalgic but relieved.